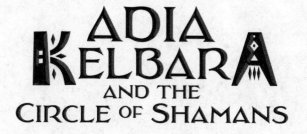

ADIA KELBARA

AND THE
CIRCLE OF SHAMANS

ISI HENDRIX

ADIA KELBARA

AND THE
CIRCLE OF SHAMANS

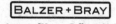

An Imprint of HarperCollins*Publishers*

Balzer + Bray is an imprint of HarperCollins Publishers.

Adia Kelbara and the Circle of Shamans
Copyright © 2023 by Isi Hendrix
Map Illustration © 2023 by Adam Rufino
All rights reserved. Printed in the United States of America.
No part of this book may be used or reproduced in any manner whatsoever without
written permission except in the case of brief quotations embodied in critical articles
and reviews. For information address HarperCollins Children's Books, a division of
HarperCollins Publishers, 195 Broadway, New York, NY 10007.
www.harpercollinschildrens.com

Library of Congress Control Number: 2022952358
ISBN 978-0-06-326633-9
Typography by Amy Ryan
23 24 25 26 27 LBC 5 4 3 2 1

First Edition

▲ ▲ ▲

For my niece and nephew, Izzy and Gabriel.
I hope you like it!

ZARIA

THE SU...

BU...

THE
ACADEMY...
SHA...

MBARI
MINES

THE
MACOBAR
JETTY

GINIAN

THE
SWAMPLANDS*

THE
HILLS

THE
WILD
PLACES

IKENGA

*the affairs of this village are not worth discussing.

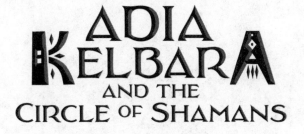

ADIA KELBARA

AND THE
CIRCLE OF SHAMANS

ONE

The Swamplands were not a place most people in Zaria ever thought about. In fact, if an atlas bothered to mention the Swamplands at all, it was sure to include a footnote stating that "the affairs of this village are not worth discussing." But the affairs of *this* particular day were of great importance to twelve-year-old Adia Kelbara.

Adia stood outside her house, clutching a letter so tightly her nails dug into her palm. A letter that could change her life and get her out of the swamp . . . so long as her aunt and uncle didn't kill her first.

"You have to go in at some point," she told herself.

Normally after school she went straight to the forest. The mosquitoes and tsetse flies were relentless in the Swamplands and even worse in the forest that surrounded the village, but it was the only place she could draw and read in peace—at home, Uncle Eric was always annoyed by the sight of her reading, and her cousin Ericson was forever hiding her sketchbook of maps. Today, however, she needed to tell her aunt and uncle about the letter. Slipping it into her pocket, Adia opened the front door.

Aunt Ife stood in the middle of the living room dusting a table and humming a hymn. Aunt Ife was *always* humming a hymn.

"Hi, Auntie."

Her aunt's only reply was a distracted nod.

Adia swallowed and took a deep breath. She might as well get it over with.

"So . . . I received the placement letter today for my year of practicality."

Every twelve-year-old in the Zarian Empire was required by law to have a year of practicality, where they worked as an apprentice and learned a useful skill. No classrooms, no teachers, no memorization of ancient epic poems or complex mathematical formulas—just practical things that would be useful when they were adults.

Her aunt spared her a glance.

"Year of practicality? Don't be silly. That's for twelve-year-olds. You're nine."

"I've been twelve for three months," Adia said.

Aunt Ife blinked.

"If you say so. Well, your uncle will be happy to put you to proper work harvesting agrias full-time. You'll be doing what you've always done, but more of it."

Almost every kid from the Swamplands *stayed* in the

Swamplands for their year of practicality—it was convenient for everyone if your family just trained you in their trade. But there was no rule saying she couldn't request to be placed overseas. And Adia wanted a placement outside the village for many reasons. The first being that she *hated* harvesting agrias. The creeping plant grew wild in the Swamplands and was so fond of creeping that, more often than not, it would creep off before anyone could get to it. But it had to be harvested because everyone in the Swamplands over the age of thirteen wanted agrias and the tonic that was produced from it—Drops.

The missionaries said it was holy communion. If you were old enough, you were given a dose of Drops before entering church to make you more receptive to the Bright Father's love. More *obedient*. But Adia had noticed some unfortunate side effects. One Drop never seemed to be enough to keep anyone calm and obedient for long, and people got downright mean if their next dose didn't come quickly enough. Her uncle and cousin more so than others. And Adia was sick of dealing with their anger.

She looked at her aunt. "I didn't receive a home placement."

Aunt Ife put down her rag, finally giving Adia her full attention—and a hard stare.

"What are you talking about? Did they mix you up with another student? Don't tell me I have to go down to the schoolhouse."

"There wasn't a mix-up," Adia said, dropping her bag

onto a chair next to a chubby orange tabby that was fast asleep. "I'm going to apprentice in a kitchen."

Adia bent down and gave the kitten her cousin had brought home to be a rat catcher a quick scratch behind his ears. The family cared so little about the animal that no one had bothered to name him, so Adia had named him Bubbles. He seemed grateful for it and had taken to sleeping in her bed.

She moved away from Bubbles and stood tall, bracing for what she knew was coming. It wasn't the thought that Adia was planning to leave the Swamplands that would send her aunt into a fit of hysterics. It was *where* she was planning to go.

Aunt Ife frowned. "Your uncle isn't going to like you not being placed at home—I know that much. No one can find agrias as fast as you." Her eyes narrowed. "No one can find *anything* as fast as you."

"I'll show Ericson the best places to go," Adia quickly replied, although she knew her cousin would be furious at having an extra chore. "I don't have any secret trick. I'm just familiar with the forest."

Aunt Ife still eyed Adia with suspicion, but she let it go.

"Well, I don't know what your uncle will have to say about this, but it's a fine enough thing to apprentice with a cook. Which chef are you training with? Elder Bunam? You've been helping him in the market after school for a while now. That man cooks better with one arm than most people do with two. You'd be lucky to train with him."

Adia picked up a pitcher of water from the table. She

poured two glasses, taking one over to her aunt as the words tumbled out of her mouth.

"No, not with Elder Bunam. I haven't been placed in the Swamplands at all. When Cousin Avery visited a few months ago, I asked if he could put in a word for me in Chelonia since he delivers goods to lots of estates there. Turns out he's friendly with a head cook and she agreed to take me on and . . . and I've been placed in Chelonia. At the Academy of Shamans."

Her aunt froze, then wheezed like Bubbles did when he was trying to cough up a particularly difficult hair ball. Adia handed her aunt the glass of water.

"The . . . the Academy. Of *Shamans*?" Aunt Ife said in between gasps for air and gulps of water. "What have I done wrong? Oh, what have I done wrong?!" She rushed over to the prized possession of her household, a white marble statue of the Bright Father that the missionaries had installed in everyone's homes.

Her aunt and uncle used to have a shrine to the Alusi—the guardian gods from the stars who protected nature and her people—same as everyone in the Swamplands. But then the missionaries showed up a few years ago with smiles on their faces and explained to the village that only uncivilized people kept shrines to the old gods. That the Bright Father was the only god civilized people prayed to. Books with the Bright Father's teachings were handed out ("for free!" Aunt Ife exclaimed), and everyone over thirteen was offered a communion of Drops. Aunt Ife had been one of the most enthusiastic converts, eager to demonize the shamans she'd always hated and be part of this modern, civilized world that promised riches, freedom from suffering, and no mosquitoes.

Not that Aunt Ife's old Alusi shrines had done anything for Adia either. The guardian goddess Ginikanwa, who was said to have vanquished evil with nothing but her pure heart and a song of love, sounded about as believable as the missionaries' promises of riches for those who did as they were told. The shrine had been pretty and full of flowers, but ultimately useless.

Adia didn't want anything to do with gods, old or new. But she knew she was about to witness a spectacle of nonsensical devotion.

Aunt Ife flung herself to her knees in front of the statue and cried, "Bright Father, please give me your strength. I've failed you. My sister's child wants to cook for demons! Demons who probably dance around and chant for Olark to come crawling out of hell and burn us all."

Adia was used to her aunt's rants about demonic juju and all the sinful things the missionaries had purged from the Swamplands, but she had hoped that the opportunity to get rid of the unwanted orphan who'd been dumped on her would be enough to keep Aunt Ife calm. Clearly, Adia had forgotten who her aunt was.

"The shamans aren't demons, Auntie," she tried to say as her aunt's wailing reached a fevered pitch. "And no one is an Olark worshipper. They're just able to go into trances and communicate with spirits, not summon the king of all evil. They relay messages from ancestors. Maybe make some tonics if they were trained as healers. It's not like they can move mountains or set things on fire. Besides, I'll be in the kitchens. I'll never even see them. And you just said cooking is a fine apprenticeship—"

"Stop speaking!" Aunt Ife shouted. She took a long, deep breath, then smiled so calmly and serenely that Adia took a step back. There was nothing comforting about her aunt's sudden display of teeth.

"We'll have no more talk of this. I'm to blame. I can see that now—I've let you get away with not going to church for far too long. You just put up such a fuss that your uncle told me to let you stay at home, but there'll be no more of that. Come now, Adia. Come here. I said COME HERE!"

Adia slunk next to her aunt, taking her outstretched hand.

"Let's sing. You remember your hymns, don't you? Of course you do. I know you're a good girl deep, deep, *very deep* down inside."

Aunt Ife began to sing, and the first note woke Bubbles from his nap, his orange fur standing on end. With an arched back, he jumped from the chair, ran for Adia's room, and gave a hiss at the door before disappearing. Adia stared mournfully after the kitten as her aunt, who had never in her life managed to land on the correct key of a song, squeezed her hand, smiling as she sang—

"Bright Father, I long to be perfectly whole.
I want Thee forever to live in my soul.
I give up myself, and whatever I know.
Now wash me, and I shall be whiter than snow.
Whiter than snow, yes, whiter than snow.
Now wash me, and I shall be whiter than snow."

Her aunt beamed, waiting for her to join in, but Adia pursed her lips and stared down at her shiny black school shoes. Any other day she would have kept her mouth shut. Years of being an unwanted presence in her aunt and uncle's home had taught her that there was no point in disagreeing with them. Aunt Ife would either tell Adia to go pray or dismiss her with a roll of her eyes. But unless her family chained her to the table, she was getting on that ship. Once she did, she wouldn't see them for a year—there was nothing to lose.

"According to my atlas," Adia said, pushing up her glasses and looking back at her aunt, "the Swamplands have never reached a temperature lower than eighty degrees. It's never snowed here."

"Why do you insist on being such a disagreeable girl?!" her aunt said, roughly dropping her hand. "It doesn't matter if it's never snowed here. The missionaries came to the Swamplands to show us the path to a better life. So we're to trust their words and their hymns without question."

"But where did the missionaries come from? All they say is that the Bright Father sent them," Adia continued as her aunt looked like she was ready to smash something. "Either way, I don't see why they're all so concerned with washing us into whiteness."

"It's a metaphor," her aunt spit out. "For piety."

Adia couldn't stop herself. "How do we know snow isn't pink?" she said as she plucked an imaginary piece of lint off her school dress.

"Oh, you this child!" her aunt snapped. She always said that when Adia was talking in a way she called *disturbing*.

Oh, you this child.

The front door opened, and Adia's desire to rebel disappeared. Her uncle was home.

Her aunt rushed to her husband. "Thank the stars. Eric, I can't deal with her anymore. I can't! You have to do something. This child managed to get herself placed in Chelonia for her year of practicality." She glared at Adia before spitting out, "At the *Academy of Shamans*."

Uncle Eric stared at Adia, and she stared back. She faked a confidence she didn't feel as her heart raced. Her aunt's theatrics, annoying as they were, didn't frighten her. Her uncle's rage, on the other hand? Terrifying.

"Ife, why are you working yourself up about something that's never going to happen?" Uncle Eric said in the calm, low tone he used when he was beyond furious. "Who's paying for the girl to go all the way to Chelonia? You? Because I'm certainly not."

Adia held her tongue. *She* was paying for it. She'd saved every cent Elder Bunam had given her for helping him with his food stall in the market—information she decided to keep to herself. Uncle Eric very well might chain her to the table if she told him she had the money for the ship. She'd underestimated her aunt and uncle's fear of anything that didn't come from the mouths of missionaries—she should have known the word *shaman* would send Aunt Ife over the edge. Along with losing a free source of labor. Her aunt reminded her about how good they were to take Adia in when her mother died almost as often as she reminded her to get back to work.

Aunt Ife stared at her uncle, then gave a relieved laugh.

"I've been so silly. Yes, of course. No one is paying for her to cross the sea." Aunt Ife gave Adia a self-satisfied smirk and pointed at the large basket on the table. "All right, then. Since you chose to be so unpleasant today, go to your precious forest and gather some agrias. They'll give us less Drops if we don't bring in a good harvest this season."

Adia's stomach growled, and as much as she wanted to remind her aunt that she hadn't eaten yet, getting out of her uncle's path was her top priority. She grabbed the woven palm basket she used to gather agrias, cautiously eased past her uncle, and then rushed out of the house. Better to be in the forest than to witness the explosion that was about to happen.

Sure enough, Uncle Eric's voice followed after her as she walked down the muddy path.

"It's not just that she won't go to church," he yelled. "It's all that reading! You never see Ericson reading, do you? No. Because I raised my boy to think for himself. He knows not to put someone else's thoughts in his head. But look at the girl—she's needed glasses since she was six because of it. It's why she's so strange! I'll have no more of this behavior. It all ends today."

Adia quickened her pace. She didn't want to hear them arguing and insulting her. But at least Uncle Eric had only called her strange. When she was younger, skinny and sickly and having tantrums whenever the missionaries came to collect them for church, he had called her something else.

Ogbanje.

A child demon. An evil spirit who was born sick, heaped misery on their family, then deliberately died young out of spite.

But Adia had a perfectly good reason for being sickly and skinny and an even better one for why she threw fits around the missionaries. And neither of those reasons was that she was a spiteful child. In fact, she was a rather lovely and remarkable child. The only such child currently living in their house. But there used to be another.

Eric Jr.

Eric Jr., first son of Eric and older brother of Ericson, was dead. And there wasn't a day since he'd died that Adia didn't miss him. Sure, he'd had the occasional episode where he'd fall in a faint while his body shook and his eyes rolled to the back of his head, but EJ had been gentle, smart, and kind. As opposed to his brother, Ericson (second son of Eric one), who was ugly, dull, and a brute.

But it wasn't being gentle, smart, and kind that had made

EJ Adia's favorite relation. It was that she'd felt a true kinship with him. Because her aunt and uncle couldn't stand EJ any more than they could stand her. His shaking episodes sent Aunt Ife into constant bouts of hysterics, and Uncle Eric couldn't believe he'd fathered a weakling as his first namesake.

EJ had vanished one day when they were at the lake. One minute, Adia had been reading a book in the grass while he swam, and the next, he was gone. Maybe he'd left to go for a walk and had one of his shaking fits and hit his head. Or maybe he'd been bitten by a spitting cobra while he lay unconscious. No one knew. Adia didn't even blame Aunt Ife when she'd called her a stupid girl for having her head buried in a book when EJ needed help. He'd always protected Adia, and she'd completely failed him. And she would have to live with that failure for the rest of her life.

The missionaries had spent days searching for him. Adia searched too, but she came back empty-handed. The missionaries came back with EJ's body.

They said he was an ogbanje. That if the family didn't find and destroy the stone totem EJ had most likely hidden somewhere in the house, his evil spirit would use the stone to travel back from the realm of the dead and return to the world of the living. And that if he did, he would bring even more misery and stress to the family.

The accusation added a level of rage to Adia's mourning. Not that she believed a word of it. She and EJ had spent every second together. He was her best friend and the best person in that house. Besides, if he'd really been some sort of otherworldly bringer of misfortune, she would have been the one who died that day, not him. Nevertheless, Adia had to listen to people attack her cousin even in death, and she and Ericson were told never to mention EJ again.

Without EJ around to protect her, Ericson upped his torture, stealing her lunch at school every day, causing her to look even more frail and catch more colds. And then the new rumors began.

Maybe Eric Jr. jumped into Adia's body, villagers whispered, not caring if Adia heard them as they pulled their children close when she passed by. *She's always looked ripe for possession. And that memory of hers, it's unnatural—she never forgets anything she reads or hears. Something is wrong with her. Mark my words, she'll be the next child to die.*

But Adia didn't die.

She started helping Elder Bunam, the one-armed cook, with his stall in the market. There she would snack on deep-fried akara and plantains to make up for the lunches Ericson stole. She went from skinny and sickly to a tall, strong girl who everyone begrudgingly admitted was turning out rather pretty. And no amount of searching Adia's room ever led Uncle Eric to an ogbanje's stone. She swept every day to make sure she never dragged so much as a pebble inside the house.

The thickening cloud of mosquitoes as she walked deeper into the forest snapped Adia back to her present situation. All right, so her aunt and uncle weren't going to walk her to the port and send her off with a smile. But did she really need their permission?

She reached EJ's grave. Uncle Eric had buried him deep in the forest, where his grave would be out of sight. Adia put down her basket and touched her cousin's headstone. An agrias vine was creeping around it. She let it wrap around her, pretending it was EJ who was holding her hand.

"How can I stay here?!" she cried. "They'll burn my books and my maps and make me go to every single prayer meeting and every sermon. That's five days a week of sermons! I can't survive it!"

Her hands lowered to her sides, clenched in two stubborn fists.

"You would run away too. Wouldn't you, EJ?"

Silence. Had she truly expected the dead to answer?

Adia gave a heavy sigh and picked up her basket, feeling more alone than ever as she walked into the forest. Yes, running away was the answer. EJ hadn't made it to twelve. He would forever be in the Swamplands, swallowed by the mud. But she was getting out.

TWO

Feeling confident, Adia walked home with renewed determination and a basket full of agrias. Just a few more days and she wouldn't have to see her family for a year, so long as she could sneak out of the house without waking anyone up. A dream come true! But her confidence faded when she opened the door.

"What are you doing?" she asked in shock.

Her hateful cousin Ericson was perched on a chair just inside, holding her schoolbag with a smug look on his face. He must have been waiting for her to return.

"Daddy took your money," he sneered. "I figured you'd have a way of getting on that ship, so I searched your bag. You think you're the smartest one in this house, but you'll never be as smart as me."

Adia lunged at him, but someone pulled her back. She whipped her head around and met Uncle Eric's angry eyes.

Aunt Ife strode into the room, along with someone else. A cold face stared at her from above a black robe.

"Why is a missionary here? Where's my money?" Adia gasped, wrestling herself free of her uncle's hold. "Isn't stealing wrong?"

"No one stole anything," Aunt Ife snapped. "You've been making money working for Elder Bunam. And you're not excused from paying a ten percent tithe to the missionaries. Your uncle thought it was time you paid your fair share, so he invited Sister Claudia over."

Uncle Eric gave Adia a patronizing smile as she furiously blinked back tears. That money had been her only chance to get out, and he'd taken it away.

Her aunt turned to the missionary and gave an apologetic bow of her head. "It's my fault, Sister Claudia, for not making sure she paid her tithes, but this will more than make up for it."

"I can see you've had quite a challenge with her," Sister Claudia said with a shake of her head as Adia glared. "What a willful girl! But you did the right thing in taking her in. Your sister's child?"

"Half sister!" Aunt Ife said, eager for any opportunity to be declared a saint. "She's not even a full-blooded relation. Sleeping sickness took her mother, and no one's heard a word from her father since she was born. I knew the Bright Father would want us to welcome this poor orphan into our home and treat her like one of our own."

If anyone heard Adia's snort of disbelief, they ignored it.

"Of course," the missionary said with a solemn nod. "But didn't you have another child?"

"We don't talk about him," Uncle Eric said quickly.

Sister Claudia's eyes narrowed, and then she smiled.

"Ah, I remember now. The child turned out to be an ogbanje, yes? While we don't know why these evil spirits come in the form of a child, I always tell parents to be grateful, for at least they die young. You didn't have to suffer for long. And once this girl learns to control herself, you'll still have extra help around the farm."

Adia didn't know if she'd ever hated anyone as much as she hated Sister Claudia in that moment.

"At least *they* didn't have to suffer?" she said quietly. "At least EJ died young?"

"As I said." The missionary sniffed. "Now, let's get to the matter of the money."

Uncle Eric finally let go of Adia so he could hand her small bag of coins over to Sister Claudia. Adia clenched her fists and tried to stay calm, but inside she felt like she was about to explode. Not for the first time she wondered how grown-ups could get everything so backward.

"Yes, yes," Aunt Ife said, eager to change the topic. "We take full responsibility and hope that you'll forgive our family if she pays her tithe as one lump sum. Along with her apologies for being a scheming, devious little—"

Something crashed through the window, making everyone shriek. Adia jumped back as glass flew everywhere. But when she saw the source of the destruction, she only rolled her eyes. An agrias vine now lay calmly on the floor among the broken glass. Sometimes the vines' creeping led to accidental acts of vandalism. A nuisance usually, though today she appreciated the timing. But then the vine began to creep in her direction.

She eyed it warily. It was taking a very determined path toward her. And it was dragging something behind it.

Everyone in the house froze as the vine deposited a stone directly in front of Adia, then slithered its way back out the window. The silence dragged on as everyone stared at the stone in horror. Aunt Ife recovered first.

"Oh dear. What a mess," she said in a strained voice. "I'm so sorry, Sister, but you know we can't control where an agrias vine decides to creep. Or—or what it decides to drag in with it." Aunt Ife was clearly worried about having *another* child in her care declared an ogbanje. Her reputation would never recover. "Adia, sweep this up."

Adia moved to get a broom, but Sister Claudia held out a pale, thin hand.

"Wait a minute. Aren't you that girl who freed the goats that were due for slaughter last week?"

"She—she has a strange aversion to eating meat," Aunt Ife said, her voice coming out strangled. "She thought the goats were her friends. I assure you she was properly punished for the chaos she caused in the market."

"But I've heard other disturbing things about her," Sister Claudia said, staring intently at Adia. "That she can look at a book for a few seconds and recite the whole thing back to you. Is that true?"

When Adia didn't answer, Sister Claudia turned to Aunt Ife.

"How old is this child?" she asked.

"Nine. No, wait. Twelve," Aunt Ife said, correcting herself.

"She's a bit young, but I think she should receive her first dose of Drops. Today."

Her family stared at Sister Claudia in confusion.

"Why?" Aunt Ife said. Adia looked at her aunt in shock. She had never heard her dare question a missionary before.

"Drops, as you know, bring you closer to the Bright Father. A gift to humanity to make it easier for us to practice his teachings and free us from sin. And what is the main teaching that we missionaries were sent here to share with you in these poor, wretched lands?" Sister Claudia asked in a singsong voice.

"Obedience without question," Eric, Ife, and Ericson said quickly.

Aunt Ife pinched Adia's arm.

"Say it," she hissed.

"Obedience without question," Adia mumbled.

"Precisely," Sister Claudia cooed. "And taking Drops helps with that obedience. It helps keep our pride in check. So I hope you will consider it a gift if I give your orphaned relation her first dose right now. You'd like that, wouldn't you, my dear?"

"Yes, of course," Uncle Eric said, answering for her. "Whatever you think is best. Our family would be honored. We obey the teachings of the missionaries. No trouble here."

For a moment, Adia felt sorry for her family. They could pretend all they wanted, but it was clear that, on some level, the missionaries scared them too.

Sister Claudia reached into her pocket. The familiar nausea at seeing the vial of black liquid churned Adia's stomach. Would those Drops turn her into someone like Aunt Ife, who could only parrot back sermons and barely thought for herself? Adia didn't know. But she knew she wouldn't be herself anymore if she let a missionary shove the contents of that bottle down her throat.

"We really should give it to newborn babies in my opinion," Sister Claudia murmured. "It would make everything so simple."

Uncle Eric looked gleeful at the prospect of a subdued niece. "Come here, girl."

"No," Adia whispered as she backed away, but there was nowhere to go. Ericson was already blocking the door, his beefy arms crossed as he smirked at her.

She didn't know why she couldn't just take the Drops like everyone else. Or why the dull look in everyone's eyes after they had a dose seemed to frighten only her. But she would kick and scream before taking them herself.

"Curious that you don't want to take them," Sister Claudia said. The missionary leaned down and pinched Adia's ear, making her wince in pain. "Scared I'll discover something you'd rather keep buried?" she whispered.

Adia shoved Sister Claudia. Hard. She wasn't proud of it, but she was delighted when the woman toppled backward over her robes, landing with her legs sticking straight up in the air. She fell on Bubbles, and Adia grinned as the cat took a swipe at the shrieking missionary.

"Adia!" her aunt screamed in horror.

A breeze came in through the shattered window, blowing in dust and leaves and adding to the chaos. Several leaves landed on Adia's hair and settled around it like a wreath.

"Mommy, she's glowing!" Ericson said.

Adia looked down at her hands. A purple light surrounded her. It narrowed into a straight line like a staff before disappearing into the floor.

"I didn't do that," she gasped. "It was a trick of the light. I didn't—"

Her words were swallowed up as the ground shook, almost to the same rhythm as her frantically beating heart.

Almost as if she was causing it.

There were screams from outside the house as people ran.

"EARTHQUAKE! EARTHQUAKE!"

"That's impossible," Adia said, shocked. "According to my atlas, we're not on a fault line. The Swamplands have never had an—"

"Ogbanje," Uncle Eric hissed. "Meant to bring misery to our family over and over again. It wasn't my son who was cursed. It's her! She's the demon! She's what killed my boy."

He lunged for her, but mud bricks began falling from the

ceiling—bricks hard enough to strike anyone dead if they landed on their head.

"Daddy!" Ericson wailed.

Uncle Eric glared at Adia one last time before running back to his family. His *real* family.

"Get to safety, Sister!" her uncle said, grabbing Ife and Ericson and, as always, forgetting about Adia.

Sister Claudia righted herself and started jumping around, trying to avoid the falling bricks. The entire house was a few seconds away from becoming nothing but rubble.

Adia couldn't believe what was happening. A few hours ago, she'd had a well-thought-out plan to get away from her family. But now that plan was literally crashing down on her head.

"I'll be back for the girl," Sister Claudia said, running out of the house. The missionary was so panicked, she didn't notice that something had fallen out of her pocket when Adia shoved her. A small pouch lay on the floor, about to be buried by mud bricks.

"My money," Adia gasped. She scooped up the pouch with one hand, grabbed a furious Bubbles with the other, and ran to the door just as a new pile of bricks came tumbling down. Her family was already outside, probably hoping she'd get killed in the earthquake.

Adia stared at the village in disbelief. Their mud house wasn't the only one in ruins. People were crying and screaming. No one looked badly hurt, but Elder Bunam, who let her work at his stall in the market, had an ugly gash on his fore-head. He was using his sleeve to stop blood from dripping into his eyes. Adia turned her eyes away from the fear and panic around her and looked down.

It wasn't the ground that was shaking—it was the roots of the plants and trees and bushes. Roots were everywhere, as if they'd clawed their way out of the dirt like a feral cat trying to scratch its way out of a house to freedom. They whipped back and forth like the vines the kids in the vil-lage used for jump ropes, moving so fast everything around them shook—the houses, the people, the ground beneath her feet. She'd never experienced an earthquake before, but she couldn't imagine this was a normal one.

"Adia!"

She snapped out of her trance. Her family was huddled in an open space with several others. Uncle Eric tried to pull her aunt back, but for once Aunt Ife pushed him aside. She stretched out her hand.

"Adia," she called again. "Get over here! It's all right; just come here where it's safe. We'll figure this out."

Adia felt a lump in her throat. Maybe she and her aunt had never understood each other—and they definitely didn't like each other—but Aunt Ife had never been outright cruel to her. Not like Uncle Eric. She gave Adia the same amount of food as Ericson (even if he stole it), and she made sure she had clothes (even if they were itchy church dresses). For the first time, Adia realized that Aunt Ife would probably protest if anyone tried to lock her up. But would Aunt Ife be strong enough to stop them? To go up against the village for her orphaned half niece?

She looked at her aunt and shook her head.

Aunt Ife lowered her hand. She understood.

Adia had to run.

She took off. To her shock and horror, the ground around her stopped shaking and the roots moved out of her way, parting as though she were their demon queen. If anyone had any doubt that she was the cause of this unnatural disaster, the ground standing still just for her sealed her fate.

Getting placed at the Academy of Shamans for her year of practicality was a bigger opportunity than she'd ever realized. Because her family was right. The village was right. The ground was shaking because she'd gotten angry. Houses were destroyed. People were hurt. And EJ . . .

"He died because of me," she whispered as tears spilled down her cheeks. If she hadn't been with EJ that day at the lake, he would have come home, same as he always did. But he'd been best friends with a literal harbinger of doom. He had never stood a chance.

"I'm a curse. I really am an ogbanje."

Bubbles had thankfully stopped squirming and purred in her arms. They were at the outer edge of the village now. No one would be able to go after them. The village was still shaking. She angrily wiped the tears from her face. This was no time to cry.

She tucked the money into her pocket and took a deep breath.

"But if anyone can figure out how to break a curse, it's a shaman."

THREE

Three days later, Adia sat in a cramped ship cabin. Bubbles was not enjoying their maiden sea voyage, and his yowling was beginning to set her teeth on edge.

Until now, she'd never stepped a foot outside the Swamplands. And she hadn't planned on venturing far from her tiny cabin either. She'd been too scared that she'd look out at the Ginian Sea and find Uncle Eric and Ericson rowing behind the ship in a dinghy, ready to drag her back home. But she had been cooped up in the tiny cabin all day, and she needed to stretch her legs.

If no one's stopped me by now, I should be fine, Adia thought, more to convince herself that no one was chasing after her as she walked above deck.

She ignored a cheerful grin from a pale boy with freckles and reddish-brown hair who looked around her age. Maybe he was bored and looking for conversation, but Adia wasn't in the mood for anyone cheerful. She carried on walking until she found an uncrowded spot.

Hanging over the ship's rail, she let the seawater spray her face. As they sailed past small villages and fisherfolk, a few smiled and waved at her and she waved back. But soon there was nothing but the vastness of the Ginian Sea and the Sunless Mountains far off in the distance.

Adia got lost in the hypnotic shimmer of the water. She pretended it was caused by multicolored jeweled fish as she sailed through the magical rain forest of Imo Mmiri. She'd been reading a legend about Imo Mmiri that day on the lake when EJ disappeared. That miserable thought shook her out of her daydreams. Nothing good ever came from them. Time to go back to her cabin before someone could ask where her parents were.

She straightened and was about to head back down, when an island with a shore covered in a thick layer of dark gray ash caught her attention.

"Burned lands?" she said in surprise, pushing up her glasses. Zaria had a dense ecosystem of woodlands, marshlands, wetlands, greenlands. But there were also the burned lands. They covered every map of Zaria like ugly smudges, as if a mapmaker had dropped charcoal on the parchment and tried to rub it out, leaving stains all over their work. Adia frowned. Either her eyesight was getting worse than it already was or a trick of the light was making it seem like sun didn't touch the scorched island.

The burned lands were ancient villages that had been

burned down during the reign of Olark the Tormentor. A demon of shadow and rot who rained fire on Zaria, only to be stopped when—according to legend—the Alusi Ginikanwa descended from the heavens and sang a song of love. Her pure heart made Olark so ashamed of his murderous tendencies that he vanished, never to be seen again.

The sight of the burned lands made Adia depressed—the Swamplands weren't exactly in great shape right now either. Olark and Adia, both destroyers of villages.

"Ugh," she said, suddenly exhausted. "Time to go back inside."

If she'd believed in the Alusi she would have asked Gentle Ginikanwa to keep her safe. But as Adia took one last glance at the island of ash, she shook her head. A goddess's songs of love hadn't saved that village from Olark any more than it could have saved the Swamplands from Adia.

Every day that they sailed farther away from the Swamplands, Adia felt a little bit safer. From the rare book about the Academy she had found in the small village library, she knew it was supposed to be one of the most impressive sites in Zaria aside from the emperor's palace. She wondered whether it would look like a museum of oddities with whatever tools shamans used to cast their souls into other realms, or more like a giant magical garden with students running around with arms full of plants as they learned how to make medicines.

By the time Adia stepped off the boat and onto the dock,

she felt something dangerously close to hope. She was going to a place in Zaria untouched by missionaries. *They* only bothered to show up in the poorer parts of the empire. But this school was a place where people still practiced the old ways of seeking guidance from nature and ancestors and the spirit world. Where a shaman might give her help, not a baptism. But as Adia stood in front of her final destination and took in the famed and ancient school, her hope plummeted.

The Academy's grounds *were* huge and intimidating, with students in colorful kaftans wandering around carrying curious-looking staffs and rattles. But the school itself was nothing like she'd imagined. It wasn't a marvelous sight. It wasn't even a decent one. It was hideous.

The wooden panels of the Academy were different colors. Some had the deep rich mahogany of the bark of khaya trees; others were a pale gray wood that could only have come from an iroko. The mismatched color pattern didn't look intentional, but more like a haphazard quilt someone had sewed together with whatever scraps of fabric they could find.

She didn't understand it. Only rich kids got to go to the Academy. For all the money the students paid, couldn't the school at least afford to hire someone to cut the weeds? It was as if the ground was trying to swallow the buildings back down into the earth.

A board flew off the side of the school as if someone had punched it straight through the wall. Then another. Then another.

"What . . . ?" Adia gasped, ducking out of the way.

All three boards landed on the ground straight up, then spun away, end over end, like tumbleweeds into the dense forest that surrounded the school, as if they were trying to escape from whatever was inside. A few students ducked out of the way but didn't seem put out to see pieces of their school trying to escape.

I guess that's why the building's so patched up, she thought in dismay.

Everything she'd read about the school's magic had made it seem like a place of wonder: a place where the walls literally breathed with possibility, filled with murals that came to life, rain that would fall inside but get no one wet, stars shifting on the ceilings, stairs that moved around and led to secret rooms full of books, games, and who knows what else.

But the school in front of her looked one strong gust of wind away from becoming a pile of rubble.

Bubbles yowled and clawed to get out of her arms. As soon as Adia dropped him, he dashed off after the fleeing boards, disappearing into the woods. She shrugged. Bubbles was half-tame, half-feral, and she didn't try to keep him contained. He'd show up when he was hungry. He always did. She was less worried about him than she was about herself.

"I think I've made a mistake," she muttered.

Adia reminded herself that she hadn't come all this way for the school's magic—she'd come for the students and the teachers, the shamans who were said to have ancient knowledge that ran through their blood, letting them communicate with the realm of spirits. They were the ones who could fix whatever was wrong with her, not some grumpy school, no matter what shape it was in.

Then another piece of the school flew toward her and nearly took off her head.

Just as she was considering running into the forest too, a flash of color caught her eye. A man in a green-and-gold uniform approached and she took an involuntary step back, but he just walked past and didn't pay her any mind. Still, she stayed frozen to the ground. Those were the colors of the capital soldiers. The Gold Hats.

She had only seen them once before, shortly after Darian Edochie won the battle for Zaria's throne a year ago. The Warlord Child had come out of nowhere, successfully defeating seasoned warriors and making everyone kneel to him. Why Emperor Darian's soldiers had appeared in the Swamplands, no one could say, and they left as quickly as they came, but the entire time they were there, Aunt Ife had been in hysterics. Well, more hysterics than usual. The minute the Gold Hats arrived, she'd sat Adia and EJ down.

"You might think you're too young to hear what I'm about to tell you," Aunt Ife had said as she paced up and down. "And you're probably right. No one's telling kids in the capital a horror story like this, but . . . you're not from the capital. And we need to have a talk.

"When I was a little girl, a boy in the village stole a plantain from a market stall. Just one plantain. A Gold Hat caught him. Dragged him to the village center for all to see and asked him, 'Long sleeve or short?'"

Aunt Ife looked at them and wrung her hands.

"Either of you have any idea what that means?"

Adia shook her head and looked at EJ. He also shook his head, shrugging.

"The boy didn't know what it meant either. He was younger than the two of you are now."

Aunt Ife took a deep breath and walked up to Adia.

"Long sleeve," Aunt Ife said, touching her wrist, then moving her hand up to the top of Adia's arm, "or short. The boy said short. Probably because it was such a hot day. Who would want to be in a long-sleeved shirt? So the Gold Hat chopped off his arm just underneath his shoulder. Gave him the short sleeve."

EJ's hand had grabbed Adia's under the table, and she'd given it a tight squeeze. She knew what EJ was thinking because she was thinking it too. The presence of the Gold Hats had gone from interesting to terrifying in the span of twenty seconds.

"That's why the two of you aren't so much as to spit on the ground when the Gold Hats are around," Aunt Ife said. "That's why you're never to make eye contact with them while they're here. And, unfortunately, that's why Elder Bunam, the cook who lets Adia help out at his stall, only has one arm."

Adia was so shaken by the memory of her aunt's story that she didn't notice someone barreling toward her until they knocked her to the ground.

"Watch it," the girl snapped even though *she'd* been the one to bump into Adia.

Adia stared up into angry blue eyes.

The missionaries might have only hit the Swamplands a few years ago, but they'd been stomping through Zaria for almost five hundred years. And right behind them stomped the filthy rich foreigners from the land behind the Sunless Mountains. Adia had thought they mostly stayed in the oil-rich capital, where they could live as far away from actual Zarians as possible. So she was baffled as to why one was attending a school for shamanism.

Adia realized the rich girl was waiting for her to say sorry, despite the fact that she was the one sprawled out on the ground.

"My apologies," she finally managed to spit out.

The girl huffed and stormed off.

"Are you all right?"

A boy with reddish-brown hair and light freckles sprinkled across his slightly crooked nose stood in front of her, holding out a hand.

"I'm fine, thanks," Adia said, ignoring his outstretched hand. She picked up her bag and the Academy map that had fallen out of it and dusted herself off.

"She must not have seen you," the boy said. "Are you a new student here? I think we were on the same ship."

The boy who had smiled at her on the deck. She remembered.

"I hate sailing," he continued. "And that was such a

bumpy ride. You just got in, right?"

She opened the map, gave it a quick scan, then tucked it into her pocket. Sister Claudia was right. She never needed more than a few seconds to commit an image or text to memory—that horrifying memory of hers that made everyone nervous. Every detail of the Academy map was now burned into her brain.

"No, I'm not a student here. I'm an apprentice cook," she said, assuming that her being a lowly servant would put him off. But if anything, he got more excited.

"You're here for your year of practicality! So am I!"

She frowned. His clothes were simple, but the material was expensive. Shouldn't kids like this do their year of practicality in the palace or at a governor's mansion?

"Really? How long have you been here?"

"Almost a year. I'm from the capital," he said, confirming her suspicions. "I have a military apprenticeship. I thought I'd be helping guard the school by now, but they're still making me do grunt work. I've been traveling, delivering luggage for the nobles and guards who are coming soon for a visit. I'll be sailing back and forth all month, but I don't mind, aside from the seasickness—I like to travel."

"Why would nobles come here?" she asked.

"Not entirely sure," the boy said. "I heard a rumor that Emperor Darian will be visiting the Academy. Nothing like this has ever happened before. If it's true, then the school is about to be overflowing with nobles and rich people, like a second version of the palace court. If you play your cards right, you could walk away with great connections. Would be nice. And I'd like to have a friend here. Especially one with connections!"

He gave her a hopeful glance, but Adia had no idea what connections he thought she would be making. If the emperor showed up, she'd make sure to stay out of his way. You don't get a nickname like the Warlord Child for being pleasant.

"Well, I'm just here to learn a trade—"

"And Emperor Darian's invested a lot of time in the Academy," the boy said, too excited to let her get a word in. "You might even get to see him. The rumor is he's got some project going on. Lots of shipments back and forth."

Adia frowned. She wasn't inclined to like Emperor Darian. He was on a mission to unite all of Zaria under his rule, but his methods for unity were brutal. Plus, the missionaries had basically ruled the outer villages ever since he came into power. She wouldn't be surprised if they gave him a cut of the new tithes to help fund his warmongering. The empire's money had to come from somewhere.

"You didn't tell me your name," the boy said, finally pausing for breath.

She didn't think anyone had ever spoken so many sentences in a row to her. At least not since EJ died last year. But this boy was relentlessly cheerful and chatty. He seemed nice enough, but she hadn't come all this way to make friends. She came to make sure she never flattened another village with an earthquake while glowing purple. To find someone who could fix her. But as much as she wanted the conversation to be over (because she was failing at it, and she didn't like to fail), she couldn't bring herself to be rude. She sighed.

"I'm Adia. Nice to meet you."

"Nami."

"Nice to meet you, Nami. So . . . you're training to be a soldier? That's what you want to do when you're older?"

"Not just a soldier," Nami said, standing up tall. "A Gold Hat."

A chill ran through. All her amusement at Nami being nice, if overly talkative, dried up. *Now* she had no problem being rude.

"I have to go find the kitchens," she said with a curt nod.

"Oh. Well, all right, then," Nami said, looking disappointed. "Nice talking to you. Maybe we can meet up for dinner?"

Adia pretended not to hear him and walked off without a backward glance.

She soon spotted a frazzled boy carrying six trays in his arms and followed him as he staggered toward a wooden door that she assumed must lead to the kitchen. Adia ducked inside after him before the door swung shut. Inside, dozens of cooks ran around, somehow managing not to crash into each other as fire and steam leaped from the stoves. A tall girl who looked about sixteen waved a spoon in the air and screamed at a young boy who stared at the floor, failing to hold back his tears. From the white scarf wrapped tightly around the screaming girl's head, Adia figured she was Maka Esiniri, the head chef.

This looked nothing like her job helping Elder Bunam with his market stall. This was chaos.

"Careful!"

"Sorry!" Adia said, jumping out of the way so someone with a tray could go through the door. She moved farther into the kitchen and cleared her throat.

Maka's eyes narrowed.

"Finally! You're Adia, I presume?"

"Yes, ma'am."

"It's Maka, not ma'am." Maka put down her spoon and walked over to her. "Well," she said, giving her an appraising look, "you look strong enough." She gave a sharp whistle. "Lebechi. Bring the kola nut."

Adia stood with her hands behind her back as another girl, who was easily balancing a palm basket on the top of her head, came up to them, bringing a small wooden plate that held a red-brown nut.

"At your command, cousin," Lebechi said with a roll of her eyes before grinning at Adia. "Nice to meet you, newbie. I'm Lebechi. I'm coming to the end of my year of practicality, so you'll be my replacement as the kitchen runt."

"Nice to . . ." Adia's voice trailed off as Lebechi handed Maka the wooden plate. "Wait. *You're* going to break the kola nut?"

Girls daring to take part in the kola nut welcome ceremony? Uncle Eric would have thrown them out of his house.

Only men were allowed to climb kola trees or break the nut.

"And why shouldn't I?" Maka sniffed.

"I . . . well, because of tradition," Adia stammered.

"Traditions invented by dead men? I don't think so. *I'm* the king of this kitchen. You'll learn that soon enough."

Adia could hardly fault her logic. She ducked her head to hide a small smile. Maka was terrifying, but she was glad to know she wasn't the only girl in Zaria who questioned the way things were.

Maka picked up the nut with her right hand and touched it to her lips, beginning the ritual. Ever since the missionaries had shoved the English spoken in the Sunless Empire down everybody's throats, only fragments of the old language remained in common use, but the words for the kola ceremony stayed true.

"Onye wetere oji, wetere udo." *Whoever brings the kola brings peace.*

Maka crushed the nut with her hands. Adia waited tensely, hoping it hadn't broken into two pieces. A kola nut split in two meant nothing but misfortune.

"Ihe dï mma onye n'acho, ö ga-afu ya." *And whoever seeks goodness will find it.*

Maka opened her hand, dropping the shattered nut onto the plate.

"Woo! Six pieces!" Lebechi said.

Adia smiled. She would have been relieved with anything that wasn't two. But six? That was practically cause for a celebration.

"In my village, my father would be running off to slaughter a goat if someone got six pieces," Lebechi said with a wink before sashaying back to her workstation.

"Let's hope you're as lucky as the kola seems to think you are," Maka said, putting a piece in her mouth and wincing. She held out the plate to Adia. "Now tell me, why have you come here?"

"To learn a skill for my year of practicality," Adia said, then took the offered piece to complete the ritual.

She grimaced at the excruciatingly bitter taste of the nut and chewed it just enough to choke it down.

"All right, then. Follow me. Usually I'd give you the lay of the land, but truth be told, three servers are down with sleeping sickness. You'll be more useful this week if you step in and help deliver meals to the students."

Adia would do anything if it meant not going back to the Swamplands. She nodded eagerly and launched into the speech she'd practiced on the boat.

"I can. I've helped a cook in my village for years. I'm honored to work at the great Academy—"

"Yes, well, I suggest you sit on that honor for a minute until you see what these so-called great students are like," Maka said with a snort. "Look. I know your cousin Avery. And I like him. More importantly, I trust him, which is why I took his letter recommending you seriously. He always delivers the best cassava flour. Other vendors I've used? They have the nerve to send me bags of flour that are full of moth eggs."

Maka shook her head in disgust as she walked up to a sweaty cook standing nervously over a pot of soup.

"Those wretched moths infested the kitchens so bad we had to throw out all the dry food."

She picked up a spoon and tasted the soup. The young cook relaxed when Maka gave him a nod of approval.

"You come from decent people, Adia," Maka continued. "A good and sensible family. But you are now working in the least sensible place you will ever see."

Adia managed to keep her cringe on the inside at hearing her family described as *good and sensible*. And she knew her skin would never betray her with a flush of anger.

She'd often wondered if that was why people treated the girls in places like the Swamplands and the Hills so much more harshly than the girls of the capital. That since their darker skin remained neutral instead of turning red with embarrassment, or pale when their blood ran cold with fear, people thought they were impervious to pain and thus better built for hard labor. A stoicism of skin was handy when you didn't want anyone to guess your feelings, but it was a curse when people assumed you were devoid of feelings altogether. Maybe that's why Aunt Ife was always weeping to the Bright Father, begging to be washed whiter than snow.

"What do you mean it's not sensible?" Adia asked. "Aren't shamans supposed to be wise? They can communicate with spirits."

She almost crashed into Maka as the cook came to a sudden halt, fixing Adia with a stern expression.

"Look around you. Besides the people working in the kitchens and sweeping the halls, have you seen anyone here who looks like you?"

The girl who'd knocked her down, the students she'd seen rushing around campus with staffs and rattles, Nami . . . no. She hadn't seen anyone who looked like her, or even anyone from Zaria. Just people with the pale skin of those who came from the land behind the Sunless Mountains.

"If you want to find a real Zarian shaman here, walk about a mile into the woods and stop when you hit the crypts."

Adia frowned. *Were all the shamans really dead? Who was running the school, then?*

Maka continued, unaware of Adia's growing unease. "All this place is now is a school for bored rich kids to play at being shamans when they don't have a drop of shamanic blood in them. How could they? They're not from this land. First the missionaries came and declared wisewomen witches, then, once they had the most powerful Zarians nice and subdued, in came the foreigners from the Sunless Mountains to steal the land. And now, in the most perverse full circle ever, everything these outsiders once called primitive? It's in *fashion.*

"Give it a few years. They might have only just hit the Swamplands, but they'll chase all of you out soon enough. If you're lucky, you'll get a job working for them on the land your family used to own."

Maka looked tired as she watched her staff work furiously to meet the incessant demands of the students.

"My grandmother used to work here when she was a girl. She told me stories. I think she was frightened of what she saw. Shamans constantly projecting themselves into different realms and more often than not bringing spirits back with them. Or channeling and speaking in voices that weren't their own, in languages that don't exist."

"Well, I'd be frightened if I saw that too," Adia admitted, and Maka nodded in agreement.

"It's a silly place now with these rich kids pretending to have abilities like those, but the school itself *is* full of power. Make no mistake about that. That's why it looks so sad and decrepit. I don't know what's going on, but it's been in a serious depression for a solid year now. Like the walls are protesting what's become of the great Academy. They were built with the bark of the ancient sea-trees, gifted to the realm of mortals by the Alusi. That's why the buildings here will . . . act up sometimes. This wood has had to witness a whole lot of nonsense.

"The ax forgets," Maka said, touching the wood walls, "but the tree remembers."

Adia looked at the kitchen with a newfound respect and a healthy amount of fear. She believed Maka about the school having a mind of its own. But surely she was wrong about the teachers and students. Adia had come all this way. There had to be *someone* here who could help her understand what was wrong with her.

"You'll shadow Lebechi for a few days until you know where all the dorms and classrooms are. When we're back at full staff, you'll move from serving to helping prep meals. But for now, focus on getting a lay of the land."

"I know where everything is already. I glanced at the map," Adia said without thinking, then winced. She couldn't believe she'd let that slip out. Everyone in the Swamplands knew she could memorize something after looking at it for a second. When she was little, she hadn't realized she should hide it. But once she realized how strange people found her, she kept it to herself.

"What?" Maka said, pausing from plating the tray to give her an incredulous look. "You just got here and you think you've memorized a school that covers eight acres . . . because you glanced at a map?"

"Oh. No, of course not," Adia said, desperate for Maka to stop looking at her like she was ridiculous. Or worse, a freak. "Who would be able to do such a thing?"

"No one natural," Maka said, looking her up and down before shrugging and handing her the tray.

"Right," Adia said with a joyless laugh, the memory of the earthquake still fresh in her mind. "That would be completely unnatural."

FOUR

"The number one rule for working at the Academy?" Lebechi said, one hand on her hip, the other holding a tray as she tapped her foot, waiting to be waved into the dining hall to clear the tables for the next course. "We're invisible. No one cares who cooks and cleans at a school like this. If you've done your job right, they'll go home telling their parents the meals were served by ghosts and the beds were made by wizards."

"So . . ." Adia said, peering into the noisy room, "they're fools?"

"Worse," Lebechi snorted. "Fools can be kind. They're *spoiled.*"

A Gold Hat snapped a finger in their direction. Lebechi glared but stood up straight.

"The Academy's probably cranky because of *those* menaces," she said under her breath. "We never had armed soldiers before, but Emperor Darian insisted the school needed to be guarded."

"Guarded from what?" Adia asked, but Lebechi shrugged.

"That is the question. I think the emperor's just a control freak and wanted his eyes everywhere. All right, the head-master has finished telling them they're the most important children who ever walked Zaria. We're up! Follow me. And don't drop anything."

Adia kept one eye on Lebechi and one eye on the students as they picked up empty plates. The students had made an absolute mess. Half the plants and flower center-pieces were knocked over, dirt covering the tables. Adia's feet crunched over broken glass, and the floor was so sticky with spilled juice that the glass stuck to the soles of her shoes. The behavior of kids who'd clearly never had to clean up after themselves a day in their lives.

"I've already mastered communicating with the spirit of fire," a boy shouted. He stood up at a table and pointed at a candle. Adia watched the flame curiously, waiting for the display. And waited. And waited.

Nothing happened.

Adia expected everyone to laugh at him, but instead his friends started cheering.

"I saw it! I saw a spirit in the fire! And it got so big!"

She caught Lebechi's eye.

"What did we tell you," Lebechi whispered as she wiped juice from the table. "They don't have a drop of power. The teachers don't either. They're all faking it."

Adia deflated. There went her plan of getting a shaman to get rid of the evil spirit inside her. It had always been a long shot that she'd be able to convince them to help her, but to find out there wasn't even anyone to ask for help? It was crushing.

"Though," Lebechi said thoughtfully, "every now and then, a student would come through who made me think maybe they had some talent. Not lately—I haven't seen anyone like that in ages. But the Academy would be in the best mood you'd ever seen too. No doors slamming shut of their own accord or tables flipping themselves over. And maybe those kids did have the gift because they usually left by the end of their first week. Vanished into thin air without even telling the staff they were leaving or cleaning out their rooms."

"Why would they leave if they were the real deal?" Adia asked.

Lebechi snorted. "Would you linger in a place full of frauds? I don't blame them for moving on. But the *tantrums* the Academy threw every time one of those students bailed," she said with a shudder.

They both winced as a student knocked over a glass pitcher, which shattered with a loud crash.

"All right, now, go take care of that table. But be careful— Mallorie Amber's sitting there. She's the richest girl here. And she's terrible."

"Which one is she?"

"That one," Lebechi said, nodding her head at a girl who

was dominating whatever conversation the table was having. Adia frowned.

It was the mean girl who'd knocked her down this morning.

"Go on, now," Lebechi said, moving to another table.

Mallorie didn't pay Adia any attention as she leaned over her to grab her empty plate. Lebechi was right—she might as well have been a ghost.

"I'm so glad I'm focusing on plant studies," Mallorie said in her haughty voice. "It's the way of beauty and love. Flower spirits and potions and whatnot."

She reached across the table and dragged the centerpiece in front of her. Adia had never seen leaves like that, red with purple heart-like spots all over them. Pretty enough, but she frowned as she collected the next plate.

"I can already hear the spirits singing to me," Mallorie said, closing her eyes and bending down to shove her nose into the leaves.

Poison.

Adia was startled. Someone had whispered what she was thinking. Poison. Not a deadly poison, but whoever picked and put those flowers on the table was going to end up in the infirmary by the end of the week. And now Mallorie had her face buried in the pot. Adia didn't know why she was so worried. She'd never even seen those flowers before, so she couldn't be sure. And she wasn't exactly inclined to help someone as nasty as Mallorie. But this was serious. Someone else had whispered they were poisonous. Mallorie just hadn't heard them.

"I think those are poisonous," Adia said, since the other person wasn't speaking up.

The table fell silent as everyone turned to her. Adia remembered Lebechi's words and cringed. Maybe she should go "ooooo ooooo" and pretend to be a ghost.

Mallorie lifted her nose from the potted plant. If she'd seen the girl walking down the road, Adia would have thought she was rather pretty. But then Mallorie Amber spoke and once again proved herself to be the ugliest person Adia had ever met.

"You *think*?" she repeated. "Who told you to think?"

Before Adia could formulate an answer to such a ridiculous question, a hand grabbed her elbow and dragged her to the back of the crowded room.

"What did I *just* tell you?" Lebechi snapped.

Mallorie Amber stared at her with an intense gaze from across the room.

"That girl was sticking her face in a poisonous plant," Adia said, bewildered by everyone's reaction. "I was trying to help."

"You're lucky I got you out of there before she ended you."

"For trying to help her?" Adia exclaimed.

"Yes. I told you, Mallorie's the richest student here. She thinks she's perfect. Pointing out that she *isn't* won't end well for you. If she wants to get covered in a rash for the next week, just let her. Or else."

"Or else what?"

"Or else you'll be packing your bags before you've had time to *un*pack them."

"That would defy the laws of physics," Adia said, pushing up her glasses, but Lebechi was too busy dragging her to the door to hear her.

"Just wait here. You're done for tonight anyway. First day and already getting in trouble," Lebechi said with a roll of her eyes as she walked away.

Adia sighed as Lebechi disappeared back into the crowd, seamlessly blending in with the other servers. The staff really did seem to have a knack for blending in with the room. Or . . . was it the room helping them to camouflage? She blinked, not sure if she'd imagined it, but when Lebechi stood close to a green tapestry waiting for students to finish their dessert, the tapestry had seemed to shift to brown, matching Lebechi's clothes.

"Maybe this miserable school *is* on our side," she muttered, leaning against the wall. She turned her head, her eye catching the life-sized portrait of the emperor that loomed above the hall.

The artist had done a good job, if it was an accurate likeness. Darian's sword was in motion, as if his muscular arm was about to lop off the head of some unseen enemy. A gaggle of girls walked by, giggling as they looked up at the emperor's beautiful image. One even clutched her hands to her heart.

Adia supposed his skin was light enough that people from the Sunless Mountains would welcome him, unlike the darker skin of the people serving the food. Darian might even have an ancestor from their side, but he was still obviously Zarian.

I guess if you're rich enough to end up with a crown on your head, even capital brats will turn you into a god, Adia thought.

But there was something about the painting that left her uncomfortable. It was his eyes—they were panicked and desperate, like a bird trapped in a cage.

Or maybe they've turned you into a mascot.

A tall, thin man stood up from the high table at the front of the dining hall. He was covered in black tattoos, which stood out all the more against his pale skin. His elaborate headdress almost fell off as he thumped his feathered staff on the floor. The room went still.

"As your headmaster, allow me to extend my welcome. And congratulations on being chosen to attend the Academy of Shamans. Your powers and abilities are so strong I can barely stand," he crooned.

The students straightened their shoulders, tossing each other smug smiles.

"It is time to invoke the great spirits who will guide you on your journeys into the shamanic realms."

The tenor of the room rose to a fever pitch as the fancy man waved his arms theatrically.

"Yes. Yes! I can already feel their presence! The wind is picking up! Can you feel it?" he shouted, his green eyes bright with excitement.

The air was thick with humidity, but the students rubbed

their shoulders as if a great gust of wind had blown through.

Fakes. Every last one of them.

"This is making my head hurt," Adia sighed, prying herself off the wall. She was too disappointed to stay here any longer. She tiptoed out of the room, hoping Lebechi would forget that she was supposed to stand there and wait. But before Adia could make her exit, she crashed into someone.

"Adia! It's Adia, right?"

It was that boy again—the Gold Hat in training who didn't pause for breath when he spoke. She wasn't in the mood to deal with him. She wasn't in the mood to deal with *anyone* now that she knew she'd come all this way for nothing. The boy cleared his throat at her silence and aloof stare.

"I'm Nami, remember?"

"I remember."

"Where are you going? Aren't you curious about all this?" Nami's eyes gleamed with excitement.

"Not really," she said with a shrug. "Where I'm from, shamanism is considered primitive. We're not allowed to have anything to do with it."

"Where are you from?" Nami asked.

"The Swamplands."

"Oh, that's . . . well, that's not your fault."

She could tell Nami was confused by her lack of interest. But she couldn't explain to him that it was irritating to watch capital kids do whatever they wanted without a missionary in sight to call them heathens. Rich people with no tie to the land turning her people's *primitive* customs into an exotic novelty act. And not a single person here who could actually help her.

She took off her glasses and wiped them clean to hide her frustration. Then she slid them back on and turned again to the front of the room. The headmaster had flung his head so far back, all she could see was his throat. Maybe she should take her glasses off again. He waved his arms wildly and stomped his feet as older students sat in a corner behind him, frantically beating on drums.

"Can you feel it?" the headmaster shouted again.

Most of the students looked confused about what they were supposed to be doing now. But horrible Mallorie jumped up, curls bouncing.

"Yes! I can feel it! I can see the spirits! They look like beautiful tree people. Beautiful pale tree spirits."

"This is ridiculous," Adia snorted.

"What was that?" Nami asked, his voice full of excitement.

"I said, 'Oh, how mysterious,'" Adia said with exaggerated wide eyes. She almost laughed at how entertained Nami was by absolutely nothing.

He barely paid attention to her as he watched Mallorie tell the room about her great visions.

"And . . . and I see mermaids! Beautiful mermaid spirits floating in the air, with skin as white as milk and hair as blond as . . . as *me*! Weaving their way through an ocean of flowers!" Mallorie screeched as she twirled around the room.

Adia looked up. There were certainly no mermaids—just

agrias vines creeping up the walls and onto the ceiling in a determined fashion, snaking their way into shapes. She hadn't realized agrias grew here too. The first shape settled. It almost looked like a letter *A*.

"I wish I could see it," Nami sighed. "All I see are the paintings on the walls."

"And the vines," she said.

"What vines?"

"The plants on the ceiling. The agrias vines."

Nami's mouth opened and closed. Then he laughed.

"When's the last time you had your glasses checked? There's nothing on the ceiling, Adia. Just a ceiling. And whatever Mallorie is seeing in her vision."

Adia glared at him. All right, fine, maybe it *had* been years since Uncle Eric had taken her to get her eyes checked and she was forever squinting to see, even with her glasses. But Nami was the one who needed his vision checked if he couldn't see the vines creeping around. She wasn't in the mood to argue with him, though. Maka and Lebechi were right. The Academy was full of frauds practicing a watered-down version of shamanism. The real shamans were exactly where Maka said. Long dead and buried in the crypts.

"I have to go," she said suddenly. She couldn't stay in the dining hall for another second.

"Why are you always running off?" Nami said.

"Just want to make a good impression," she said as she walked away. "It's only my first day, after all. I shouldn't stand around doing nothing. I'll see you later."

Adia slumped in disappointment as she left the dining hall. She would have to figure out another way to get rid of the evil inside her.

The agrias vines continued their snakelike movement. When they finally settled, a word was spelled out on the ceiling. But Adia didn't look back, so she never saw the word above her. Or the warning.

FIVE
...

Adia held back a yawn. She'd been at the Academy for almost a week now, but she still hadn't adjusted to waking up at the crack of dawn to get everything ready for the students' breakfast. The tray wobbled as her nerves threatened to take over. She was to deliver morning tea by herself for the first time before the students went to class.

"You'll be fine," Lebechi said as she stacked a pitcher of tigernut milk and puff-puff pastries onto the tray Adia was carefully balancing. "And apologize for the lack of tea if they mention it. Tell 'em the stoves are acting up. They should understand."

I doubt it, Adia thought.

She'd peeked her head into a few of the classrooms, but it was always a chaotic scene, with students flinging themselves on top of tables that wouldn't stay put or something equally absurd. Last time she'd gotten caught staring at them in horror and a student had snapped, "What are you looking at?" which sent her fleeing back to the relative safety of the kitchen. After that, she tried to keep some distance between her and the bratty students.

Lebechi gave her an encouraging smile and helped her steady the tray.

"Just go slow."

Adia went so slow she was amazed none of the students screamed at her for being late with their morning sweets.

"Excuse me," she murmured, climbing over a student who had just been dumped out of his wooden chair *by* the chair and now lay sprawled on the floor.

Glancing at the pile of papers on his desk and all the wrong answers written on them, she could understand why the school was annoyed with him.

She closed the door behind her, but it flung itself back open. The small room she shared with Lebechi in the servants' quarters might not be much compared to the students' rooms, which were covered in velvet throw rugs and tacky bronze statues. But at least the furniture in her room was happy to stay in one place. Bubbles had even stopped his roaming and was starting to sleep there too. Lebechi kept giving him scraps from the kitchen, and now he slept in her bed more than Adia's, the traitor. Adia sighed and left the door alone. If it didn't want to stay closed, she wasn't going to fight with a building.

It had been like this all morning. Something—or someone—had the Academy in a *mood*. And the school's theatrics made for a difficult work situation. She'd been up before the sun dusting and wiping down the kitchen counters, but the cobwebs kept reappearing no matter how many times she dusted them away. It was exhausting.

When she returned to the kitchen with an empty tray, the staff was in a state of chaos.

"All right, everyone. I have an announcement," Maka said. "Emperor Darian is coming for a visit next week."

Maka allowed giddy screaming for exactly three seconds before slamming a rolling pin onto the counter. Adia sneezed as flour flew all over her.

"That means from now on *everything* is going to be horrible," Maka continued.

The excited expressions on everyone's faces drooped one by one as they took in Maka. Her arms were crossed, her face was pinched, and her eyes were scary.

"Or did you think you too would be sitting down with the emperor for malt drinks and chin chin snacks? Ha-ha-ha!"

Lebechi was the only one who dared roll her eyes at Maka's cackling as the head chef stomped around the room.

"The professors will act as if every meal is a test for what the emperor is going to eat. Which means that for the next week we will eat, sleep, and breathe in this kitchen. Every waking moment will be dedicated to making sure the food is perfect. And I guarantee you," she said, stopping in front of Adia and poking her in the shoulder, "these capital brats will still find something to complain about."

So Nami was right about Darian's upcoming visit.

"Why is he coming?" Adia asked.

Everyone turned to look at her, and Adia shifted uncomfortably. Was it such an unreasonable question?

"I don't know," Maka sniffed. "Who cares? *We're* never going to lay eyes on him."

Disappointed sighs filled the room as everyone realized they might not get a glance at the famed Warlord Child. Adia pursed her lips.

"I have a few more rooms to serve," she said.

"Go, then," Maka said, already distracted. The rolling pin she'd slammed down was now zipping around the room on its own accord, tripping people as it rolled around, causing chaos. Adia hopped over it and rushed out the door.

For the next week, everything went along well enough. Adia delivered food and cleared food, and sometimes even helped prepare food when Maka was in a particularly good spirit. She stayed largely invisible to the students and out of the way of the faculty. And most importantly, the darkness inside her hadn't reared its head again. She could almost pretend it had never happened, but then she would have a flashback to her house toppling down around her and demonic light coming out of her hands and the guilt would come back. But whatever had happened that day, maybe it had been a one-time occurrence. Her hands shook less and less. Her nerves steeled, just a little. No one had noticed anything strange about her so far, and she was doing a good job. The

Academy's furniture hadn't even dumped her on the floor. Not even once.

And mostly it was nice enough being here. Nicer than the Swamplands, at least, where she also had to work—find agrias, pick agrias, deliver agrias to her aunt and uncle and thank them for the opportunity. But back there, instead of being ignored by the people who benefited from her hard work, she stuck out like a sore thumb, or, as her cousin more often said, like a pain in the butt.

Her coworkers were mostly nice too. In the kitchen, they had even started gossiping with her a little, or at least around her: about the headmaster and his penchant for having a little liquor in his morning coffee, about the teacher who supposedly snuck into the pantry late at night and ate them out of cake batter (they'd had to hide it), but mostly about Emperor Darian and his upcoming visit.

"It's so exciting," said one.

"Such an honor," said another.

"He's so handsome," said a third, putting the back of one hand over her forehead like she was about to swoon.

But all Adia could think was *It's odd.* Why was the emperor so interested in this sad school with its fake shamanism, its crumbling walls? What kind of project could be going on in a place like this? If Emperor Darian was interested in the Academy to the point that he'd had Gold Hats guarding it for the past year, then maybe this school wasn't as silly as it seemed. Maybe there *was* information in here that could help her. Adia might not have caused any more catastrophes since the earthquake, but she couldn't pretend she wasn't still scared of what was inside her.

She needed to find out more about why Darian was interested in this place. The emperor clearly knew something about it that she didn't. And she knew just who to ask.

She only had to take care of six rooms that morning, and all six students were still asleep in their beds. No doubt they would wake up thinking fairies had placed the milk on their golden nightstands. Several of the snoring students had long wooden staffs now leaning against their walls. Shamans used staffs to concentrate their connection with the spiritual realm and focus its power to their purpose. But the ones here were nothing more than glorified walking sticks for students like Mallorie, who'd been screaming their heads off about their great connection to whatever spirits the headmaster imagined he'd conjured.

Adia gently put down the last cup, taking care not to let it make a sound.

Instead of going straight back to the kitchens, she took a different trail that went to the main field. She'd seen Nami training there most mornings and usually ignored him when he waved hello. But today she wanted to talk to him.

Nami was doing some sort of training exercise with a sword, carefully avoiding low-hanging branches. She realized he was taller than her. Most boys weren't. The cheerful expression that was usually on his face had been replaced with a look of fierce concentration, to the point that she felt awkward seeking him out just to dig for information.

"Hello!"

Adia jumped. She felt herself heat up.

"Are you working?" he asked.

"Yes, but I was looking for you," she admitted.

His eyes widened, and he gave a big smile.

"You were? The way you kept running off, I thought you hated me."

"Don't be ridiculous. I barely know you," Adia said.

Nami raised an eyebrow and looked as though he was trying not to laugh. Adia winced at how awful she must sound. She tried again, making her voice friendlier.

"I mean . . . it's confirmed. The emperor is coming soon. Did you hear?"

Nami dropped his practice sword and rushed over to her.

"I knew it! No, I haven't received any news or orders, but whispers started last week that he was on the move."

"Why? What happened last week?" she asked, shifting uncomfortably.

Other than me causing an earthquake and flattening a village.

Nami didn't notice her unease. He practically jumped up and down with excitement.

"I don't know, but whatever it was, it must be what set this visit in motion. I told you he's got some project happening here, right? At least that's what the rumors say. Maybe he's on the hunt for a new adviser. Someone powerful and wise—perhaps one of the professors?"

Adia thought of the headmaster stomping his foot and yelling with Mallorie about mermaids.

"Seems unlikely," she muttered under her breath.

"And shamanism is all the rage these days," Nami continued. "Even the emperor is interested. He has to be, to visit the Academy."

"How nice for him," Adia said dryly. "Maybe he should tell the missionaries in the Swamplands."

"I don't think anyone could change the missionaries' minds," Nami said with a laugh, not realizing Adia was completely serious. "They're a force of their own. Besides, they serve the Bright Father, not the emperor."

Adia raised an eyebrow. As if they couldn't serve both. But she kept Maka's words about the missionaries being another cog in the empire's wheel to herself.

"I'll let you know if I find out anything about Darian's visit," Nami said. "You'll do the same, right? My room is in the Blue Hall with the other Gold Hats if you ever need to find me. You can come over anytime."

"Sure," she lied, not wanting to be rude by telling him she would never willingly enter a room full of Gold Hats. She gave him a wave and turned back to the trail, but he fell in step with her.

"We cross paths a lot, don't we?"

Adia adjusted the tray underneath her arm and frowned.

"Well, there are seven different paths at the Academy and most of them intersect. Statistically, it's bound to happen."

"Wow, you're really practical," Nami said with a laugh. "So where are you headed? I need to get luggage from a student. She's not even traveling, just needs adjustments made on some of her gowns and only wants a capital tailor to do it. But once I deliver them, I'll get right back on the ship to make sure I'm here for the emperor. Someone else can bring them back. They're for Mallorie Amber. Wasn't she incredible at orientation?"

"Incredibly fake, maybe," Adia said under her breath.

"What?"

"Nothing. Her room's over there," she said, pointing to the dorm surrounded by flowering coffee plants. "She's my last stop for tea. Lebechi told me to save her for last because they have to make her tray extra special. Her father donates a lot of money to the school, so I guess she's pretty important."

Nami's eyes lit up. "I see. Well then, I'd better get cleaned up. I want to make a good impression; she could be a good connection. Maybe I'll see you there?"

She was tempted to ask why he cared so much about making a good impression on these people, but she just nodded.

"I should be there in a few minutes," she said before racing back to the kitchen for Mallorie's special tray.

Maybe Nami wasn't on the same rung of the social ladder as the students here, but it wasn't like he was from the Swamplands. There had to be a reason why he was trying so hard to make these "connections." But she didn't want to start asking personal questions. He might turn around and start asking questions of his own. Questions she didn't want to answer. The less he knew about her and why she'd chosen a year of practicality so far away from home, the better.

▲ ▲ ▲

Adia stood outside Mallorie's door. She hated to admit she
was nervous about going through it. All week, Mallorie had
looked as though she wanted to end Adia's existence for daring to warn her about the plant, even though five days later
her face was still an angry scab.

Adia gave a sharp knock.

Nothing.

She waited a full minute before knocking again. Still no
answer. She sighed and opened the door.

Mallorie sat at a table, her head, including half her short
blond curls, buried in a bowl. She shot up suddenly, and Adia
bit back a scream. Green goo dripped down Mallorie's face
and onto her neck. She looked like a monster from the Horrorbeyond. None but the most gruesome of creatures were said
to inhabit the cursed land that had once been the lair of Olark
the Tormentor, chosen by the demon for its impossible location at the edge of a river full of serpents the size of boats.
The concoction on Mallorie's face made her look like she'd fit
right in with the creatures of that nightmare realm.

"I said be careful with that, you fool," Mallorie snapped.

Adia froze, not sure what she'd done wrong. She'd barely
stepped foot inside the room.

"I'm—"

"I'm sorry," someone said.

Adia winced. So Nami *had* beaten her there—and was
getting his first taste of the incredible Mallorie Amber.

"You'll be sorry if any of my gowns get so much as a stain

on them. Did you even wash your hands before touching my things? Everything I brought to the Academy was strategically chosen to get Emperor Darian to notice me. My father had inside information that he's coming," Mallorie sniffed. "I knew before everyone. Something happened last week that made him drop everything and plan a visit."

Adia frowned. The fact that the earthquake had happened right around the same time Darian decided to come here *was* unsettling, but she shook it off. Even if Uncle Eric decided to contact the capital about what happened, no one of importance would bother reading a letter from a nobody farmer in the Swamplands. She was being overly suspicious. Maybe being around Mallorie Amber just made her extra tense. Adia snuck a glance at her.

Mallorie stuck her hands into the putrid-smelling green goo, smearing more of it on her face. Adia would know that rotten-egg smell anywhere—but what she didn't know was why a noble girl was smearing sulfurous plow mud all over herself like it was shea butter. Maybe she thought it would cure the angry-looking red scars running all over her skin.

Told you it was poison, Adia thought, holding back a smirk.

"And Darian *will* notice me," Mallorie continued, sighing happily as she painted her face green.

"Of course, my lady," Nami said. "The emperor is wise."

"He is. Wise, brilliant, *and* handsome," Mallorie said. "Which is why I must have daily facial treatments for my complexion, so I am at my most beautiful." Her eyes narrowed. "And it's why you must stop hurling my clothes around like a farm boy throwing sacks of yams."

Adia risked a glance at the pile of luggage, and Nami shot her a wide, friendly smile. Mallorie's meanness didn't seem to dampen his spirits. She was about to smile back when a flash of orange dashed out from behind one of the suitcases.

"Bubbles!" she gasped, dismayed at the sight of her perpetually shedding cat rolling around in the frilly dresses that covered the floor.

"Did you say something?" Mallorie said, turning from Nami to glare at her.

"No," Adia said, eager to get Mallorie to turn from the pile of clothes before the mean girl spotted Bubbles frolicking around in her dresses.

"No, *my lady.*"

"What?" Adia asked.

"I am the daughter of a duke, so you're to refer to me as 'my lady.'" Mallorie's eyes flashed with annoyance. "Say it!"

"No, my lady," Adia said slowly. What a terrible person.

"And you're not allowed to speak to me unless I've asked you a question. Be careful with that!" she said, storming over to Nami and grabbing a frilly dress he had been attempting to fold.

Adia took the opportunity to try to shoo Bubbles toward the door before Mallorie noticed him. But instead Bubbles hopped onto the table with the putrid-smelling mud Mallorie thought was face cream. He plopped his fat bottom down.

"Oh no," Adia whispered.

Lebechi must not have given him extra scraps this morning. He was probably still hungry. She supposed the mud did smell like his favorite stinky treat of dried stockfish.

"Bubbles," she said under her breath. "Don't you dare."

But she could only watch in horror as Bubbles lapped up the green goo. She continued to keep one eye on her kitten as she carried the tea tray to a small table by the window. Maybe she could grab him and fling him outside before Mallorie noticed.

"And careful where you put that tray!" Mallorie called out without looking at her. "My shaman tools are on that table, and *I'm* the only one allowed to touch them."

Adia grit her teeth to stop herself from calling Mallorie a brat to her face but made sure the tray was far away from the feathers and crystals and small statues as Mallorie resumed yelling at Nami. Glancing back at Bubbles, she covered her mouth in horror. She recognized the look in his green eyes. And she knew what came after it.

Bubbles hunched over. And then, after a few seconds of dramatic gagging, a stream of green vomit spewed right back into the bowl.

As soon as he'd finished emptying the contents of his stomach, he jumped down from the table, licked his paws, and pranced out of the room.

Adia sighed. At least Mallorie's tantrum had drowned out the sound of it and no one else noticed.

She was so lost in her relief that she barely noticed something rolling in her direction across the table. A wooden stick with bells attached to the end—some sort of rattle.

The sound of the bells was hypnotic, and for a moment, she had the strongest urge to pick it up. She reached her hand out, but then another sound broke through her trance—Nami, clearing his throat. He gaped at her in horror and frantically shook his head.

Adia quickly lowered her hand and jumped back. Had she lost her mind? The rattle rolled off the table and onto the floor, the sound drawing Mallorie's attention. Their eyes met, and Adia knew she was about to be in a world of pain.

Mallorie's eyes flashed with anger.

"What did I just say about touching my things?" she hissed, walking away from Nami.

"I didn't," Adia said. "It just rolled off the table."

"All by itself?" Mallorie said in a singsong voice dripping in sarcasm. "Now I have to clean up after a servant? Can you imagine such a ridiculous thing?"

Mallorie stomped over to where the rattle had fallen and bent down to pick it up, but the rattle rolled away, hurling itself at Adia's feet. Adia hopped over it and made for the door, but the telltale sound of the rattle made her glance back. The wretched piece of wood was *following* her!

She was almost at the door when Mallorie called out.

"Wait just a minute!"

Mallorie's voice had lost all its fake sweetness. The sheer chill of it froze Adia in her tracks. She turned around slowly. Mallorie stared at her, then glanced down at the rattle, which was now sitting by Adia's heels like a happy puppy whose human had returned after a long day at school.

"I know you. You're the ugly little servant who's always where she shouldn't be."

"I'm actually several inches taller than you," Adia said without thinking.

Mallorie's jaw dropped. This time, the rage in her eyes made Adia take a step back. She'd never had a person look at her with such anger before, not even Uncle Eric.

Nami was gesturing frantically behind her. He made a bowing motion and mouthed the words *I'm sorry.*

"Uh, that is . . . I'm sorry," Adia said, suddenly understanding how dangerous her situation was. "I'll just be going, then."

"Going? But I haven't dismissed you yet. Why are you so eager to leave when it seems my shamanic tools love you so much?" Mallorie said with a pinched smile. "I have a few requests I'd like to make."

Adia stole a glance at Nami, but he only grimaced and gave her a helpless shrug. Mallorie sat back down at her table.

"I'm sick of having cold meals in the hall," she said as she unknowingly smeared cat vomit onto her face. "I want a piping-hot bowl of soup delivered to my room in the next twenty minutes."

"But the stoves in the kitchen won't stay lit," Adia replied. And even if they did, how was she supposed to return to the kitchen, have someone make soup, and then bring it back all in the span of twenty minutes?

"Then fix them," Mallorie said, slamming her goo-green hands onto the table. "I'm not eating cold sandwiches again.

And my room is too hot. I want another window put in. But first, fix the stoves. I want hot egusi soup and farina for breakfast. Now."

"I can't fix them." Adia hoped she sounded more patient than she felt. Maybe Mallorie didn't know about the school's ill temper? "The Academy has mood swings," she explained. "No one can make the stoves stay lit if they don't want to. And I have nothing to do with your room. You'll need to talk to the groundskeeper about that."

Mallorie's mouth dropped open. "What did you say to me? Are you denying my requests?"

"Well . . . there's nothing I can do about them," Adia said slowly, as if placating a two-year-old throwing a tantrum. Did all children from the capital act like toddlers? "Now, if you'll excuse me . . ."

"Don't you dare walk away from me!" Mallorie yelled.

Adia looked at Nami, but he was staring at the pile of clothes. So much for going to him if she ever needed anything. As usual she was on her own.

Maybe she'd said the wrong thing, but what else should she have done—lied and promised the impossible?

"What's your name?" Mallorie snapped.

Adia frowned. "Why do you want to know my name?"

"That's none of your concern. What is it?"

Now it was Adia's jaw that dropped. But she had a feeling that if she didn't answer, Mallorie would follow her back to the kitchen, hollering her head off the entire way.

"Adia Kelbara."

"Thank you, Adia," Mallorie said with a wicked smile. "I'll be discussing your unpleasant behavior with the headmaster. No doubt he'll agree with me that you're not well suited to work at the Academy. That will be all, thanks."

With that, Mallorie stomped back to her chair and sat down, looking very satisfied with herself as she smeared more cat puke on her neck.

"And Adia, dear," she called out.

Adia paused with her hand on the doorknob. She was practically shaking with anger, but she kept her face blank as she turned back to Mallorie. A lifetime with Uncle Eric had taught her to stay quiet when someone was raging. It was her mistake for not realizing just how awful Mallorie was.

"You might want to try these skin treatments yourself. I hear they have wonderful bleaching properties. A bit of lightening and brightening would do your complexion good, don't you think?"

Adia rushed out of the room to escape the sound of Mallorie's cruel laughter. She stood in the hallway, her feet glued to the ground.

What . . . what had just happened?

Adia had barely been at the Academy a week. Maybe there were no shamans here to help her, but she'd at least had a safe place to live and was learning a trade. If Mallorie got her thrown out, would there even be time to find another placement for her year of practicality? Would her entire future be ripped away because a spoiled rich girl who'd never heard the word *no* had a meltdown?

She tensed as Mallorie's door opened.

"I'm just going to get some rope to tie your bags together," Nami called out before shutting the door behind him and stepping into the hallway with Adia.

"Hey, now," Nami said, giving Adia a sympathetic look. "Don't look so defeated. I don't think Mallorie can go more than an hour without screaming at someone. She was yelling at me right up until you came in. But I always tell myself that even if something seems terrible, everything happens for a reason. Bad stuff is just how we learn. At the end of the day, it's all perfect!"

Adia gaped at him, briefly shaken out of her shock and misery by his privileged words. Only someone who'd never had anything genuinely bad happen to them would be able to say something so obtuse.

"Adia?" he said, his grin fading as she glared.

"I have to go," she said.

"Adia, wait!" he cried, but she rushed down the hall, wanting to get away from both him and Mallorie as quickly as possible.

Everything happens for a reason? It's all perfect? This is how we learn? Easy for him to say! A rich capital boy who could do and say whatever he wanted with no repercussions. Meanwhile she was about to get sacked. What about this situation was *perfect*?

After everything she'd done to get here, she would have to go crawling back to the Swamplands barely a week after she'd left. Best-case scenario, she'd be right back with Aunt

Ife and Uncle Eric. Picking agrias until her fingers bled and *paying* the missionaries to do it while they drowned her in never-ending baptisms for the rest of her life.

But then there was the worst-case scenario.

Maybe Aunt Ife would take her side. Claim the earthquake was just a freak occurrence. But if she didn't, Adia would be dragged away and thrown into a dungeon for being an ogbanje. Or worse.

Perfect? It was pathetic!

She stormed down the hall and rounded a corner, past a small decorative table with a single blue vase full of violets and, above the flowers, a portrait of Emperor Darian, waving a sword at what looked to be a group of terrified peasants. But it wasn't the silly picture of Darian that startled her out of her anger. The vase rocked back and forth, then started shaking so hard the entire table wobbled.

"Good grief," Adia muttered.

This was a new type of tantrum from the Academy. Or had she stomped so much that she was making furniture tremble? She reached out her hands to try to steady the vase, then gasped.

"Oh no," she whispered.

Her hands. It wasn't as dramatic as last time, yet there it was. Her fingertips were taking on a decidedly purple tint. She stood completely still, terrified to move, as the vase continued to wobble on the table as if something—or *someone*—was shaking it.

"Stop it," she said desperately. The vase rocked back and

forth a few more times, then stilled, and Adia gave a sigh of relief. But her relief was short-lived as, in the very next moment, a crack formed at the bottom, snaking its way up the side, until with a *crack* the vase shattered, breaking into six pieces that fanned out around the violets they had once contained. Just like the earth in the village had cracked open the last time she got angry.

"Did somebody break something?" a voice called from one of the dorms.

Adia had never felt so overwhelmed in her life. She wanted to cry, but she couldn't cry her way out of this situation. Tears weren't a privilege afforded to girls from the Swamplands.

Getting in trouble with Mallorie was bad enough. But if she got accused of breaking Academy property? There was no time to think. She quickly swept the broken vase and flowers onto the empty tea tray.

Classes were about to start. The students would rush out of their bedrooms any minute.

"I know!" she exclaimed, spinning on her heels and running in the opposite direction, not slowing down until she hit an abandoned dorm room.

She double-checked that no one was looking, then opened the door and rushed inside. Lebechi had pointed this door out when she'd been shadowing her, so Adia knew it was an empty room. It had belonged to one of those students who'd ditched the Academy after a week. No one had gotten around to cleaning it out, so the student's things were still there. Strange that they never even sent a family servant to retrieve their possessions after they cut out. But she didn't have time to think about that.

Adia's heart raced as she dumped the broken shards and violets into a waste bin. Hopefully the servants who cleaned the dorm rooms would continue to forget about this one. And even if they did, they'd assume the vase had been broken by a student who'd left long ago.

SIX

...

For the next two days, Adia barely said a word, not that anyone seemed to notice. It wasn't as if she'd ever been chatty anyway, and right now she was too terrified of herself (and Mallorie) to even speak. She'd gotten another server to take Mallorie her tea, but every time she saw her in the dining hall, Mallorie would give a small smirk, as if she was enjoying dragging out the torture. Whatever calm Adia had felt about being at the Academy was gone, replaced with barely concealed panic.

She delivered the wrong meals to the wrong rooms; she called her coworkers the wrong names; she even dropped a tray two separate times at dinner and had to go back to the kitchen to replace the ruined food. Thankfully, the Academy was also at peak foulness, and she hadn't gotten yelled for her mistakes because they were hardly the worst of the staff's problems. When a tap burst and sprayed water in five different directions, drenching Maka, everyone fell silent No one dared laugh.

"I've had it!" Maka snapped, her eyes blazing. She untied her soaked apron and flung it on the floor. "I'm calling it a night. Adia, clean up this mess as best you can. Everyone else, you're dismissed."

"Just wipe down the counters and lock up," Lebechi said, barely holding in her laughter as her furiously soaked cousin stormed off. "Oh. Almost forgot. Mallorie Amber's having tea with the headmaster tomorrow morning, so you're off the hook. He has a personal servant who'll take care of that."

Off the hook? Sure, Lebechi—off the hook and straight into the oven to get roasted alive like a peanut. Adia wanted to fall through the floor. She wouldn't even mind if the Academy helped her along and created a hole right there for her to fall into and die from humiliation. So it was to be tomorrow morning, then. Mallorie was done toying with her and was about to ruin her life.

Lebechi didn't notice Adia swaying on her feet and wishing for sinkholes as she went to finish cleaning up.

Once everyone left for the night, Bubbles came out of hiding and followed Adia as she locked up the kitchen.

"Let's walk around a bit, Bubbles," she sighed. "I'm pretty sure this is our last night here. Or would you rather stay with your new best friend, Lebechi? Maybe you'd be safer here with her than following me around, since I'm about to lose my home for the third time. My mother, the Swamplands, and now the Academy . . . I think at this point I need to accept that the problem is me being an abomination."

She hadn't been walking in any direction in particular as she babbled to Bubbles about her hopelessness, but when she came to a staircase covered in a thick layer of dust she paused. She had the strangest urge to go down these stairs. She had been curious where they led, yes . . . but this feeling was more than curiosity. There was always a unique energy at the Academy. A side effect of living in a sentient school, no doubt. But she'd never felt this mood before—like it *wanted* her to go down here. And thanks to her map, she knew where these steps led.

The libraries.

Judging from all the dust on the steps, no student had ventured down here for quite some time. Adia shrugged. If Mallorie was about to strike and Adia's days at the Academy were coming to an end, why not make her last moments here count for something? Maybe there was a book in the libraries that explained what was wrong with her and how she could fix it before she caused any more earthquakes. Or broke any more vases. And it really did feel like the school *wanted* her to go forward. . . .

"Stay close, Bubbles."

Adia walked down the stairs but hesitated when she reached a door. Should she really be in here? The Academy had always been nice to her and the other servants. She didn't think it would put her in harm's way, but still.

"Oh, what's the worst that can happen?" she muttered. "Mallorie's already ruined everything."

She pushed the door open. It creaked and groaned, but when she shoved hard enough, it gave.

"Oh!" Adia gasped.

At the center of the room stood a life-sized bronze statue of an old man on top of a pedestal, and beneath it, on each side, were four long study tables, arranged around the statue like a T. Books lined every wall and covered the tables. Adia read the plaque beneath the statue.

FATHER OVIE, KEEPER OF SHAMANIC KNOWLEDGE

Ovie was believed to be the first shaman, having been given incredible powers by the Alusi. Other shamanic lines came after, gifted with various abilities from the guardian gods, but Ovie's now-extinct line was the first and the strongest. Of course the Academy's current residents would have repurposed him as some sort of scholarly paternal figure without mention of the fact that he'd been the favored helping hand of powerful deities.

Like he would ever be caught hanging out with the students here, Adia thought, walking away from the statue to take in the rest of the room.

The Swamplands library—if you could call it that—consisted of a moldy box in a closet at the schoolhouse. And she'd read every book in it several dozen times. Once she got her job helping Elder Bunam, she'd been able to buy her own, but it was never enough. Even in the village bookstore, it was near impossible to find a book that *wasn't* missionary approved. But *this* library? It was incredible!

The plush burgundy carpet beckoned her to kick off her shoes, which she did. She let her toes sink into the carpet for a moment before walking past the shelves. She stopped when she came to a wall of atlases.

She'd studied every map of Zaria she could get her hands on back in her village. Not only had she always seemed to understand maps, she'd always instinctively known when certain islands and queendoms were drawn incorrectly. If the wrong lands were placed in the center of the world. Or if a kingdom was drawn twice as large as its actual mass. She'd taken to redrawing maps in her journal the way she felt was correct. She'd always considered it a little game. It was almost laughable that it took her causing an earthquake to realize that it wasn't a normal ability.

She took a few atlases that she'd never seen before off the shelf and piled them on a table, along with a pretty blue copy of a book about legends of Imo Mmiri. Maybe she'd have time to take a quick peek and read some stories about the mythical rain forest. She continued walking along the library shelves, only a little afraid of what she might find within them. Maybe these books would tell her how to stop being an ogbanje. Or maybe they'd tell her that removing an evil spirit wasn't possible. That it was just a darkness inside her that could never be exorcised.

Adia pulled down a thick book titled *The Ogbanje Next Door* and began to read, but it only contained example after example of ill-tempered spirits that reincarnated repeatedly, bringing their families endless misfortune, even ruin. And then, further along, ideas for how to *deal* with them, each more horrible than the last.

Her eyes filled with all the tears she'd held in since the earthquake, and she flung herself facedown on the couch, beating her fists into the cushions. This was officially more than she could handle. Whatever force she'd felt pushing her to come down here was either the wishful thinking of a desperate person or the Academy having a laugh at her expense. There were thousands of books in this library—even if the answers were in here somewhere, it could take her months to find them. Months she didn't have anymore.

"My entire life ruined because of a spoiled, angry brat," she said through her sobs. "I'll have nowhere else to go."

For the better part of an hour, she lay there crying and would have kept going if not for a sudden thump. Wiping her face, she tilted her head. She heard it again. Louder now. Footsteps.

I don't believe it, she thought. *Who's coming here now, when all I want to do is cry in peace?*

Her irritation was replaced with fear as she thought about her predicament. She couldn't imagine how much more trouble she would be in if she was discovered in a library that was undoubtedly off-limits to kitchen apprentices. If she got fired tomorrow, it would be bad enough, but if a Gold Hat on night patrol found her now and thought she was a thief, she might lose an arm.

She had to hide.

Bubbles was already ahead of her. He dashed inside a wooden cabinet behind one of the couches. It was small and she was long, but it was her best chance of avoiding the Gold Hats' machetes and keeping all her limbs. She flung herself inside after Bubbles, folding her body in on itself and pulling the doors shut just as someone entered the library.

Maybe I'll get lucky, Adia thought, chewing on the inside of her cheek. *Maybe it's a friendly staff member coming to do one last round of cleaning.*

She cautiously peeked through a crack in the cabinet to see who'd come in, then pulled her head back in horror. They weren't servants or teachers or students.

They weren't even human.

SEVEN

Adia covered her mouth to prevent herself from shrieking as she watched the three creatures arrange themselves in the room.

When the missionaries had first arrived in the Swamplands, Aunt Ife's wooden figures of the guardian Alusi were
thrown in a pile out back by the compost heap. It made Adia
sad to see them there, tossed in the mud as if they didn't
matter. A lot like she herself had felt when she first showed
up to her aunt and uncle's house, freshly orphaned. But Aunt
Ife and Uncle Eric had made it clear that if Adia or EJ tried
to rescue the wooden statues from their food grave, they'd
quickly come to regret it.

Adia had no intention of trying to save the statues. She'd
preferred to read stories about Imo Mmiri anyway. It was
EJ who'd been fascinated with the stars and the Alusi, especially horned Ikenga, the Alusi of victory. EJ had kept a small

statue of him hidden under his bed—Adia wasn't sure where he'd gotten it—as if some of Ikenga's strength would trickle into him and stop his seizures. Of course, Uncle Eric would have beat him if he'd found it, but EJ loved the little carving of Ikenga holding dual swords. Adia had accidentally stepped on it once, piercing her foot on the sharp horns carved out of the top of Ikenga's head.

Those horns were even more terrifying in person.

Adia couldn't believe it. As she had grown older, she'd accepted that the Alusi were mythical stories meant to explain the inexplainable: the odd properties of the wood that grew along the south side of the Ginian Sea, the powers of the shamans, how Olark the Tormentor had been so easily defeated five hundred years ago once the Alusi supposedly decided to help in the fight. Stories and myths. Except now she was trapped in a cupboard and *actual* Alusi were floating around the library.

Another one came into view. Her floor-length locs touched her feet and tiny sparks crackled in the air around her, and she carried a large staff covered in gold flowers, similar to the gold flowers woven through the crown on her head. Adia shivered. Beautiful as the Alusi was, the power coming off her was so strong it bordered on chaotic. Adia's head hurt to look at her—a clear sign that no one was supposed to lay eyes on these creatures—but she couldn't turn away. This had to be Gentle Ginikanwa, the divine daughter. Only right now she wasn't so gentle.

"I've had it!"

A burst of fire shot out of one of Ginikanwa's eyes. Adia clutched Bubbles and tried to burrow deeper into the cabinet. As the trail of fire rapidly approached, the temperature inside the cabinet rose by several degrees.

"Gini," Ikenga said, holding out a hand with outrageously long fingers. "Please don't burn down the room."

Water sprang from his fingers, not as a gush but as a smooth, ribbon-like wave. It met the fire and put it out without so much as a scorch mark left on the carpet.

Gini stopped setting things on fire. Instead she floated to the ground and kicked a trash bin, sending rubbish flying across the room.

Adia let out a squeak, then slapped a hand over her mouth. Hopefully if the Alusi noticed the sound, they would assume it was a mouse.

This was Ginikanwa? It wasn't possible. The divine daughter—or heretical myth according to the missionaries—defeated demons with nothing more than a song of love. She didn't kick rubbish bins and set things on fire! Adia wanted to weep. Forget the Gold Hats. She was going to be ended by a pyromaniac goddess she had never believed existed.

The smallest Alusi floated away from the flying trash and sat on the couch Adia had been sobbing on.

"Is this wet?" he muttered.

Adia watched, mortified, as he tried to mop up the dampness with his robes.

From his long beard and small stature, Adia could surmise that he was Mbari, the Alusi of art. His statue had been the tiniest in the pile, and yes, in the flesh, he was half the size of Ginikanwa. Adia shook her head. It was too much to process. It was good she'd skipped dinner; if there had been any food in her stomach, she might have thrown up. And Bubbles had done enough throwing up this week for both of them.

"The school really has fallen into decay," Mbari continued, wiping his hand on his robes. "So damp and musty."

"Of course it has," Gini said with an angry huff that Adia worried was going to be followed by more fire fingers. "What else would happen to a shamanic school with hardly a shaman in sight?"

"Lower your voice, Ginikanwa," Ikenga said, his voice deep and serious.

"Oh, no one will hear me. The students are all tucked away in their beds, fast asleep. It's why I called you down here."

Adia shook her head in exhaustion. She had thought the pull she'd felt to come down here was the Academy trying to help her find a safe space to hide. Clearly she'd just been drawn to getting into even more trouble.

"And would you stop pacing! You're making me dizzy," Mbari replied.

"You feel dizzy?" Gini snapped. "I feel like I'm about to explode. And we certainly don't have time for that. I can't deal with accidentally creating a new universe right now. Not when Olark has possessed the emperor of Zaria for over a year and not one person has noticed! He's choosing places that won't be missed, but the fires have already begun. Burned lands creeping up all over the place. And now the headmaster's even invited him to the Academy."

All thoughts of being discovered fell out of Adia's head. Fires? Those burned lands she'd seen from the boat. And Gini thought the person who had done that was *Olark* walking around in Darian's body?

"Something must be done," Gini snapped, shaking Adia from her shock. "Are we supposed to sit on our Star mountains—"

A throat cleared loudly. Gini flung Mbari an impatient glance.

"—or dwell in the Star mines," Gini added, and Mbari looked pacified, "and do nothing? Pretend this isn't happening? It's an abomination that the throne is now occupied by . . . by . . ." She was shaking in fury and her mouth seemed unable to form the words before she finally spat out, "Emperor Darian! Or I suppose I should call him Emperor Olark-as-Darian. After all, it's not the poor boy's fault that he went and got himself possessed."

Mbari stood up from the damp couch with a glare.

"And what exactly do you propose we do, Ginikanwa? The mortals are convinced Olark was destroyed. *We* convinced them! History has turned into mythology. Half of them don't even believe he ever existed!"

Adia couldn't argue with that. She'd always wondered whether Olark really was a shape-shifting fire demon or just a man who people had turned into an undefeatable monster.

It was more comforting to believe only a demon could commit all those atrocities than to accept it was a person just like them. But if Olark was still alive and possessing people five hundred years later, that meant he was clearly just as supernatural as the squabbling Alusi in front of her.

"Second," he said as he moved closer to Gini, "you saw the curse Olark spun when he took hold of Darian's mind. The monster made sure to spell it out for us in starlight across the night sky: '*Hear my words throughout the world and read them in the skies*'!"

"Do not repeat that curse in my presence, Mbari!" Ikenga thundered.

The cupboard rattled at the vibration of his fury, and Adia hugged Bubbles tight to try to stop herself from shaking too. Bubbles let out a pitiful meow. Thankfully no one on the other side of the cabinet heard him.

"He is right to speak it, Ikenga," Gini said, her voice weary. "Go on. You might as well finish."

Mbari continued, whispering now.

> "*Hear my words throughout the world*
> *And read them in the skies.*
> *No mortal will believe the truth,*
> *So do not think to try.*
> *If you tell them who I am,*
> *They'll simply think you've lied.*
> *If you tell them I am back,*
> *The thought will leave their mind.*"

"I tested it out on the headmaster a few days ago, since he's been cozying up to the emperor," Gini said.

"Gini," Mbari groaned.

"Oh, it's fine," she sniffed. "I was in disguise. I mentioned that Darian might not be who he seems. That he's Olark returned. It was quite the spectacle. First, he started screaming at me for telling such a lie. Then he was quite disoriented, like someone who'd been hit on the head and forgot their own name for a minute."

"All right, then. So let's not bother trying to talk to the mortals any further about possession or curses," Ikenga said thoughtfully. "You know how fond I am of them, but they *are* incredibly simple-minded. Very small brains, you see."

Gini and Mbari nodded their agreement, and Adia tried not to feel offended.

"I've been looking at the decisions that Darian—that is, Olark-as-Darian," Ikenga corrected, "has made as of late. They are positively incompetent. Surely his advisers and the wisewomen of this world have noticed their so-called emperor is behaving like a complete imbecile."

Mbari snorted and shook his curly gray head.

"You're thinking like an Alusi, Ikenga. These are *mortals*. The higher your position of power, the more you are allowed to be incompetent. As far as I can tell, it's expected. A king or queen or emperor can do things and behave in ways that would get a kitchen maid removed from their post."

Adia shrank into the closet at that particular analogy.

"Which is why we have to intervene," Gini said. "Even

if the odds are against us. I have no idea how we'll get close enough to exorcise Olark from Darian. I can't get within fifty feet without him knowing and sending innocent, mindwashed people to fight me—he knows I would never hurt them just to get to him. But I still mean to find a way. This is my fault, after all." Gini headed over to the tables covered with maps and atlases. She tapped a piece of parchment that was spread open on one of the tables, and though Adia couldn't see it from her hiding spot, she remembered it was a nautical map of the Ginian Sea. "I'm heading to the Serpentine Pass tomorrow. There's only one object strong enough to contain Olark once I exorcise the boy, and I mean to find it."

"The blood-stained stone?" Ikenga said slowly. "Gini, are you sure about this? You know how volatile it can be."

Adia frowned. In all her reading, she'd never heard of any blood-stained stone.

"I'm sure," Gini said. "But despite being the wisest and most clever of the three of us, I cannot act unless the decision is unanimous."

"You forgot the most humble," Mbari muttered.

If Gini heard that, she chose to ignore it.

"We all know that if he isn't stopped he'll burn the surviving half of Zaria down to finish what he started. We all know what those fires mean. What he's trying to find. And he has to be stopped before he does. So do I have your support?"

Mbari sighed and waved his hand in agreement.

Ikenga looked miserable, but he nodded his horned head as well.

"Fine," he said. "This is your mess, so I guess that makes it yours to clean up. But you need to act fast. You know what will happen if you're away from the stars for too long. That's why Mbari and I came down here. You're getting dangerously close to surpassing your limits. I know this is personal to you; don't pretend it's not. But if you stay here for much longer, Zaria will have a far greater problem to deal with than Olark."

Whatever that meant, it didn't seem to concern Gini.

"Don't worry, I have it under control," she said dismissively.

"Sure you do," Mbari said, rolling his eyes. It was unsettling for Adia to see such a human expression on a star being. "And only travel by mortal means while you're here to conserve your power. Take boats, use doors, ten toes on the ground at all times."

"I have transportation taken care of," Gini said. "I'll set sail on a midday ship tomorrow and connect with Ferryman from there."

"Very well," Ikenga said. "We'll see you off tomorrow, and then we'll return home. But if you take too long, we'll be back."

The Alusi stood and headed to the door. Ikenga paused. Adia held her breath, scared they'd spotted her, but instead he fixed Gini and Mbari with a pointed stare.

"And remember to always use your mortal names when we're in this realm," he said. "Even when there are no humans present. Remember when the two of you were squabbling a few thousand years ago and Mbari accidentally called Gini by her true name? The power of the vibration turned a desert into a sea."

Gini sniffed. "Yes, that was very badly done of you, Mbari." The purple stardust surrounding Mbari turned red. "She didn't seem to mind when they named the damned thing after her," the smallest Alusi grumbled as he followed after them. "The Ginian Sea indeed."

Adia was once again in an empty room. There was no sign of the Alusi, but she was too frightened to leave her hiding space. She replayed the entire conversation over and over again, word for word, trying to come up with a rational explanation for what she'd just heard—but there was none.

Should she try to send a message to the capital? Warn them that a demon was on the throne? She's seen those new burned lands from the ship. That was physical proof that the emperor was sneaking around, destroying Zaria for who knows what reason. Maybe if she got back on that boat and pointed them out to the ship's captain, they could send word that something was amiss. Or maybe if she told Maka or . . .

"Wait a minute," she groaned. "I can't tell anyone anything."

The words of Olark's curse came rushing back to her.

If you tell them who I am
They'll simply think you've lied.
If you tell them I am back
The thought will leave their mind.

But nothing's left my mind, she thought in confusion. And

she wished it would. How was she supposed to walk around knowing something like this? "Oh!" she cried as the closet doors flung themselves open.

The wretched piece of furniture wobbled, then tipped itself over, sending Adia tumbling out in an ungraceful heap. Bubbles yowled as he went flying. Before Adia could right herself, books flew off the shelves, pelting her in the head as they whizzed around the room.

"Ow!" Adia yelped, jumping up and ducking behind a couch before anything else in the room could attack her.

"Is this my punishment for eavesdropping?" she groaned, rubbing her head. "It was an accident, all right? I didn't mean to overhear. It was . . ."

Her voice trailed off.

If you tell them I am back.

If you tell them . . .

If you tell . . .

Adia's eyes went wide.

"They didn't *tell* me anything!" she realized in shock. "I eavesdropped!"

A thick book hurled itself at her head, and she glared at it in indignation.

"Accidentally!"

The sun would be up soon. She'd spent the entire night in the library, trying to make sense of what had happened. As a personal rule, Adia didn't believe in anything she couldn't see. It was why she'd refused to accept that EJ was dead even when the empire's missionaries brought his body back wrapped in white cloth. She didn't see a corpse, so it wasn't true. She had waited for him every day for a month at the swamp, confident that he would show up having escaped from an alligator's den or chagrined that he'd dragged out this "I've gone missing" prank for too long.

A swamp was hardly an ideal place for swimming—the water was too murky and the plants too thick. But that had never bothered EJ. He was the braver one, but everything else about them was so similar, down to their matching silver-rimmed glasses. But no amount of persuasion could keep her cousin out of the dark waters. EJ had needed to swim like most people needed to breathe. She remembered their last conversation. Her shaking her head as he bounded toward the lake.

"That's why I only swim here when I'm with you," EJ said as he handed his glasses to her before wading into the water. "You're good luck. All the plants move out of the way like some great hand is holding them back. I have a clear path. So relax and read one of the three books I know you have in your bag, all right?"

It was their ritual. He'd dive in as she stood on the shore, nervously waiting for him to resurface, terrified he'd be dragged to the bottom by a visiting alligator. Then he'd pop up and wave and she would lie down to read until he exhausted himself. No alligator could take down EJ. He always came back.

Until he didn't.

Even when the missionaries returned with his shrouded body, she still went to the water, expecting him to pop up with a cheerful wave and tell her it had all been a prank. She wished he were here now. EJ would help her make sense of what she'd overheard. Because there was no denying what she'd seen.

The map library was a mess. Books and atlases flung all over the place. She'd been too scared to go back to her room and so had spent a restless night buried in maps, trying to distract her brain. She ran her hands over one of them. The Serpentine Pass snaked its way through the bottom, ending at the corner.

"There's nothing beyond it," she said, baffled. Where could Gini be planning to go? *Unless . . . No, it couldn't be real.*

The Horrorbeyond. Olark's old lair.

Grown-ups in the Swamplands loved to threaten to leave bad children on the side of the road for garbage disposal with a note that read, *This child is more rotten than a mushy mango full of maggots. Please throw them away in the Horrorbeyond. They can be a snack for the wraiths, or a new playmate for Hiroma, the headless girl.*

Adia had never in her wildest dreams considered that the Horrorbeyond might really lie at the edge of the snake-infested Serpentine. But she'd never thought she'd see ancient gods in the flesh either.

"Maybe it was all a strange dream," she said, giving denial a try. "A really vivid nightmare."

A nightmare made a lot more sense than Zaria being under the rule of an emperor possessed by a demon.

"Just a nightmare," she said more confidently, standing up and stretching. But then she spotted an overturned trash bin and garbage all over the floor. Right where Ginikanwa had kicked it.

It *wasn't* a nightmare. She took a deep breath and climbed back up the dust-covered stairs. She'd learned something shocking, seen something unbelievable. But as much as she wanted to stay hidden in the library forever, there was no escaping what was waiting for her. It was time to deal with whatever Mallorie had in store.

EIGHT

"Good morning," Adia said hesitantly as she walked into the kitchen.

A few of the cooks nodded, but most paid her no mind as they rushed around. Everything seemed normal. No one had any idea they were whipping the kitchen into shape for the arrival of a demon. Even without a curse to make them forget, who would believe her if she tried to tell them what she had seen last night? Mallorie wouldn't need to do anything; Maka would probably send Adia packing on account of her not being of sound mind.

Adia sighed and went to her station to tackle the pile of coconuts that needed to be hacked open, but Lebechi whistled for her.

"You're on serving duty today," Lebechi said, handing her a tray. "I don't know why, but the kitchen is in a good mood for once. The stoves are working and everything!"

"That's good," Adia mumbled, too distracted to fake enthusiasm. "Er . . . did Maka say anything about me?" Adia had asked the same question each morning since her run-in with Mallorie three days ago, but now she really needed to know what was happening. Would she even be here when Darian arrived?

"No. Why do you keep asking me that?"

"No reason," Adia said quickly.

Lebechi raised an eyebrow but let it go. "You're covering the faculty wing today too, so don't dawdle. Say, are you feeling all right? You look queasy."

"I'm fine," Adia said weakly, but Lebechi had already moved on to catch a frying pan that was flying through the air.

Adia managed to get through the morning tea service without incident. She was heading back from the faculty wing to the kitchen when she was startled by loud banging. She turned around and winced. Mallorie Amber, wearing long diamond earrings and a smirk on her face, pounded her fist against the headmaster's door.

"Come in!" the headmaster shouted from the other side. But Mallorie didn't enter. Instead she squeezed her eyes closed.

What's she waiting for? Adia wondered, pushing up her glasses.

Mallorie's eyes opened, and tears began spilling down her cheeks. She pulled out a pocket mirror, examined her watery eyes, and gave her reflection a smug smile. Then she snapped the mirror shut and fixed her face into a sad pout before opening the door and disappearing into the headmaster's office.

It took Adia a minute to process what she'd just seen, but when she did, she was furious.

"Oh, what a hateful girl," Adia muttered in disgust, "and what a performance. Crying on command? Who does that?"

She returned to the kitchen but couldn't focus on anything. Baking the morning bread wasn't at the forefront of her mind, and it showed. Possessed emperors, fires no one was noticing, Mallorie in the headmaster's office. She was a mess.

"What has gotten into you?" Lebechi exclaimed when Adia spilled flour onto the table instead of into a bowl for the second time that morning.

"I'm so sorry, Lebechi."

She quickly salvaged what she could of the flour, redoubling her attempts to focus.

"I thought we were going to have a good day, but things are getting foul again," Lebechi said with a sigh as she helped free a panicked dishwasher from the giant cobweb that had him trapped.

"At least the stove's still working," Adia said.

"For now," Lebechi said, rubbing her hands on her apron. "Come with me. I need your help in the vegetable garden. We need to pick more callaloo for today's stew."

Adia quietly followed Lebechi through the tall maize field, but after a few minutes, she couldn't stay silent any longer.

"Lebechi?" she asked. "What's your opinion of Emperor Darian?"

"The emperor?" Lebechi repeated, handing Adia the basket as the cornfield gave way to the field greens. "Well, it's only been a year since he took the throne. But he's won every battle he's been in. I mean, he's also *started* every battle he's been in. Ruthless for someone so young. He's only thirteen, you know."

Adia didn't know. She knew the emperor was young, but his battle prowess at thirteen made a lot more sense after what she'd learned last night. *Darian* wasn't the one calling the shots.

"Why do you ask?" Lebechi asked with a sly grin. "You have a crush on him like everyone else here?"

"No, no," Adia said quickly as she picked the callaloo. "I've never paid him any mind but . . ."

She was going to burst if she didn't tell somebody about what she'd learned last night. Nami had already proven he was useless, just standing there, letting Mallorie go off on her. Which made Lebechi the closest thing she had to a friend here. She had to try.

"What would you say if I told you that Darian *wasn't* Darian," she said, the words tumbling out of her. "That he was possessed? By Olark."

Lebechi tripped over her skirt. She knocked the basket from Adia's hand with a hard strike. Adia stared at the spilled greens in shock, then backed up when Lebechi loomed over her looking furious.

"Olark? Have you lost your mind? I should have Maka toss you out on your ear for having the audacity to spout such lies and wickedness! She should send you to the Horrorbeyond and let Hiroma have you! Olark is gone and can never come back, and for you to stand here and spout such vile, insensible, ludicrous things—"

"Lebechi," Adia cried, alarmed at her friend's sudden rage. "It was just something I overheard—"

"Overheard lies!" Lebechi shouted. She ripped her wrap from her head and slammed it to the ground, beads of sweat flying off her as she hurled insults at Adia. "Nothing but despicable, evil lies, spread by a hateful, wicked girl who—"

"Lebechi, calm down!" Adia cried.

She grabbed her hands and held them down.

"Stop it! Pull yourself together!"

As quickly as it had come, the fevered fury left Lebechi's eyes and was replaced by a dull expression as she stared above Adia's head for a moment.

"Sorry, Adia, what were you saying? My mind wandered off for a bit."

Adia gaped at her. Lebechi's appearance was completely disheveled, but her eyes were calm.

"And stars save me, how did my wrap come undone?" she said, touching her head. "Help me tie it. You do know how to tie a wrap, yes?"

"I—I do, but it won't be pretty." Shaken from what she had just witnessed, Adia moved to retie Lebechi's scarf.

This was what Gini had described. The curse in action.

"No worries about that. I'm here to cook, not be pretty," Lebechi said. "Just make sure my hair is off my face. And how did all the vegetables fall out of the basket?"

Lebechi was too confused to be angry as she stared at the mess she'd forgotten she made.

"Oh, great. Something stung my face. It better not have been a tsetse fly. I was bit when I first got here and caught the sleeping sickness. I had a fever for three weeks, and Maka didn't show me a drop of sympathy, can you believe it? Her own cousin."

Lebechi droned on about Maka's unsympathetic nature as they walked through the fields, but Adia was too shaken to do more than make occasional sounds of agreement. Lebechi showed no signs of having another outburst. It was exactly as the curse said—everything Adia had tried to tell her had completely left her mind. Unfortunately, Adia's mind felt like it was about to leak out of her head with all the unwanted information flooding her brain.

They returned to the kitchen, but Adia didn't have time to process what just happened with Lebechi. A Gold Hat was talking to Maka.

Oh no.

Mallorie had really done it. Instead of wasting her time trying to tell Lebechi about Olark, maybe she should have admitted what happened with Mallorie. Not that Lebechi could save her, but maybe she wouldn't have felt as helpless and alone in this moment if she'd had someone to hold her hand.

"Oh, what now?" Lebechi muttered, unaware of Adia's growing panic.

"Chef Esiniri," the Gold Hat said. "The headmaster requires your presence. There's been a complaint about one of your staff."

The kitchen came to a screeching halt. Adia was amazed her legs held her up when, inside, she wanted to fall to the floor in disgrace.

"A complaint about—" Maka sputtered as she whipped around to glare at everyone in the kitchen. "All right, out with it. Which one of you didn't know better than to hide when you saw Mallorie Amber coming?"

Adia's head jerked up in surprise.

"How—how do you know it's about Mallorie?" she asked in a tiny voice.

Maka sighed. "Ah, of course. Is that why you've been such a mess the last few days? Well, no matter. It's my fault. You're new. I should have warned you."

Maka took off her apron.

"I'll be back in a few minutes. The rest of you, make sure Adia doesn't faint. Everything will be fine."

When Maka left, Adia turned to everyone, letting hope creep in. Was her Mallorie Amber encounter really not as bad as she thought? She'd completely given up on finding a shaman to help her, but if she wasn't getting thrown out, that meant she could snoop around and learn more about Olark and see what he looked like in the flesh. *Or Darian's flesh*, she thought with a shudder.

"Oh, you poor thing," one of the older girls said.

"No wonder little sister's been dropping dishes for days," a dishwasher said with a sympathetic look.

Lebechi threw an arm around Adia. "My first month here? I called Mallorie *Mallorie*. She ordered the headmaster to fire me for my insolence."

Adia frowned in confusion. "But . . . her name *is* Mallorie."

"Yeah, no kidding," Lebechi said, rolling her eyes. "But that week? She insisted the great spirits came to her and said her true name was Mahalia and everyone had to call her that from now on."

More than a few people in the kitchen snickered.

"Great spirits?" Adia muttered. "You mean the spirits of the people who died mining the diamond fields for her necklaces?"

Now the snickers turned into outright laughter, and the knot in her stomach loosened.

"That's better," Lebechi said with a grin. "Show some attitude. We can't let these people turn us into drudges."

The boy who was always near tears whenever Maka came too close spoke in a shy voice. "My second month, I saw one of Mallorie's rivals slip something into her tea. I warned her. So she wouldn't get sick, you know?"

"Well, of course you did," Adia exclaimed, thinking back to the orientation dinner. "What else were you supposed to do? Let her get poisoned?"

"Apparently, yes," the boy said with a bewildered expression, "because Mallorie slapped me in the face for daring to insult her friend. She ended up in the infirmary for a week from whatever her *dear sister* put in her drink."

This time Adia joined in the laughter as she remembered Mallorie covering herself in green mud to rid herself of red splotches.

"The headmaster knows that if he fired everyone Mallorie told him to fire, *he'd* be the one cooking and scrubbing the toilets, because there would be no servants left," Lebechi said. "That girl's eyes are constantly looking for someone to yell at. Like that'll justify the anger that lives inside her. But the headmaster has to pacify her since her father donates a ton of money to the Academy. We have to keep her happy. You'll most likely just get suspended for a few weeks."

Adia's newfound relief deflated. If she was gone for weeks, she'd never see the Alusi again, let alone get a look at the emperor. Her shoulders drooped as she stared at the ground in disappointment and humiliation.

"It's embarrassing and completely unfair," Lebechi quickly said, "but it's also kind of nice. You'll have a vacation after only a few weeks of work! I'm certain your family will be happy to see you."

Adia was certain they would not.

Maka came back into the kitchen. Everyone rushed back to their stations, giving Adia encouraging grins and thumbs-up.

"Besides," Lebechi whispered, "a battle with Mallorie is a rite of passage. You're one of us now. We're family." She gave

Adia a wink as she went back to her stew station.

Family?

She didn't believe Lebechi meant that. It was just one of those things people say. Adia had learned that lesson years ago when a new family had moved to the Swamplands. The daughter was in the same grade as Adia, and for one week, when she didn't know any better, the new girl had declared Adia her best friend. By the end of the week, after being properly informed by the other students that Adia Kelbara was *not* the sort of girl you were friends with, the girl never spoke another word to her. So she wasn't going to get her hopes up. EJ was still the only friend she'd ever had. And EJ was gone.

She stood with her hands behind her back as Maka approached. Adia took a deep breath. Suspension wasn't so bad. Well, it wasn't great, and it was definitely embarrassing. And there was no way she could go back to the Swamplands. But she could explore nearby towns. Process the fact that she had seen Alusi in a library. Maybe Gini would have healed Darian by the time she came back and everyone would have a story to tell about whatever went down. It could be worse. It could be—

"Expulsion," Maka said with a bewildered shake of her head.

Stars swam in front of Adia's eyes. Stars like the ones that swam around Gini's pupils. The kitchen fell silent.

"Ex-expulsion?" Adia managed to wheeze out.

Maka awkwardly put a hand on her shoulder. The pity in

the head chef's eyes made Adia feel even more embarrassed.

"I tried to get it down to suspension on account of it being my fault for not warning you," Maka said. "It's always been a suspension! But the best I could do this time was get the headmaster to pay for your ship passage and enough money to get you safely home. You should catch the afternoon ship. Better to get you out of Mallorie's sight as soon as possible."

Maka held out a small satchel of coins, her face apologetic. Adia stared at it in shock for a minute before wordlessly taking the money and putting it into her pocket.

"Maka!" Lebechi said, rushing over. "This is going overboard! It's Mallorie Amber. The headmaster knows what she's like. Go back and tell him to give Adia a week's suspension, same as we always get!"

"I can't," Maka said, obviously exasperated. "Mallorie really has it in for her. She made a lot of threats about telling her father to take back money if the headmaster doesn't have her permanently removed. And she made some pretty wild accusations too, about Adia having dark powers."

Adia's stomach dropped.

"Dark powers?" Lebechi repeated. "Who? This girl who's too sensitive to eat meat? You should see how queasy she gets when I'm plucking the chickens."

"She says Adia was causing her shamanic tools to act up and brought dark energy into her room. Nonsense, I know," Maka said when everyone in the kitchen grumbled, "but Adia could end up in actual danger if she doesn't get out of here, and fast. We don't need her getting tossed into the dungeon.

"Here." Maka shoved a basket at her. "Take some food for the ship. Who knows what they'll feed you."

Something rubbed against her leg. Bubbles looked up at her and purred. Of course he would show up at the mention of food. She blinked back tears. Was it even fair to keep dragging him around with her when all she did was cause chaos? She'd miss him, but he'd be happier and safer here with the other kitchen cats and Lebechi. Maybe she could have been happy here too.

"I'm sorry, Adia. I wish there was something I could do but . . ."

Adia didn't know what to say. Maka wasn't the one who should be apologizing.

Adia having dark powers was the only thing Mallorie Amber hadn't fabricated out of thin air. What had she been thinking, coming here? That she could fix whatever was wrong with her and change her future? Everyone in the kitchen looked miserable. Of course they did—she brought misery wherever she went. No wonder the school had burst at the seams the second she arrived, boards hurling themselves into the woods. It was trying to protect itself from an ogbanje.

She gasped. Her expulsion had almost made her forget about Olark-as-Darian for a minute. Another evil thing was set to arrive in a few days' time. An evil that sounded far worse than her.

"Adia?" Lebechi said.

Adia might not have broken her own curse, but she'd broken Olark's. She knew he was alive and well and possessing the body of the emperor. It sounded like the Alusi had some plan to stop him, and maybe no one would even notice what was going on when Olark-as-Darian arrived— according to the curse, they wouldn't even remember if they did see anything—but gods and demons sneaking around the school at all hours? Maybe getting out of here *was* the best option.

"It's all right," she said quietly. "I understand."

"Mallorie won't be at the Academy forever. Maybe you can come work here when you're older."

Everyone was still giving her concerned looks. They may have been nicer than her aunt and uncle and Ericson, but Lebechi was wrong. They weren't her family or friends. She didn't have friends. She didn't have anyone. She had gotten herself into this mess, and she would get herself out.

"Maybe," she said with a shrug, aiming for a nonchalant tone. She couldn't linger in their pity and her own embarrassment for another minute. "I'll send word when I'm back home. Thanks for everything."

"Adia, wait—" Lebechi said, but she rushed out of the kitchen.

Students were all over campus now, knocking servants out of their way as they rushed to class. Even though the servants were being shoved aside, it was the students who seemed clumsy to her, awkwardly carrying their new rattles and staffs. She couldn't bear to be around them, not even to walk to her room and pick up her sad little bag. At least she could put her knowledge of the elaborate secret tunnels and passageways of the Academy to good use. She might not be using them to snoop around and figure out what the demon emperor was up to, but she could use them to avoid anyone seeing her cry as she left the school in disgrace.

NINE

..

Port Warri was the busiest seaport in Zaria. At least it was supposed to be. But there were no fish sellers out and no vendors hawking trinkets to people about to set sail. There were barely any people at all. Just crates. Piles and piles of red and blue crates.

Maybe most people catch the early morning ship, Adia thought.

She spotted a sign with a list of destinations. Two old men sat in front of it, hunched over a chessboard. She should just buy a ticket for whatever ship would take her as far away from here as possible. Forget what she learned and put as much distance between her and the Academy before Olark-as-Darian showed up. It wasn't like there was anything she could do with this information anyway. Lebechi having a fit at the mention of Olark's name proved that.

"Where are you headed?" one of the men snapped, taking her from her thoughts. "You're interrupting our game.

Not that you care, but I'm about to win in six moves."

She opened her mouth, then paused.

Going back to the Swamplands wasn't possible. But was hopping around looking for another place to work that much better an option? The exhaustion she'd felt over the past few weeks hit her all at once. There was the dangerous matter of Olark and the Alusi, but there was also the dangerous matter of *her*. Mallorie had got one thing right in her smear campaign—something dark *had* come out of Adia. The vase breaking might not have been as destructive as the earthquake, but just like Uncle Eric had said, there was an undeniable wrongness about her. And she had no idea how to make it stop. Which meant no matter where she ran, she'd always end up in the same situation—unwanted, alone, and cast out.

The man whistled sharply, startling her. Did he think she was a dog?

"I said, where are you headed?"

"Sorry. Which ship is sailing for . . . ?" Adia trailed off as an idea began to form.

"I'm waiting," the man snapped.

She ignored him. *She* might not have any idea how to get rid of the evil inside her. But there was someone currently stomping around Zaria who did—Gini. The Alusi might have come to exorcise Darian, but maybe if Adia stuck by her, she could see how an exorcism worked and then replicate the process on herself. All she had to do was stay close to Gini and not get caught.

She knew where Gini was headed. This could be the answer to all her problems.

"Which ships sail through the Serpentine Pass?" she said quickly, before she could overthink her new plan.

"Only one. Head over to the Macobar Jetty dock and you'll find it," he said. "Either pay the fare or move along."

Adia quickly handed over some of the money Maka had given her. The man ripped a ticket off a roll, handing it to her. She thanked him and began to walk away. Then she paused.

"By the way," she said, calling over her shoulder, "*he's* going to beat *you* in three moves."

The man sputtered as he stared down at the chessboard.

"What—what—" His opponent chuckled and tipped his hat to her as she dashed off.

As the ship left the dock, Adia took in the smell of the sea. She didn't love the water like EJ had, but she liked that it could take her anywhere in the world. She knew she should start looking for Gini, but for one moment she would embrace having complete freedom. No family, no chores, no year of practicality. Just her, the sea, an exorcism to sneak her way into, and—

"ADIA!"

She flinched at the cheerful, booming voice. There could be only one person on this ship who would know her name. Only one person who could be so *loud*. And she wasn't in the mood to talk to him.

"What are you doing on this ship?" Nami exclaimed, rushing to her side. "The water sure is rocky, isn't it? I'm half-scared I'll get tossed overboard. And I can't swim, so you'd have to save me! Can you swim? Hey! Where are you going?"

He chased after her as she walked. It would have been better if he thought she had run off like those Academy students who got sick of the school. At least it didn't matter now if anyone ever found the broken vase she'd hidden.

"Adia, wait! What happened?" Nami jumped in front of her, forcing her to come to a stop.

She fixed him with an icy stare. "What do you think happened? Mallorie got me expelled!"

The cheerful grin that seemed like a permanent fixture on Nami's face fell. He reached out a hand and put it on her shoulder.

"I didn't know. That's . . . that's . . ."

"Perfect?" she said in a dull voice, shrugging his hand off her.

Nami turned red. He ran a hand through his hair. "No, of course not. It's—"

"How I'll learn?"

"Well, no. I guess that came across as a pretty thoughtless thing to say. I only meant that . . ."

"That everything happens for a reason?"

"Adia, I'm trying to apologize! Are you all right? Do you have somewhere to go? You could always come with me back to the capital to drop off Mallorie's things."

A twinge of guilt pinched her heart. None of this was Nami's fault. Deep down she knew he didn't deserve her coldness. Still, she hardened her face. She was sensible enough to know that her story didn't end with being rescued by the prince and whisked off to a palace. She wasn't even being offered a prince, just a wannabe Gold Hat with a habit of putting his foot in his mouth.

"Don't worry about it, Nami. It's not like we're friends. You didn't say anything while Mallorie went off on me, and now you're carting around her old clothes."

"I *couldn't* say anything!" Nami said, but she took some satisfaction in his guilty expression. "Even if I'd wanted to, what good would it have done? I'd have gotten tossed out too!"

He was right. But she wasn't going to admit it.

She suddenly felt exhausted. Too exhausted to be angry. Too many things were happening—Alusi, demons, expulsion, Nami's irritating presence.

"Just leave me alone," she sighed.

She walked off, not wanting to look at his crestfallen face for another second. She was so distracted that she didn't notice someone was in her path until she crashed into them.

"I'm sorry," she said, then froze.

Ginikanwa.

Looking . . . mortal. Her face was still relatively the same, but the Alusi had done something to herself—she no longer glowed with stardust, and both her feet were firmly planted on the ground, not floating above it. Her hair was piled on top of her head instead of pooling at her feet, and she wore a colorfully patterned print outfit like everyone else in Zaria. She could pass for a young noblewoman. Extraordinarily beautiful, but mortal enough.

"I—" Adia tried to speak but withered under Gini's annoyed gaze. She quickly stepped to the side, and the Alusi swept past her without so much as a nod of acknowledgment. *Everyone* stepped to the side as Gini walked by, instinctually behaving as though they were in the presence of a queen. One sailor was even in the middle of a bow before he realized what he was doing and straightened up in confusion.

This was Gini's idea of inconspicuous travel? Adia sighed as the Alusi headed below deck, no doubt to lock herself in her room. But then Gini paused on the steps. Adia gulped as the Alusi marched forward, but Gini wasn't walking toward her. Instead, she put her hands on the rail and stared out into the sea. Adia followed her gaze. There was nothing but water and the surrounding woodlands. . . . No. Something else was out there. She pushed up her glasses. It was so faint you might not spot it if you weren't looking, but Adia could make out an orange glow through the dense trees.

Flames.

Gini's eyes narrowed. She was the picture of elegant fury as she spun around and stormed down the stairs, disappearing below deck. Adia remained where she was until the burning forest faded from view as the boat sailed on. Olark-as-Darian really was quietly and determinedly razing Zaria to the ground.

But why? she wondered.

In the library, Gini had said the fires had some purpose. Maybe it had something to do with the project Nami said Darian was working on. But what purpose could fires have other than creating a barren world of smoke and ash?

Adia spent the next two days avoiding Nami's gloomy face and keeping an eye on the incognito Alusi. It was a fascinating thing, watching a goddess pretend to be a human. Gini spent most of the morning below deck in her quarters, so there was nothing for Adia to do except bide her time until she could get close to this exorcism and learn how to do one on herself. She should have grabbed a few books from the Academy library. Instead she watched as dolphins jumped at the bow of the boat; as the clouds gathered overhead, threatening rain but never delivering on it; and as passengers moved between their cabins and the galley, all entirely clueless that their emperor was possessed, a goddess was on the ship, and an ogbanje had inserted herself into all of it.

Someone's yelling spilled across the deck, shaking Adia from her thoughts.

"Gini."

She moved in the direction of Gini's voice, which was growing more irritated by the second.

Adia edged closer, ducking behind a pile of precariously stacked crates of Drops when she spotted her. Gini was staring down the ship's captain.

"I *know* where my stop is," Gini yelled, pointing to a run-down-looking dock in the distance. "And it's there."

"Well, actually," the captain said, giving Gini a conde-scending look, "you're wrong about that. You don't want to get off there, trust me. Nothing but a wasteland."

"Are you telling me that *I'm* wrong about where I want to go? Because I see a dock over there as clearly as I see that furry thing on your head that I suppose you call a hat."

"I'm saying you've made a mistake," the captain said with a glare as he adjusted the dead animal on his head. "Yes, there's a dock there, but that village is abandoned. There was a drought five years back, and the land's never been the same. Completely untenable. The people moved on. If I leave you there, you'll only end up stranded until another ship passes by. And they'd only see you if you built yourself a signal fire.

"Now," the captain said with a placating smile, "*do* you know how to build a fire?"

It happened so briefly that if Adia hadn't known who Gini was, she would have assumed it was just a trick of the light. That it was the sun reflecting off the water that made it look like the top of the captain's furry hat was on fire.

The fire disappeared as quickly as it came, but bits of smoke rose from the captain's head and he frowned.

"Do you smell something burning?" he asked.

"Burning?" Gini asked, eyes wide. "Not at all."

She put her hand on the captain's arm and gave him a dazzling smile. He was so flustered that he let Gini steer him in the direction of the helmsman.

"Thank you, Captain. Your concern for my safety is touching. So *very* touching. But I assure you that island is *exactly* where I need to be. Now, if you would be so good as to tell the helmsman to pull into shore, I'll be right on time for my little appointment. I'm there to inspect the land, you see. Checking to see if the soil hasn't become a bit more . . . tenable."

"What? Oh, yes, yes, of course," the captain said, reaching up to pat his burnt hat. "Did it get hot all of a sudden to you?"

"Oh, who can tell when one's on the sea, directly in the sun!" Gini said with a chime-like laugh. "Everything about being on this vessel is so hideous, is it not?"

"Hideous?" the captain repeated incredulously as Gini kept pushing him forward.

"Yes, quite hideous. Now, to the helmsman we go, Captain," Gini said. "I mustn't be late."

"Yes, of course," the captain said as he approached the helm, looking as dazed as Adia felt.

The sunny smile faded from Gini's face as soon as the captain wasn't looking at her. It was replaced with a glare and smoke—actual smoke—coming out of her ears.

Adia stood up so fast that the pile of luggage she'd been hiding behind toppled over. Gini was on the move. And if she was serious about following the Alusi, she needed to be on the move too.

"Hey!" said an annoyed sailor.

"Sorry, sorry," Adia called out as she raced to her cabin.

She flung open the door and ran in to grab her bag. It held next to nothing—just a few dresses and the meager change she had left after buying her ticket—but it was all she owned in the world. She pulled the bag over her shoulder. Then her hand stilled on the door.

It wasn't too late to turn back around. She could always get off at the next stop. Go back to her original plan of finding work somewhere instead of following Gini.

The ship's horn blew, signaling they were about to dock. If she was going to go after Gini, she had to move. Now.

By the time she returned to the deck, the ship had pulled into shore. Almost everyone on board leaned over the side, shaking their heads in disbelief as Gini got off. Several sailors snickered at the rich young lady strutting off the boat like a queen. Adia waited until Gini was off the plank, then followed after her.

"Hey!" a sailor cried out. "This isn't a stop, girl! That lady's being wild getting off here!"

Adia ignored the crew's panicked yelling, as well as Nami, who was waving frantically from the deck, also yelling something she couldn't hear.

Her nose wrinkled as her feet hit the mud. She knew what droughts looked like, and it wasn't this. And they certainly didn't smell like this. She jumped as a hot gust of sulfurous yellow gas erupted from a spot to her left, almost burning her legs. Untenable soil was right. Nothing would grow in a place like this, but it wasn't because of any drought.

Adia took off her head tie and held it up against her nose

to try to block out the smell of rotting eggs. She should tell Mallorie about this spot. The spoiled brat could cover herself in plow mud to her heart's content. Adia spotted Gini up ahead and discreetly followed her through the bushy flora.

Gini walked with purpose and was so fast Adia could barely keep up. After an hour of trailing after her, she was tired and hungry. Just when she thought she would have to stop to rest, Gini came to a halt.

Adia dove headfirst into a bush, hiding in the dense brush. They must have walked to the north side of the island, judging from the sun's position and the tide. There was nothing on the small beach except a rickety boat that was so decrepit it looked like it could sink right there on the sand.

Mushrooms were growing on it, she noted in dismay. *That's* how Gini planned to row herself to the Horrorbeyond?

A lone star was visible in the sky. Alusia. It was so bright that it was always visible, even when the sun was up. Gini raised her hand and pointed at the star from where she came.

Whatever Gini had done on the ship to dull her appearance fell away. Now that Adia wasn't squinting at her through a crack in a cupboard, Gini was even more dazzling than she had been in the library. Adia's eyes burned from the brightness of the stardust illuminating Gini's dark brown skin. She closed them for a moment to adjust. When she opened them again, Gini was no longer alone on the shore. A tall person in a bright fuchsia cloak stood next to her. Adia stumbled back. They'd appeared out of nowhere.

"Ferryman," Gini said briskly. "I'll need you to take

me down the Serpentine Pass. I need to enter the Horror-beyond."

Adia leaned forward, but she couldn't hear what the hooded figure said.

"Yes, of course it's just me," Gini replied with a raised eyebrow. "Why would you think I was traveling with someone? Do you see anyone else . . . ?"

Her voice trailed off, and a deep frown settled on her flawless face. The Alusi sniffed the air and turned, walking toward the bushes, sparks of fire popping up near her feet with every step.

Realizing how dangerous a situation she was in, Adia began to back up, but her ankle snagged on something.

She looked down and saw an agrias vine wrapping itself around her leg.

"Not now, you wretched thing," she hissed, clawing at her ankle trying to free herself from the creeping vine.

"Who's there?" Gini said as she walked forward. "Show yourself. Or I'll *make* you show yourself."

Adia covered her face with her hands and groaned. What did you say to a goddess you'd never believed in?

Fake it.

The branches parted, and she slowly looked up.

"Gentle Ginikanwa," she squeaked out like a mouse as Gini gaped at her in horror. "So nice to meet you. I'm a huge fan of your work."

Gini closed her eyes and let out a loud exhale that caused a gust of hot wind that seemed to scare even the agrias vine.

It released her ankle and crept away. Adia scrambled to her feet, unsure whether she should bow, curtsy, or fling herself to the ground while begging Gini not to set her on fire.

"I'm afraid you have me at a disadvantage," Gini said through clenched teeth that looked slightly sharper than the average human's. "You know who I am. But who—or what—are you?"

TEN

...

"Followed me off the ship?" Gini asked, incredulous. "What do you mean you followed me off the ship? Why would you do such a thing? Did the stench of this island appeal to you?"

"Of course not," Adia snapped, then flinched at Gini's murderous gaze. "My lady," she quickly added, remembering who she was in the presence of. "I thought I might . . . I thought I might offer my assistance!"

"Your assistance?" Gini repeated as she looked Adia up and down. "Your assistance with what exactly?"

"Well . . ." Adia paused. Gini had her reasons for exorcising Darian. A demon was ruling Zaria through his body. Of course that had to be taken care of. But Adia was nobody. If the Alusi knew she was an ogbanje, would she be kind? Or would she incinerate her on the spot? Just because Adia had been discovered didn't mean it was safe to tell Gini the real reason she was following her.

"I knew that no one lived on this island, and I thought you might need help finding your way," she said, thinking fast. "I have every map of Zaria memorized."

"How prodigious of you," Gini said dryly as she leaned close and peered into Adia's eyes. She stood up sharply. "But you're lying. And I'm out of patience. Truth be told, my dear, I have very little to begin with. So let's try this once again. Who, or what, are you? And why have you followed me?"

Adia rubbed her forehead. All right, so lying to a goddess didn't seem to be possible. She would have to tell the truth.

Just not the whole truth.

"My name is Adia. Adia Kelbara. I'm no one, really, but I know . . ." She looked at Ferryman, not sure if Olark's curse affected him. She didn't want to risk a repeat performance of what had happened with Lebechi when she'd tried to tell her the truth.

She leaned in close to Gini. "I know who you are. And . . . I know about the emperor," she whispered.

"You know about the emperor," Gini repeated slowly.

"I do."

"You know *what* about the emperor?"

"That he's possessed. By Olark."

Gini nodded. "I see. I see."

Adia was surprised and relieved that Gini was reacting so calmly, but her relief faded as quickly as it had come.

"Ferryman!" Gini shouted.

Adia screamed as the cloaked figure flew up from the

ground and threw itself on top of her.

"Get off me!" she cried. She pulled at it and bit back a scream when she realized she wasn't dealing with a person—it was only a cloak, with no figure inside it. "Oh, you creepy thing. Get off!" But the cloak held her so tight, it was like trying to escape knotted ropes.

"You're not a mortal. No mortal would know that information. Which means Olark has grown stronger than I realized if he can create such a lifelike Soulless."

What on earth was Gini talking about?

"Reveal yourself!" Gini thundered, aiming her staff.

Nothing happened.

Gini blinked. She gave the staff a few knocks with her fist and lifted it again, clearing her throat.

"I said," she shouted, again pointing the staff at Adia, "reveal yourself!"

Adia tilted her head in confusion. The cloak poked her on the shoulder. She glared and slapped it away.

"I did reveal myself. My name is Adia. I was doing my year of practicality at the Academy of Shamans and was in the library when you and those other two Alusi came in. I didn't mean to eavesdrop. I didn't know what to make of it. So I told Lebechi—that is, my friend at the Academy—and she forgot everything I said in less than a minute. So I know—"

Adia stopped rambling as Gini's staff fell to the ground and the Alusi stared at her with wide eyes.

"You're mortal. But . . . this isn't possible. Wait. Start

again. Tell me from the beginning."

Adia eyed the cloak, which had righted itself and was again standing next to Gini.

"Don't worry about Ferryman," Gini said. "He's a Soulless. You may speak freely."

"What's a Soulless?"

"A creature I gave life to. I just didn't give him a soul, so he has no loyalty to anyone except me and can never be swayed from my command."

"You also didn't give him a face."

"Miss Kelbara," Gini said, her voice clipped. "Your explanation. I'm waiting for it."

Adia sighed.

"I overheard your conversation about the curse. Not on purpose, of course," she quickly clarified when she saw Gini's sharp gaze. "But I didn't forget what I'd heard. I think the curse must have a loophole."

She tried not to squirm under the intensity of Gini's stare as she continued.

"*You* had no intention of telling me, and *I* had no intention of hearing it. And the way the curse was worded . . ."

"A loophole," Gini repeated, her voice shocked. "Of all the clumsy mistakes—though Words of Power never were Olark's strong suit. I can't believe I didn't see it. We finally have an advantage. Thank you."

Gini stumbled over the words like she was unaccustomed to thanking anyone. Adia appreciated the effort.

"Thank you, you extraordinary, nosy little child."

And moment ruined, Adia thought with a roll of her eyes. "I'm not nosy," she muttered. "And I'm quite tall for my age."

"Are you? And here I thought you'd been grown incorrectly. But I haven't walked among mortals for centuries. I suppose you've all shrunk since I've been gone."

Adia shook her head, trying to make sense of what was happening. "Wait. What do you mean you have the advantage?"

Gini began pacing. The starry glow she'd done such a good job of hiding was now waxing and waning, like she was too excited to keep ahold of herself. "Yes, yes. Quite the advantage."

Gini stopped and stared at her. "I have no right to ask this of you, child—Adia was your name, yes? But the truth is, you are now the only mortal in Zaria who knows what's going on. Not even Olark could imagine that you exist. And that means you are going to be useful. I'll have to ask you to come with me."

Adia's mouth fell open.

Gini actually thought *Adia* could help *her*? She couldn't even help herself. That's why she'd snuck after the Alusi—to watch from a *safe* distance while Gini freed Darian from a demon so she could replicate the process on herself. If Gini wanted someone to go into battle with her, there was a whole school of kids with no sense who'd jump at the chance at a glorious death quest. Adia was trying to survive this world, not leave it.

"Come with you? Come with you where?"

"Well, to the Horrorbeyond to start with," Gini said, "but that's only the first step on our journey. I'll need to make a completely new plan now that I have you. A better plan. I had no idea how to get close enough to Olark to exorcise him from Darian's body, but you're the solution. He'll never suspect a mortal girl is helping us, because you're not even supposed to know he's alive! Now, after we come back from the Horrorbeyond, I'll need you to—"

Adia held up a hand. No. This was impossible. Watching Gini perform an exorcism from afar was one thing, but actually getting close to the demon emperor? That was too much.

"Listen," Adia said. "I'm sorry, but I can't help you with that. I never meant to eavesdrop. It was an accident, just a ridiculous coincidence—"

"There's no such thing as a coincidence," Gini snapped.

Adia flinched, then patted her head just to make sure Gini hadn't set her hair on fire like the ship captain's furry hat. This was clearly not someone used to being contradicted.

"Why would you need me anyway? You're an all-powerful goddess, aren't you? Just do what you did when you got rid of him the first time."

"First of all, no one is *all*-powerful," Gini sniffed. "And I'm certainly not all-powerful down here. This is a mere fragment of my true glory. But my aura is still strong enough that Olark-as-Darian would know the second I was within fifty feet of him. *I* can't get close to him. But a mortal can.

You can lure him to me."

Adia put a hand to her stomach, feeling her breath go in and out, regretting every decision she'd ever made.

"Second of all," Gini continued, unaware of Adia's panic, "contrary to popular belief, I didn't defeat him last time. I didn't do anything. He just . . . vanished. And I didn't have the sense to make sure he was truly gone."

Adia stared at her in confusion. How did someone like Olark vanish?

"Well, if you couldn't get rid of him then, what makes you think you can now? And what's the blood-stained stone?" Adia asked. "You said you were going to the Horrorbeyond to find it."

Gini exhaled, clearly exasperated that Adia wouldn't do what she wanted. But Adia didn't care. There would be no *obedience without question* happening today. If Gini wanted her to go demon hunting, she was going to have to give her some sort of explanation—and she could start by telling her what this blood-stained stone was.

"This stone is something that can defeat Olark?" she pushed. "Some sort of magical object of good?"

"It's the shriveled-up remains of a star Olark destroyed, stained with the blood of the beings who once lived there before he blew them to smithereens," Gini said in a clipped tone.

Adia blinked. All right, so . . . not exactly a magical object of good. "Ummm . . ."

Gini muttered something under her breath, then flopped

down on the sand, her feet peeking out from under her long dress.

"Fine," she finally said. "You're asking me to tell you something very few know about. If I do tell you, and you decide to go running through the streets spreading this information, I'll have to deal with you. Are you sure you want me to continue?"

Adia paused. *Deal with her?* She was sure there were a great number of ways Gini could deal with her. Most would probably end with her roasting over an open fire.

But she was already in the middle of this. It's not like things could get any worse.

"Go on."

Gini gave her an appraising look, then nodded. She held out a hand and small sparks shot out, catching on some underbrush. In a matter of seconds, it turned into a roaring fire.

"I've known Olark since he was just a fledgling spirit," she said. "He was always a gifted creature. Intelligent. Powerful and shrewd. When he chose, he could bring so much clarity to a situation. But he could also sow the worst confusion you've ever seen, and frequently did so if it suited his purpose."

"Like the curse?" Adia said, sitting down next to Gini, but maintaining a safe distance between them. She held her hands out, warming them by the fire.

"Yes. He was always fast to use a curse. Especially a confusion curse."

"So . . . you're all up there," Adia said, pointing at the sky, "flinging curses down on us?"

"Oh, only on those who deserve it!" Gini said with a smile that Adia assumed was meant to be reassuring. She edged a bit farther away. She couldn't for one second forget how dangerous this creature she was dealing with was.

Gini's smile faded.

"But he had a reckless personality and was so spoiled. Honestly, he was a terrible young spirit."

Adia shrank just a little. She'd been called a terrible child more times than she could remember. Maybe if everyone hadn't told Olark he was terrible he would have tried to be something *not* terrible.

"And it didn't get better as he got older," Gini continued. "It stopped him from attaining the power he truly wanted. He wanted to be given a star to bind with and become a true Alusi, but he couldn't be trusted with that kind of power. He wasn't ready, not with the way he behaved, so we didn't let him into our sphere."

"So instead he took a star by force," Adia said.

Gini gave a grim nod. "When we saw what he'd done, how he'd annihilated an entire species, I was sent to destroy him. I cast him and his blood-stained star out of the sky. . . ." Gini paused, a strange expression on her face that almost looked like shame. "My mistake was in not realizing he would survive the fall. And that Zaria would be the next place he tried to conquer. The star shriveled into a stone when it landed here, but it still had enough celestial energy to keep Olark alive—in a shadow state, but alive nonetheless. And with enough powers to possess people. He survived by jumping from body to body, burning Zaria down as he did."

So that's why Gini was hell-bent on stopping him, Adia realized. In the library, she'd said that all this was her fault. Although Adia thought the Alusi was being a bit too hard on herself. She'd made a mistake in flinging him down here, but Olark was the monster, not her.

"When he vanished all those years ago, the stone stayed behind. He must have thought it vanished too, because he's never searched for it. I'm not sure how he's managed to possess another person without it, honestly."

Adia squirmed on the sand.

"Do you think he's found another power source?"

"It's possible," Gini said with a frown. "Although I have no idea what object in Zaria could have the kind of energy he would need to keep himself not just alive but strong enough to steal bodies. But once I get that stone, I'll be able to use the blood of his victims to bind him."

Gini stood and started marching to the water, clearly impatient to get going.

"Wait," Adia said, chasing after her. "This is all properly horrifying, and it's not every day you learn your emperor is possessed by a demon long thought dead, but I still don't see why you think I can help you."

"You can help me because you've broken through the curse," Gini said, looking a little too gleeful at the idea of now having bait. "He'll never suspect that a girl could be part of a plan to bring him down because he'll assume you're under his curse. You'll lure him to me, and then I'll exorcise Darian the Warlord Baby—"

"The Warlord Child," Adia corrected, but Gini ignored her.

"—and trap Olark inside the blood-stained stone once and for all. Plus, you're positioned at the Academy, so your presence won't even be questioned."

Adia stared at her shoes. "About that . . . I sort of got expelled."

"Don't worry about such trivial things," Gini said with a dismissive wave. "I'll take care of the little details."

"Little details?" Adia's voice came out a pitch higher than usual as she followed Gini through washed-up old fish bones and seaweed.

How could Gini think she would ever be allowed to set foot in the Academy again, let alone survive a minute in the Horrorbeyond?

Now that she knew it was real, all the stories of the Horrorbeyond came rushing back to her. Stories of people who were never seen or heard from again. Of Headless Hiroma collecting skulls to carry around with her own.

"And never mind me somehow strolling back into the Academy after I've been thrown out. How exactly are you getting into the Horrorbeyond?"

"With Ferryman, of course."

The offensive fuchsia cloak made a low bow, and even though Ferryman didn't have a face, Adia swore he was mocking her.

"So, if you're ready, we need to go now. The energy of the Horrorbeyond is so warped, it's barely a part of Zaria at this point. It's only visible when the veil is at its thinnest at dawn and at dusk. And you've delayed our voyage long enough."

Adia looked at the sun as it sank lower in the sky, the horizon growing inky shades of red and orange, and somewhere past that, a world of waking nightmares. If they didn't go now, they'd have to wait until the next day.

"I didn't say I was going with you," Adia reminded her. Gini gave her an assessing look, but Adia steeled herself and tried to stand just a little taller than she felt. She had run away to the Academy so that she could rid herself of the demons within her—she wasn't exactly looking for a mission that would bring her closer to the most murderous demon in the known universe. "I'm sorry for your sake that I'm the one who found the loophole in the curse, but I'm . . . I'm . . . well, I don't know who I am. But I know who I'm not. And I'm not the hero."

She was the demon.

Gini thumped her staff on the sand and glared, unaware that she was trying to get one demon to help get rid of another.

"The Alusi have helped create thirty-three universes— did you know that, Adia?" she asked.

"I didn't." She didn't even know there *were* other universes.

"Zaria is hardly the first place we helped breathe life into, and it won't be the last," Gini continued. "We don't stay in the lands we create as queens and kings and rulers. That's not our place. But we do like to peek in every now and then to see what's going on with these worlds. How they're developing, who ended up in charge. Some worlds are ruled by the wisest of creatures. Most are not. But they all have one thing in common. Out of all the worlds born from my stardust, not one was inherited by the meek."

"I'm not meek," Adia protested, not wanting to think about every time she'd apologized to Mallorie Amber. "I just don't want to put myself in danger for people who would never do the same for me. If anything, everyone would want to hurt me if they found out that I'm . . ."

Her voice trailed off. She couldn't tell Gini that she was an ogbanje and a bringer of misfortune. Best-case scenario, Gini would leave her standing right there on the shore. Worst case, she'd destroy her along with Olark. But this was Adia's chance to never have to worry about any curses ever again. Yes, she would have preferred her original plan of just sneaking after Gini and watching from afar, not to have an actual role in this exorcism, but helping this volatile goddess was her ticket to freedom. The exorcism might even rub off on her if she was close enough. Plus, the money Maka had given her would only last so long. And Gini had said Adia would be rewarded. . . . She just had to make sure Gini didn't know she had her own agenda for joining this mission.

"All right," she said after a few seconds of pretending to mull it over. "I don't think I can be of any help to you in the

Horrorbeyond or in freeing the soul of the emperor. In fact, I know I can't. So you can't say I didn't tell you so. But I *can* help you sneak around the Academy. I memorized every map in the library that night, and I know where all the secret passages are. But my fee is high."

Gini looked taken aback. Then she flashed Adia an approving smile. "My, my. I didn't realize that you were such a sensible creature. You're quite right. This isn't a fairy tale, and you're not the hero. Which doubles our chances for success. You'll get paid for your work, I promise. Enough so that when you're of age, you can buy yourself a house right away and study whatever trade you'd like. Or never learn a trade and spend your days eating chocolates, doing nothing. I promise you'll never have to work a day in your life if that's what you want. That is, as long as Zaria doesn't end up as a pile of ashes and you still have a life. Does that make the decision easier?"

It briefly crossed Adia's mind that she should be selfless and help save the world for free. But she quickly crushed that thought. So what if she was going to help save the world and hopefully expel the demon inside her? If she succeeded, she was still coming out of this with no home to go back to. She needed money, and work was work.

She crossed her arms, fixed Gini with what she hoped was a tough expression, and prayed her voice wouldn't crack.

"I'll need an exact amount. In writing, if you please."

ELEVEN
· · ·

The once-fuchsia cloak called Ferryman was now a long fuchsia boat. Adia was certain there wasn't a more ridiculous way to travel. But as silly as it was, she couldn't deny it was frighteningly fast.

The waters of the Serpentine Pass lived up to its name. Snakes and eels flung themselves out of the murky water and into the air as the boat raced forward at an impossible speed. Adia moved this way and that, but no matter where she turned, a snake's tail whipped at her arms or smacked her in the face.

"Move around all you like," Gini said, looking obnoxiously serene as a snake flew over her head, "but it won't make you any more comfortable. It's better to be still."

Adia grabbed a small eel that had fallen into her lap. She tossed it back into the water and sighed when a snake landed in her lap to replace it.

"So," she said as she watched the snake slither around in her lap, "there's no other way to get to the Horrorbeyond?"

"There are many ways, but this is the most discreet. Now, Adia," Gini said, her voice stern, "in the Horrorbeyond, you must do as I say. Focus on your breathing as often as you can. Trust me when I say your breath will be the only thing you can guarantee is real. I've only been there once before, and even I barely made it out in one piece. I was immediately set upon by creatures begging for help, and my compassion took over. They almost bled me dry before I realized what they were."

"Creatures that bleed you dry?" Adia repeated.

Her cousin Ericson enjoyed telling her stories about hairy beasts with pink skin and hooked feet that hid in the trees of the Horrorbeyond, waiting to rip out your throat with their iron teeth. Waiting to gorge themselves on your blood. He found it funny how scared those stories made her. After EJ died and there was no one to stop him, Ericson would hold her down and tell her how Uncle Eric planned to send her off to the Horrorbeyond with all its monsters, from the iron-teethed bloodsuckers to Headless Hiroma herself.

"The asanbosam?" she whispered.

"No, not exactly," Gini said, "though I suspect they might be what inspired the stories of the asanbosam. These unfortunate creatures couldn't care less about your body. They're Energy Thieves. What they want is the energy that fuels your soul. Many of them are mortal. Or at least they *were*. But being trapped in the Horrorbeyond for too long will drain you of your soul. You slowly lose your ability to feel. And when they sense someone who can still feel and care? They latch on in the most subtle of ways: by asking for your help. That's how they capture energy. And they're constantly on the hunt for a new source."

"But who would even get close enough to get captured? How many people sail down the Serpentine Pass? I mean, look at it," Adia said, gesturing at the reptile-infested waters.

"As I said, this is hardly the only way to enter the Horror-beyond," Gini said. "And the Energy Thieves will be waiting at every port of entry, looking for someone to snatch. They'll slink up to you, a picture of kindness and friendship, and the second they know they've got you on the hook? They'll latch on and begin to bleed your soul."

Gini leaned down and whispered something to Ferry-man. The boat made a sharp right turn.

"We're at the entrance," she said sharply. "Keep your wits about you. Energy Thieves aren't the only things waiting to attack you in the Horrorbeyond."

To Adia's shock, the temperature rose at least twenty degrees the second they climbed out of the boat.

"The only thing pleasant about this place is the weather," Gini cooed, extending her fingers and letting a few sparks of flame dance around her palm.

"Let's get this over with before I faint," Adia said, ripping her scarf off her head and using it to mop her face. Barely ten seconds in the Horrorbeyond and she was drenched in sweat. She hadn't been seasick at all on the boat to and from the Academy. Maybe being in a smaller vessel made a difference, because she was definitely queasy now.

"Faint? Oh, yes, of course. I always forget how delicate you mortals are. Delicate and simple. Ferryman, help the child."

Ferryman immediately went back to cloak form and draped itself around her. The cloak was freezing. It perfectly balanced the blistering heat.

"I guess you're not so bad after all," Adia said, gratefully patting her new fuchsia garment and looking around the beach and at the tall palm trees in the distance.

"It's pretty," she said in shock.

"It won't be for long," Gini muttered.

"What do you mean—" Adia clamped a hand over her mouth. "Excuse me, I—I think . . ."

She bent over and proceeded to hurl up her last meal.

Gini rubbed her back sympathetically.

"I forgot to warn you about that part," she said. "The Horrorbeyond likes to collect sadness and pain. It makes you purge it up. But you can use that to your advantage, since we're not going to be staying. Get it all out and let it stay here."

In the short time she'd known Gini, Adia had only understood maybe half of what came out of the Alusi's mouth, but she understood this. This wasn't like being sick. Something besides digested food was coming out of her. She could even see it. Streams of black and gray smoke wafting out of her mouth as she vomited.

Gini whistled at the smoke and rang the bells on her flowering staff. Some of the streams disappeared, some blew away, and a few turned a bright purple and floated back into Adia. She felt better every time the purple ones came back in.

She wiped her mouth and eyes as Gini helped her up. As Gini's skin touched hers, Adia hissed, quickly pulling back. The Alusi burned like a thousand suns. No wonder she was enjoying the heat of the Horrorbeyond! It probably felt like palm fans stirring up a cool breeze when her regular body temperature was an inferno.

"Feel better?" Gini said.

"Much," Adia said, hoping her face didn't betray how unnerved she was at Gini's unnatural heat signature.

"Good. We'll need to move quickly. I'm on a bit of a deadline, you see."

"A deadline?" Adia repeated, shrugging the Ferryman cloak off her now that she'd cooled down. He glided into the water, a lone strange figure as Gini headed out. "What do you mean?"

"Did I not mention it?" Gini said as she marched down the beach toward the trees. "I can't stay in Zaria indefinitely."

"Why not?" Adia said, slightly out of breath. She was struggling to keep up with Gini's purposeful gait as they entered the dense forest.

"For the same reason Olark shouldn't have been able to survive here as long as he has. My home is in the stars. This is the mortal realm—anything alive here is fated to die, because that is how the Alusi who created Zaria designed it. The problem is, if an Alusi—or any celestial for that matter—is on the ground for longer than two, maybe three months, our true age starts to catch up to us. Quite frankly, we lose our minds first, our mortality next. I'd be dead within the year."

Ikenga and Mbari had said they'd come to check on Gini because she was close to surpassing her limits. *That's* what they meant?

Adia sputtered in disbelief. "And how long have you been down here?"

"I came to monitor the situation with Olark-as-Darian a little over a month ago, before I decided to intervene. Or has it been two? Ikenga's better at dates than I am. Well, no matter. They'll come find me if I start to go on any sort of rampage," Gini said, blissfully unaware of how stress-inducing her personality was.

Adia rubbed her head. What a nightmare. If Gini was still in Zaria a few weeks from now, she'd have to make sure she was as far away from her as possible.

The sound of a branch breaking behind them made Adia turn.

"Are there animals in here?" she asked. "I didn't think a place like this would have wildlife."

Gini didn't answer. Adia turned back around and gasped in shock. There was nothing but empty space where Gini had just been.

"Gini?" she said. Her heart raced. What had happened? How had she vanished into thin air? Had Mbari and Ikenga decided to snatch their wayward sister and take her back to the stars because she was spilling secrets to a mortal girl?

No. Gini wouldn't have let them take her so easily. But she was nowhere in sight.

What horror had taken her? Was it coming for Adia next?

"Gini, where are you?" Adia whispered, her voice pitifully small. Desperation had made her brave when she followed Gini after getting thrown out of the Academy, but now she was just scared. Left alone in the Horrorbeyond.

"Think," she said as she quickly mulled over her options.

Go deeper into the woods by herself to try to find Gini? No. Adia was no fool. She had no intention of running toward monsters with no way of defending herself.

Make her way back to the beach and hoped Gini came back to find her? Also no good. She could end up waiting around for the rest of her life if Gini had indeed been taken back to the stars.

"Ferryman!" She spun around and raced back to the mouth of the Serpentine. Gini had said the Soulless answered her command. He would be invested in helping find her.

Her feet touched the sand as she reached the beach, but the rest of her collided with someone, and she was knocked down. Thank goodness. She'd panicked over nothing. Gini had already come back.

"Gini! What happened?" she said as she quickly pushed herself off the sand. "You were there one second and then you were— Ah!"

She bit back a scream. It wasn't Gini.

A woman stood in front of Adia, tears running down her face. Seaweed clung to her, highlighting the strange and sallow green tint of her skin. Her eyes were large and black, and as they focused on her hungrily, Adia felt cold.

"Don't come any closer," Adia said as she scurried away.

The woman gawked at her. "Do I look like I'm going to hurt you? Did you get stranded too?" she asked, wringing her hands. Her voice was soft, but it did nothing to lessen the chill running through Adia's blood. "I thought I was the only one in here. I was on a fishing boat, but we sailed into a horrible storm and our boat capsized. I don't know if anyone survived besides me. I had to swim through a sea of snakes. It was horrible," she said with a shudder. "I've been completely alone for three days. Do you have any idea where we are?"

Guilt replaced Adia's fear.

Adia would look terrible too if she'd gotten stranded alone in the Horrorbeyond for three days. She gave the woman an apologetic look. But she didn't let her guard down. This was still a stranger.

"No. It's just me," Adia said cautiously. "And my companions. They went to look around."

Better to make it seem like she was traveling with a big group of people. People who would notice if something happened to her.

"Your companions? Where's your boat?"

"We docked on the other side," Adia lied.

The woman sagged in relief. "Then we can get out of here! I'm Sinachi, by the way. What's your name?"

Adia didn't answer. She wasn't agreeing to anything until she found Gini.

The silence dragged on for so long it became uncomfortable.

"Umm . . ."

Sinachi blinked. "What's wrong with you? Don't tell me you're not going to help me! Please—"

"Of course I'll try to help," Adia said quickly. "But I'm not in charge."

"In charge? In charge of what?" Sinachi's voice was still soft, but a hard edge had crept in.

Adia took a step back.

"How hard is it to bring me on your boat with you?" Sinachi said, her voice pained. "You don't have to take me where you're going, just get me off this cursed island. Something's not right here. Ever since I got stranded, I've felt exhausted. Something in the air."

She rubbed her eyes and stepped closer, closing the distance Adia was trying to keep between them. Was it the setting sun that made Sinachi's eyes appear to go from black to yellow? This place had made her sicker than she realized. Her mind felt foggy. As if she had a high fever.

"My mother is sick, and I heard there was a plant here that could help her. It's been three years of taking care of her, and I've sacrificed so much. I was supposed to get married, and my fiancé left me because I didn't have enough time for him. And I keep getting fired from jobs, so coin is hard to come by."

"I'm sorry—"

"And then I had to sell all my goats to pay the medicine

woman. Even when I had enough money to buy them back, the farmer I sold them to wouldn't sell them back to me."

Sinachi's eyes brightened as she continued her tale of woe. Adia rubbed her head. She needed to sit down. Or stick her head in the water to cool off. The heat was really getting to her. But Sinachi was relentless.

"None of it is my fault. I tried so hard to be a good daughter, and now look at what's happened to me. Stuck in the Horrorbeyond and—"

"Wait," Adia said, shaking her head trying to clear the fog that was now covering her brain. She felt dizzy, as though Sinachi was sucking away her strength the more she dumped her misery on her. "How do you know that?"

"How do I know what? That none of it's my fault? Because it isn't," Sinachi hissed.

"No," Adia said slowly. She could kick herself for being so dense. "How do you know you're in the Horrorbeyond? You said you haven't seen anyone for days and don't know where you are."

Sinachi's mouth formed a thin line. "Oh. I slipped up there, didn't I? No matter. You're already weak enough for me to take you."

Adia could only watch in horror as Sinachi's arm stretched and stretched toward her. She no longer looked like a helpless traveler—instead, her limbs were the dead branches of trees, her glowing eyes hungry and malicious. Adia's insides screamed at her to act, to move, to shove Sinachi like she'd shoved Sister Claudia . . . but the Energy Thief was right.

She was so weak she could barely stand.

What had Gini said? Focus on your breath? It seemed too late for breathing to save her.

The same panic that had taken hold of Adia in the Swamplands with Sister Claudia took over now. And for the third time, quick bursts of purple light shot out of her hands, forming a straight line into the ground before disappearing.

Something wrapped around her ankles. Heart in her mouth, she looked down, expecting to see a snake. But it was a piece of seaweed. Even more came out of the ocean, moving toward Sinachi. Adia frowned. Was this part of the Energy Thief's magic? But it didn't *feel* evil.

"You've got such wonderful energy. I can feed off you for days," Sinachi said. She hadn't seemed to notice the light or the seaweed. "I wasn't lying when I said something is wrong here. No good game for ages. Probably the fault of that wretched girl—the one who guards the stone."

That startled Adia out of her fear. Someone was guarding the blood-stained stone?

"Girl? What girl?"

"It doesn't matter," Sinachi said. Her voice came out warbled now, all trace of humanity gone. "Although, you should consider yourself lucky she's not the one who found you. She put an arrow through my toe last year. But enough chit-chat. Time for dinner!"

Adia remembered the day of the earthquake in the Swamplands. She didn't know how she'd caused it or why, but her body was tingling again the exact same way. Suddenly she knew this wasn't over. Not by a long shot. "No," she said firmly. "You're not eating me."

Adia braced herself for an earthquake, but the sand was still beneath her feet. Some of her confidence faded. Had she made a mistake? Were her demonic powers not going to get her out of this? But then the seaweed on the shore whipped around Sinachi's legs, making her topple over with a scream. Adia could feel the plants like they were an extension of her own hands, wrapping around the energy thief like a mummy.

"What is this?" Sinachi said, panic creeping into her voice as the seaweed crawled up her body. "What are you?"

That question made Adia falter. What *was* she? How was she doing this?

Sinachi took advantage of her hesitation and clawed at the seaweed with a frustrated growl and ripped it off. Adia put her hands up into two fists, ready to fight, but Sinachi glared at her.

"You're not worth it," she hissed. The Energy Thief ran away from the water and disappeared behind the tree line.

Adia nearly collapsed on the sand with relief. For the second time, her powers had saved her. She didn't know if she should feel guilty, or ashamed. . . . After all, if her powers were part of being an ogbanje, and being an ogbanje was decidedly bad, how could her powers be a good thing? But mostly, she was just glad to have survived. She might have lain there forever if she hadn't been so scared that another Energy Thief would show up and drain her unconscious body.

"Ferryman," she said. "Something's happened to Gini. Turn back into a boat so we can sail around and search for her. Going into the woods isn't safe. It swallowed her up."

She waded into the water, but Ferryman held out a sleeve, pushing her back.

"What now?" she groaned, peering over his shoulder. "How much more nightmarish can this place get?"

She immediately wished she could take back her words. Headless Hiroma would be pretty nightmarish. But then she saw what Ferryman was trying to shield her from. And it wasn't Hiroma.

A boat so rickety it looked ten seconds away from sinking sailed into the Horrorbeyond. She recognized it—it was the boat that had been on the shore growing mushrooms when she'd first met Gini.

Whoever was rowing the boat definitely had a head. But she couldn't quite make out the face attached to that head. She pushed up her glasses and squinted. Her stomach sank as the captain of the decrepit vessel became clear.

TWELVE

Nami was always loud, but Adia was amazed his booming voice didn't send every Energy Thief in the Horrorbeyond running in their direction.

"The next snake that touches me is getting sliced, diced, and roasted for dinner!"

"Nami!" she gasped. "What? How? WHY?"

She was too mad to form a sentence. Of all the things she'd thought she would find in the Horrorbeyond, *Nami* wasn't one of them.

"Adia, what are you doing?" Nami said as he pulled up in the boat. "What were you thinking getting off the ship?!"

"What am *I* doing?" Adia yelled. "What are *you* doing? You shouldn't have followed me!"

Nami glared up at her.

"Of course I followed you! I lose you for one minute, and you go sailing off with a stranger! The captain said you were heading to your death! You're my friend—"

"I barely know you."

"—even if you don't want to admit it," Nami said stubbornly. "I wasn't going to let you go running off into danger. It's my fault you're in this situation."

The guilt on Nami's face made her stop yelling. He really came all this way because he felt bad about what happened with Mallorie? Her anger slowly fizzled out.

"It's not your fault," she said quietly. "You were right before. If you'd tried to help, you'd have gotten fired too. So you don't have to feel bad about it, all right? Just turn your boat around and go. I mean . . . you should probably patch it up a bit first. I don't know how you even managed to get this far in that thing. But you're going to get in trouble with the Gold Hats for leaving your post. So go home now."

Nami seemed taken aback by the lack of yelling. "I shouldn't be in too much trouble," he said, but he frowned as if he'd only just considered how bad a situation he'd put himself in. "There were other Gold Hats guarding the ship. Maybe they won't even notice I'm gone. We'll catch another one tomorrow and try to meet up with them. But you're right. We need to go. Now."

Adia couldn't pretend there wasn't a part of her that wanted to leave, but she couldn't abandon Gini when she'd agreed to help her. The Alusi had said she wasn't at full strength when she wasn't in the stars. Maybe she wasn't a match for the Horrorbeyond. Adia needed to help her. She just had to get Nami out of there first.

"I can't go. I took a job with . . . with the rich lady," she said, edging back to shore.

Nami frowned.

"It's a great connection," she said quickly.

He looked curious. "Well, she's definitely rich. I don't know who she is, but even the way she walks is so regal that she's obviously *somebody*. And that's good that you'll have some money coming your way after . . . after everything that happened at the Academy."

"Exactly," Adia said, relieved he was buying all this. "I'm taking care of myself. So you'd better go now."

She was completely exasperated when, instead of turning around, Nami hopped out of his boat.

"No," he said. "I'll wait here till she comes back. I'll introduce myself so she knows you have friends. Plus, you can put in a good word for me."

Adia didn't know if she should be annoyed or touched. It was brave of him to follow her. And she couldn't imagine he would do that if he didn't care about her. Still, Nami had switched from panic and concern for her to wanting to help himself pretty quickly. She couldn't figure him out.

"Why do you care so much about impressing rich people anyway? Aren't you a capital kid? If your apprenticeship is with the Gold Hats, you're hardly a peasant."

Nami went red. "My family has a good name," he admitted. "Or at least we did. My father's been gambling everything away for as long as I can remember. He used to win it back or a friend would help him out if he didn't, but . . .

his luck ran out a long while ago. And I think his friends are done with him at this point. No one will lend him the money to cover his debt."

Adia felt terrible. "I'm sorry. I shouldn't have said anything."

"No, it's all right. The only reason you don't already know is because you're from the Swamplands. Everyone from a civilized place knows about the Watsons' family shame."

If she didn't feel so guilty for yelling after he'd come all this way to try to help her, she would have snapped at him about that *civilized* comment.

"So . . . you want to restore your family's honor?"

"Honor, finances, social standing. I don't have any siblings, so it's all on me. My mother's like a shadow spirit at this point—she just stays in her room and won't talk to anyone. But I can fix that if I become a Gold Hat and make connections in high places to replace all the friends my father lost. I know I can," he said, his face more serious than she'd ever seen it. "Then everything will be perfect again."

"I see."

For once, Nami seemed uncomfortable with the volume of words that had come out of his mouth.

"I'd better go tie the boat," he said, giving her a slightly embarrassed grin before pulling the dinghy toward a few small trees that lined the shore.

Adia paced up and down the sand, occasionally throwing seashells into the water while Nami dealt with the wood scraps he called a boat. His circumstances explained why he walked around insisting that bad things happened for a reason and that it was all perfect. His life had trained him to think that failure was just another step forward toward a great destiny. But *her* life had trained her to know hope and a catchphrase wasn't enough to get you out of a bad situation.

She couldn't say she wanted Nami to become a Gold Hat. She didn't know who she considered more of a menace to society, them or the Bright Father's missionaries. But Nami could get in trouble for leaving his post. Coming after her had put everything he'd been working toward at risk. But he still had done it.

Maybe he really was her friend.

Nevertheless, she had to find Gini. It didn't seem like she could shake Nami, so he would have to join her search, if he would only hurry up. As the minutes dragged on, she frowned. Nami was never this quiet.

"Honestly, Nami," she said, exasperated. "How long does it take to tie up a boat?"

She tossed a seashell in his direction.

It hit Sinachi instead.

"NO!" she cried.

Nami was on the ground with Sinachi's hand around his throat. Seashells fell all around Adia as she jumped up and ran toward them. The Energy Thief tossed her a gruesome smile before dropping to all fours like an animal. She galloped off behind the tree line, dragging Nami's unconscious body behind her.

The air left Adia's lungs.

Again. It had happened again. Too lost in her head to notice as something evil snatched her friend. An evil that was attracted to her, though her friends were the ones who kept getting hurt. First EJ, now Nami.

No. Not Nami.

"Not this time," she said, taking off after Sinachi.

She hadn't been able to save EJ, but she would save Nami.

The ground sloped down and the light grew dimmer the deeper Adia went into the Horrorbeyond. She'd caught one glimpse of Sinachi dragging Nami away when she first ran in after them, but that was ages ago. She had no idea which way they'd gone. The sound of the waves from the Serpentine Pass gave way to disembodied voices floating through the humid air from all directions as she moved farther and farther away from the shoreline.

"A fresh meal?" one moaned plaintively. "Please, I'm so hungry."

"Won't you feed me, little girl?" another whispered. "Such a kind child. You wouldn't want us to starve, would you? Won't you help us?"

Adia fought the urge to turn back. The memory of searching for EJ both pushed her forward and made her want to curl up in a ball and cry. The sadness she'd thrown up earlier crept back in. Maybe if she'd spent one more day searching, it would have made a difference. Maybe she'd been close to saving him when she'd given up. Maybe—

"Pleassse, little girl—"

"Oh, would you SHUT UP," Adia snapped, irritated at the interruption of her self-pitying thoughts.

To her surprise, the voices stopped. She snorted. Forget Gini's talk of breathwork. Maybe the best way to get an Energy Thief off your back was to just say no.

But even with the voices gone, the Horrorbeyond earned its name. Gini had been right—the beach was deceptively pretty, but inside was a forest of rot and decay. Moldy branches wrapped around trees instead of growing upward, giving the gray trees the appearance of being strangled. And thankfully it wasn't raining, but there was still constant thunder, which made Adia jump every time it clapped. A bolt of lightning struck the ground in the distance. It seemed to be hitting the same spot over and over again. A highly unnatural occurrence.

Maybe it's Gini throwing a tantrum, she thought. That seemed like something she would do. There was too much ground to cover by herself. And Nami was running out of time. Hopefully she was right and an irritated Gini would be at the center of this storm.

Adia was so focused on following the lightning that she didn't notice the protruding roots at her feet and tripped, crashing into a decaying tree and knocking her glasses off. She squinted, trying to find where her glasses had fallen.

"There you are," she said, stepping into the bramble surrounding the tree, ignoring the scratches her legs were getting. Something snagged her dress. She turned to get it off and shrieked.

A branch with five bony tree fingers had her in its grip and was pulling her back against the tree. She tugged at her dress. Gini had warned her Energy Thieves weren't the only thing that would try to get you in the Horrorbeyond.

She pried herself free with a shudder, grabbed her glasses, and started running again, this time in the direction of the lightning.

After a few minutes, a burnt smell hit her nose.

"Gini?" she whispered. "Nami?"

No one answered, though the burning smell grew stronger. Then she saw it—a house. The burnt smell was a patch of scorched earth in front of the door where the lightning was striking over and over.

Hopefully she could quickly peek her head in to see if Sinachi and Nami were inside. If they weren't, she would get out of here. If they were . . . she'd have to fight an Energy Thief to save him. Adia counted how long it took for one lightning strike to end and another to come. She would have to run for it.

"Just hang on, Nami," she said. "I'm coming."

As soon as the next bolt of lightning struck, she ran as fast as she could.

When she reached the door, she hesitated. She might have rolled her eyes at Ericson's horror stories before, but she was traveling with a goddess. If the Alusi were real, and the Horrorbeyond was real, and curses and Energy Thieves . . .

What if this was the home of Headless Hiroma?

The next lightning strike would come any second. She

could either stand there in fear until she got deep-fried like a plantain or she could go through the door.

She took a deep breath and turned the knob.

Adia exhaled in relief. There wasn't a headless girl braiding her own hair inside the cottage. There was just a bald girl, staring her down.

And aiming an arrow at her head.

THIRTEEN

· · ·

There wasn't much inside the cottage by way of furniture. A table with hundreds of lines carved into it, a few chairs, a mat on the floor. But what it lacked in home decor, it made up for in filth.

Weeds grew out of a sink full of dirty dishes, branches had shot their way in from outside and acted as hangers for dirty clothes, and the floor was full of crumpled paper and trash. The girl at the center of the mess calmly held her bow and arrow in place.

"Well, well, well," the bald girl said. "What do we have here? The two of you don't have the look of those disgusting wraiths to you. But this hell dimension is full of tricks."

Adia took in the girl's living situation. "I'm not sure *you* should be tossing around the word *disgusting.*"

She was as tall as Adia, which was a rare thing. And the lack of hair made her ears all the more noticeable. They were pointed at the tops. Not too much, but enough to get a second glance. If not for that, she could pass for a village girl. She had the same brown skin and brown eyes as anyone born in the Swamplands. But those ears. And her *clothes*. She wore a patternless black tunic and a similarly bland pair of pants, tied with a black belt and an angry dagger strapped to her waist. But as strange as her appearance was, and even though she had an arrow trained on her, the girl didn't set Adia's teeth on edge like Sinachi did.

Wait. What had the girl said?

"What do you mean the two of us?" She whipped her head around the cottage.

There he was, lying unconscious in a corner.

"Nami!"

She rushed forward, but the girl stopped her.

"Uh-uh-uh," the girl said, moving forward with the arrow trained on Adia. "One of you showing up at my house is suspicious enough. But two? How do I know you're not a wraith?"

"You mean the Energy Thieves? I'm not. One tried to get us. I managed to get away. Nami didn't."

"How did you get away? I can tell you're not carrying a weapon."

"Then why are you aiming one at me?" Adia asked.

The girl pursed her lips but didn't budge as she eyed Adia cautiously. "So you're telling me you got stranded here too?"

"No, not stranded. I was traveling with someone, but we

got separated. We came here to look for something."

"What are you talking about?" the girl scoffed. "You came here on *purpose*? Nobody comes here on purpose."

"We did," Adia said. "And as soon as we get what we came for, we're leaving."

"Leave? Leaving this place isn't possible. You're trapped here now, same as me."

"It's true," Adia said stubbornly. As if she would have set foot in the Horrorbeyond if she didn't think Gini could get them back out.

She forced herself not to flinch as the girl moved closer, never lowering her arrow.

If Adia ended up with an arrow in her arm, she was going to ask Gini to double her fee.

"You know how I've managed not to end up like those creatures outside? I don't trust anyone. I did once," the bald girl said, looking put out by the memory. "It was the perfect trick too. I heard a dog crying—I've always been a fool for dogs. I thought maybe some helpless animal got trapped here, so I took it in. Three days and he almost had me. I was half-dead but still giving it a share of my food so that he wouldn't starve. Then I caught a flash of yellow in one of his eyes, and I realized what was happening—the dog was really a wraith, bleeding me dry. Eventually I tricked him into going back outside. I still see him sometimes, trying to cross the threshold."

The girl's grip on the bow tightened.

"I should have put an arrow through that eye."

Wonderful, Adia thought, *an Alusi that sets things on fire and a hairless warrior looking for dogs to blind.*

"Then why is Nami in your house?" she asked.

The girl let out an irritated huff. "I saw him getting dragged off, so I fought off the wraith and brought him here. I don't know how far gone he is, but if he shows any sign of becoming one? I'll end him. It would be an act of mercy, I assure you."

Adia slowly moved closer to Nami. The girl sighed and nodded, finally lowering her arrow and putting down her bow. It was immediately replaced with a loosely held dagger, but she let Adia enter the room. Adia had to climb over piles of trash to get to him.

"Nami?" she whispered. She leaned down and touched his forehead. "Nami, it's Adia. Are you awake?"

No answer. But Gini would be able to help.

Gini.

What with all the chaos, Adia had almost forgotten what Sinachi had said about a girl guarding the blood-stained stone. This had to be her. But before Adia could figure out where the stone might be hidden, she'd have to get the girl to stop talking about ending Nami and blinding dogs. She had to prove to her she wasn't an Energy Thief.

"Tell me," Adia said. "What do all these wraiths have in common?"

"What do they have in common?" the warrior girl repeated. "I don't know. They make you think they're lost and helpless and trick you into wanting to save them. Then they begin to steal your energy till there's nothing left of you."

"Exactly," Adia said. "But I'm not lost or helpless. *I'm* offering to help *you*. I'm getting out of here, and you can come with me."

The girl thought about it for a minute, then slowly tucked the dagger back into her belt.

"All right. I'll trust you just this once. But one wrong move and . . ."

"An arrow through the eye?" Adia said coolly.

The girl smirked. She stuck out her hand.

"The name's Thyme. Champion of Nri and killer of the Quillfire."

Adia blinked. She knew from Thyme's tone she was supposed to be impressed with this nonsensical statement.

"Nri?" Adia repeated as she shook Thyme's hand.

She had every map of Zaria memorized. She knew the name of every kingdom, queendom, village, and city in Zaria, as well as their capitals. And none of them was named Nri. At least not anymore. The only Nri she'd ever heard of was—

"Do you mean the *Queendom of Nri*?"

"What other Nri do you know?" Thyme said incredulously. "It's the greatest queendom in the world."

Adia blinked, remembering reading *Nri: the Definitive History* while EJ swam. It *was* the greatest queendom in the world. . . .

Until Olark destroyed it five hundred years ago. Another

land consumed by fire.

Adia was baffled.

"How long did you say you've been here?"

Thyme pointed at a table. It contained hundreds upon hundreds of notches on it. "Don't know why I still bother to mark the days. Gives me something to do, I guess. One year. One bloody year."

Adia frowned. This didn't make any sense.

"I don't understand. How did you end up here?" she asked.

"We were under attack. It's Nri—we always have our tribal wars," Thyme said with a shrug. "But the queens usually resolve them within a few months. It's more like sisters squabbling, only, you know, with soldiers involved. But then this warlord showed up out of nowhere with an army of pale-faced soldiers from behind the Sunless Mountains. He said he would burn Nri to the ground if we didn't hand over some girl he was looking for."

"A girl?"

The warlord Thyme was talking about had to be Olark. But Gini hadn't mentioned him hunting for a girl.

"What did he want with her? Who was she?"

"Who knows," Thyme said, bewildered. "But I'm guessing she was a shaman. Maybe he needed her to do something for him and she refused."

Again, Adia was startled. So much had happened in the past few days she'd almost forgotten the reason she was in this mess to begin with. Running away to the Academy of

Shamans. Why were shamans always at the center of these messes she got herself into?

"Why do you think that?" Adia wondered.

"Well, when we said we didn't know who or where this girl was—what was her name again?" Thyme muttered, thinking for a few seconds. "Ah, Viona! When we said we didn't know who or where this Viona was, he did everything he could to lure her out—threats, bribes. Then he threw out one of the strangest curses I've ever seen. I guess it was meant to protect her until he could get to her, but it would have hurt us if we touched her."

"What do you mean?" Adia asked. "What was the curse?"

Thyme frowned. "How did it go again . . . ? *Hear my words throughout the world and read them in the skies.*"

Adia's blood turned cold. Nothing good ever came after those words.

> "*She of Ovie is protected*
> *By the good and wise.*
> *Her name will be a Word of Power*
> *In a world of lies—*"

Thyme paused, trying to remember the last lines. She grimaced when it came to her.

> "*And anyone who brings her harm*
> *Will be the one who dies.*"

"That's why I'm guessing she was a shaman," Thyme said. "He died before I was born, but my parents told me Ovie was the greatest shaman in the known world. She must have been related to him."

"I know," Adia said. "I work at a school for shamans. Or at least I did. Ovie's statue is in the library."

"Well, if this relation of his was in Nri and she was the shaman he was looking for, she never came forward," Thyme said with a glare. "That's when the Bright Father declared war on us and said he had no choice but to burn everything down."

Adia stood up with a start.

"The Bright Father?" she gasped.

"That's what he calls himself, dark as his soul is," Thyme said. "You know him?"

"I know him," Adia whispered.

Olark. The Bright Father. They were one and the same. Only, Olark was remembered as a ruthless demon to Zarians, but his followers had rebranded him as a benevolent god. Whether or not Olark lived or died, in some ways he'd already taken over Zaria: the soldiers he'd brought with him from behind the Sunless Mountains never left after the war ended; they had just rebranded themselves too, as missionaries, and installed statues of their Bright One in every living room, replacing the Alusi. He may not have a star in the sky, but he had reinvented himself as a god all the same.

"That's when I was assigned my mission to help take down the warlord," Thyme continued, not noticing Adia's shock. "We'd learned that wherever the Bright Father went, he wore this ugly stone around his neck, and sometimes he'd even talk to it, as though it was giving advice. Our spies told us he never took it off, not even when he slept—so one night, I snuck into the camp and stole it while he was sleeping. We knew it had to be something important."

"Why did you bring it here?" Adia asked.

"I didn't," Thyme snapped. "It brought *me* here. It's a cursed object. The only useful thing about it is that the never-ending lightning storm it causes outside my door keeps the wraiths away. Anyway, I was running away from the Bright Father's camp, hideous necklace in hand, next thing I know I'm here, trapped in this inferno for a year."

"Yes," an annoyed voice said. "That would happen if you touched a celestial object. Its power could potentially take you out of space and time. The blood-stained stone has always been volatile like that."

Adia spun around. A cranky goddess stood in the doorway, a fuchsia cloak draped down her back. Ferryman had found her.

"Gini!"

Thyme's bow was back in her hand, arrow notched, but Gini walked up to her without a drop of fear. Thyme was so taken aback she dropped her weapon.

"Gini, what happened to you? You vanished into thin air," Adia said, rushing over. She couldn't believe how relieved she was to see her.

"As did you. I turned around and you were gone. I've

been looking everywhere for you, and it turns out you found the blood-stained stone all by yourself."

"Well, not exactly," Adia said, slightly put out that Gini hadn't warned her the Horrorbeyond could disappear people. "This is Thyme. She's had the stone all along. Although . . ." Her voice trailed off. Adia was still confused about how Thyme had been the one to take the stone from Olark when he'd lost it centuries ago.

"I could never explain it," Gini murmured. She leaned down and peered into Thyme's wary eyes. "One minute, Olark was causing chaos, razing villages to the ground, and then he just vanished. It must have been you, taking the stone away from him and jumping through time with it."

"How can a stone have that much power?" Adia said in shock. Should they really be trying to track this thing down?

"Not a stone," Gini said sharply. "A star. Not a full-strength one since Olark stained it in blood and dragged it around in the mud with him, but it will always be a star."

Her voice softened as she turned back to Thyme. "I'm sorry to tell you this, but five hundred years have passed since you took the stone. The Queendom of Nri was destroyed."

Thyme gave her a blank look.

"What are you talking about? What happened?"

"Olark happened," Gini said. "The dark tyrant, the Bright Father, whatever you want to call him. He's gone by many names over the years. Nri was one of the lands he decimated with fire."

"So you're saying five hundred years have passed since

my mission," Thyme said, incredulous.

"Yes."

Adia waited for Thyme to cry. Or scream or smash something. That's what she would do if she woke up five hundred years from now. Instead Thyme laughed. It went on for so long Adia started to get concerned.

"Adia," Gini said, leaning into her.

"Yes," she said, assuming Gini had a suggestion on how to get Thyme to calm herself.

"What is that thing snoring in the corner?"

"Oh, that's Nami," Adia said. "He followed me off the ship. He's . . . my friend?"

"Are you asking or telling me?" Gini snapped.

"Telling," Adia said quickly.

Thyme's laughter had turned to a hiccup. Adia used the pause to cautiously approach her.

"Thyme?" she asked. "Is there anything we can do?"

Adia knew well enough that nothing anyone said would take grief away. But there were things you could do to avoid making it worse. Like not telling someone how they should feel about it. If denial and uncontrollable laughter were going to be Thyme's reaction to finding out everyone she'd ever known was dead, that was perfectly fine.

"So I'm Thyme, the time traveler?" Thyme said, still doubled over. "What a laugh! Thanks, I needed that. This day really couldn't get any more ridiculous."

Adia didn't press the matter. Denial it was.

"And what do you want with this stone?"

"Zaria's emperor is possessed by the Bright Father, as you call him. Gini says the stone can trap him and free the boy he's possessing."

"Possession." Thyme shuddered. "Nasty business. Most hosts can't survive it."

Adia looked up at Gini. This was the first she was hearing about that. "Is this true?"

Gini nodded.

"When a person is possessed, their body fights back. Everything in this world has a certain vibration. A flower, the water, a person, a star. Some of those vibrations work together. Others were never meant to coexist. For a being as powerful as Olark to possess someone, he is, in essence, poisoning his host because it's too great a clash—the body revolts and tries to rid itself of the outside invader, like fighting a virus. But the outcome is always the same and the host never survives."

Adia suddenly felt ashamed. This whole time she hadn't given a thought to what Darian must be going through when they were in a similar situation. If Gini didn't exorcise him, he would die young, same as ogbanjes were said to.

"I still say this stone is a relic of evil," Thyme protested, stirring Adia from her thoughts.

"And I'm telling you there's no such thing," Gini said. "It's not good or evil. It's just energy. Just power. Olark chose to use that power in a horrific manner, but I'll use it to contain him once and for all."

Adia did a double take as something hit her. Gini had said

Olark's name more than once now. But Thyme hadn't gone into a fit.

Adia waited for the telltale signs of Olark's curse in action, for Thyme to start screaming like Lebechi had, but the warrior girl remained unimpressed.

"Does that name mean anything to you?" Adia asked.

"Never heard of him." Thyme shrugged.

"Gini," Adia said urgently. "The curse?"

"Will have no effect on her," Gini said, looking pleased. "She's from a lost era and clearly not mortal. Look at those ears."

Thyme glared at her.

"You can leave with us or you can stay here," Gini said, "but the blood-stained stone comes with me. I can only remain on Zaria for a few more days, so I don't have a moment to lose. I can feel Ikenga getting cranky with me."

Adia glared at Gini.

"I thought you said you had weeks."

"Did I? I'm terrible with dates. But no matter! The sooner Olark is dealt with, the better. But first," she said, "I'll need to see the stone. I know it's here."

"I swore after that dog that I wouldn't trust anyone in this world," Thyme muttered. But she reached into the collar of her shirt and pulled out a necklace.

A black stone streaked with dark red lines hung below Thyme's collarbone, secured to the chain with a thin metal wire.

"Ugly, right?" Thyme asked, misreading Adia's unease at

seeing the stone. "These dirt marks are permanent."

"It's not dirt," Adia said quietly.

Thyme frowned and shook her head in disbelief. "How did I not realize that? It's blood, isn't it?"

"Yes," Gini said. "The blood of the beings whose lives Olark took. And that blood is what will bind him. Their souls want justice."

Gini reached out her hand for the stone, but Thyme took a step back, slipping the chain under her shirt once more.

"It stays with me until we're actually out of this place," Thyme said. "*If* we can get out of this place. Agreed?"

Gini frowned but nodded.

"Agreed."

FOURTEEN

...

I t became immediately clear that among Thyme's apparent virtues—courage, fortitude, strength—patience was not one of them. Perhaps when you've been stuck in a shack surrounded by Energy Thieves with nothing but weeds to eat for a year—or five hundred—you grow a bit eager, because once Thyme believed she had a chance of freeing herself from the Horrorbeyond, she was hard to contain. She was strapped with more weapons than Adia could count and ready to run out the door, but Gini dragged her back by her collar.

"Not so fast," the Alusi said.

Because one could only traverse the boundary of the Horrorbeyond at sunrise and sunset, they would have to spend the night here and wait until dawn to leave.

While Thyme got out her various pointy weapons— knives, spears, blow darts, stars know what else—and started sharpening them, Adia set about figuring out what they could eat. The house was overgrown with weeds, but weeds were just overeager, unwanted plants, after all, so Adia felt some kinship with them. And if you knew which ones to pick, they could feed you.

Gini looked at her curiously.

"What are you doing?"

"Getting stuff for dinner. I assume you don't need to eat, but Thyme and I do."

"And do you know what you're picking? We'll have to drag your friend Nami out of here if he doesn't wake up any time soon, but I won't be able to carry all three of you if you poison yourself."

Adia rolled her eyes.

"I won't poison myself. Even at the Academy I stopped a girl from—"

She caught herself before she said more. That day with Mallorie at the welcome ceremony, she had wanted to believe she'd just overheard another person speaking. But she knew in her heart that that warning had sounded in her head and hers alone. There was no reason to admit to Gini she'd heard voices telling her Mallorie was about to poison herself. There was no reason to tell that to anyone.

"You stopped a girl from what?" Gini said, her eyes narrowing.

"Nothing," she said, putting the greens on the table. "I'm just good at recognizing plants."

"How did you get away from an Energy Thief all by

yourself?" Gini tried to sound casual, but Adia could see the suspicion in her eyes. "You never explained that."

"I did what you said," Adia lied. "Kept calm, took some deep breaths. Eventually she moved on." She picked up a stem with a cluster of small bushy white flowers.

"This one can be turned into a sleeping agent," she babbled, hoping to distract Gini. "I used to prepare it for my aunt if she got too worked up. She was pretty excitable. It has no taste, so I would just dip some cocoa fruit in the medicine. She'd be asleep within the hour."

"Yes, what a sweet child you are," Gini said dryly. Her eye narrowed. "You also didn't explain how you made it all the way through the Horrorbeyond alone, completely unscathed. It's not just Energy Thieves that can attack you here. Quite frankly I'm amazed to find you in one piece."

"I guess the monsters were having a quiet evening," Adia said, pushing aside the memory of Sinachi.

Thyme spared her from having to continue trying to deflect this uncomfortable line of questioning when she flung a knife into the wall, narrowly missing Adia's ear.

"Thyme!" she shouted.

"What?" Thyme asked, seeming confused by Adia's reaction. "Oh, don't worry! I was just making sure it was sharp. It wouldn't have touched you. I was always the best at knife throwing at training camp. I've gotten even better here since I've had nothing but time to practice. Wait till my friends see how good I've gotten. Wait till they see *me!*"

"Oh, Thyme," Adia said sadly under her breath. The girl

truly didn't believe everyone she'd ever known had died centuries ago. And judging from her ears, whatever Thyme was, she was probably the last of her kind. A living example of how much Olark had taken from the world. How much he was still taking.

Thyme picked up some of the plants on the table and cautiously bit off a piece.

"I had no idea these were edible. How'd you get mixed up in this anyway?" she said, taking a bigger bite. "You're obviously not a warrior."

Adia couldn't argue.

"I was in the wrong place at the wrong time," she said. "Or right time, if you ask Gini." She gave Thyme a brief summary of eavesdropping on the Alusi and getting thrown out of the Academy.

"Sounds intense," Thyme said. "All right. So let's say you two hold up your end of the bargain and get me out of here. You really think the blood-stained stone can trap the Bright Father? Or whatever he's calling himself now. Olarkestarian?"

"Olark-*as*-Darian," Gini and Adia said at the same time.

"Ugh, that's terrible," Thyme muttered. "All right, then. How are you going to get close to *Olark-as-Darian* if he's gone and declared himself an emperor now?"

"Gini wants me to lure him to her," Adia said grumpily. "Even though no one is letting a servant anywhere near the emperor unless they're bringing him food or helping him get dressed, so you better come up with a good plan."

Gini's eyes went wide.

"Oh, how clever you are!" she exclaimed.

Adia was relieved Gini had stopped interrogating her, but what had she said that was clever? That the only way a servant was getting near the emperor was if . . . *no*. She couldn't be serious.

"Gini," Adia said through gritted teeth. "Remember I've been fired. And even if I hadn't been, why would he follow a lowly Academy servant?"

"I don't know. Maybe you can pretend you need to escort him somewhere?"

"The Gold Hats would do that," Adia said. "Or his personal guard."

"Hmm. We'll think of something. For now, you two should eat and rest. But be a dear first and make me some of that medicine you give to your aunt to help her sleep. A hefty dose. Being down here is so trying for my nerves. Ferryman, a word," Gini said as she and Ferryman went off into a corner together.

Adia sighed and began pulling apart flowers. She was grinding the plant into a paste when Thyme slid up to her.

"Here. Take this." She held out one of the small daggers she'd been sharpening. "You shouldn't wander around defenseless, especially if you're planning to take on a demon."

"I have no idea how to use it," Adia said, carefully taking the blade, "but thanks."

"So does your family know where you are? Mine probably thinks I got sent on a quest. They know not to expect much communication from me, but a year is pushing it. My father won't care, but my friends are probably worried."

Adia stayed silent. *By tomorrow Thyme will figure out that she's as alone in this world as I am.*

She wiped her hands on her dress. "The medicine is ready," she said, still not sure how to talk to Thyme. She brought the clear paste over to Gini, who was huddled with Ferryman, talking in a hushed tone.

"Ah, thank you," Gini said, straightening up. "And I can just dip a piece of fruit or a nut in this and I'll be asleep soon?"

"That's right," Adia said suspiciously, but Gini was the picture of innocence.

"Excellent. All right, eat up," Gini said. "We have to be up in a few hours, so try to get some rest if you can."

Thyme pulled out the chair next to her, but Adia took her plate and sat in a corner, ignoring Thyme's disappointed expression. It was the same look Nami had given her when she'd pulled away from him too. But if he'd listened when she told him to leave her alone, he wouldn't be unconscious in the Horrorbeyond now. Proof of what happened to anyone who got close to her. Hopefully Gini could help Thyme after they got out of here, but Adia would only hurt her.

Adia didn't know how Thyme had managed to live in a place like this for a full year. The moans and screams of the Energy Thieves outside the door kept her wide awake and staring at the ceiling all night. Every time she got close to falling asleep, the sound of something clawing at the walls to get inside made her sit up in terror. But then one of Thyme's booby traps or a bolt of lightning would send the creatures retreating into the darkness.

Adia was relieved when Thyme jumped up and started strapping weapons to her back. The sun must have been about to rise. Nami was still out of it in the corner, and Gini floated up and down the room in the Alusi's version of agitated pacing, but she stopped when she saw the two girls.

"Good. You're awake. Now listen, you two," Gini said. "We have to be smart. These creatures might not attack with fire and knives, but they're going to get more aggressive the closer we get to leaving."

"I've lived here for a year," Thyme said with a sniff. "I know what we're dealing with better than you. The second you think you've found a way out, you just end up right back where you started. I stopped trying months ago."

"Well," Adia said, "this time you're not alone. Besides, getting out of here will probably be easier than dealing with Olark."

"What's going on?" a sleepy voice asked.

Adia turned to the corner of the room where Nami was sprawled out.

"Oh, good. Your friend's awake," Thyme said. "We were just saying that getting out of here will be easier than dealing with Olark."

Nami sat up now and stared at the three of them as if they were performers at a carnival.

"Did you say Olark?"

Nami had gone completely still. Could it be possible? Had he been able to see through the curse like Thyme was? Maybe being in the Horrorbeyond would make it so that the curse wouldn't affect him and he wouldn't—

"AHHHHHHH!" Nami screamed.

"Oh no," Adia said, rubbing her head. He'd finally woken up from whatever Sinachi had done to him, and now she'd gone and sent him into a fit. His poor brain.

"What's wrong with him?" Thyme asked, staring at him in horror. "Has he turned?"

"No, no," Adia sighed. "Lower your arrow. So there's this curse—"

Nami stomped up and down, screaming his head off.

"A broom! I need a broom!" Nami shouted.

Adia backed up. Was he looking for a weapon to attack them? Not that she didn't think Thyme could handle him, but she didn't want anyone getting hurt.

"Making up such nonsense! You have a nasty mind because you live in filth! Everything in here needs to be cleaned. Immediately!"

Nami started picking up piles of garbage and putting them on top of other piles of garbage.

"What is he *doing*?" Thyme said. "He's messing up my room!"

"Honestly, I think he's improving it," Adia murmured as Nami cleaned with a fierce passion.

"Terrible," Gini tutted. "Absolutely terrible. People's

reactions can vary. A stronger mind will forget within a minute and go back to normal. The boy is weak."

"He's not weak," Adia said defensively. "And if he is, it's because he got drained by an Energy Thief and dragged by his neck through the Horrorbeyond."

Gini sniffed. "Well, no matter. We need to leave. And we can't have this boy screaming his head off while he searches for a duster."

"What do you propose we do?" Thyme asked.

"We'll just wrap him up and roll him out," Gini said, picking up the fuchsia cloak, which was draped across the back of a chair. She flung it at Nami, and Ferryman immediately wrapped around him like a carpet. Nami's head stuck out as he toppled to the ground, his mouth still going a mile a minute about germs and dirt.

"Oh, for the sake of the stars," Adia said. "Thyme, don't you have a wheelbarrow or pushcart or something? We can't *roll* him out of the Horrorbeyond!"

"But of course we can," Gini said. "We'll take turns giving him a little nudge with our feet."

She demonstrated, pointing a dainty foot forward and giving the Ferryman carpet a shove, sending Nami rolling around the room.

"See? You just walk and kick and walk and *kick*. Then one swift kick into the boat, and off we go!"

"Sounds like a plan," Thyme said, strapping more weapons to her back.

"This isn't a plan," Adia moaned.

"Are you both ready?" Gini asked. "It's time."

Thyme bounded forward as Adia followed them grimly.

Dozens of Energy Thieves lay in wait outside the safety of Thyme's house—yes, even puppies. The puppy monsters fixed their large yellow eyes on Thyme, who glared at all of them, an arrow nocked on her bowstring.

Gini held out her staff in warning. The creatures remained at a safe distance but followed as they moved away from the house.

"There's so many now," Adia said nervously.

"The stone around Thyme's neck is calling to them," Gini said. "And I can feel it stirring. The creature that rules this place. It can sense that the stone is moving."

"What creature?" Adia asked, through gritted teeth. "You never mentioned a creature."

"We all answer to someone," Gini murmured. "These wraiths have a leader."

"I've never seen it," Thyme said, looking surprisingly nervous. "But sometimes there's this sound. A wail like you've never heard before. And whenever it happens, all the wraiths disappear as though they're being summoned or something. If that thing is on the move, we should get moving too."

Gini walked the way they had come, but Adia hesitated. It *was* the same path they'd come down and *should* lead back to the beach . . . but it was all wrong.

Even when her mind was focused on finding Nami and blocking out hissing Energy Thieves, she'd still made a mental map of the landscape. She couldn't help it. It was how her brain worked. Plus, this was unexplored, uncharted territory—it would be a remarkable achievement to have a map, even a partial one, of the Horrorbeyond. So she'd paid careful attention to everything around her. And something about this was wrong. So this was how the Horrorbeyond has separated her from Gini before—Gini hadn't disappeared so much as the path they were on had shifted and taken her somewhere else. And if they got separated again when all the creatures of the Horrorbeyond were looking for them—

"Gini, stop!"

Gini and Thyme came to an immediate halt and turned toward her.

"This isn't the right way."

Adia waited for them to tell her she was wrong, same as the ship's captain had tried to convince Gini she didn't know her own mind. Girls in Zaria weren't exactly treated as people who had anything important to say, who should be listened to. But Gini's gaze was serious.

"What is it, Adia?"

"It's the same path . . . but it's also not. There were low bushes over there before, but now it's a pit of sand. And look over there. *That* used to be a pit of sand and now it's bushes. See?"

Thyme narrowed her eyes. She bent down and picked up a rock, then tossed it a few feet ahead, right where Gini had been about to step. It landed with an angry hiss, as if a cup of water had been flung into a pot of boiling oil, and then it sank into the sandpit.

"What an extraordinary memory," Gini murmured. "You did say I would need you as a guide. Well then, by all means take the lead."

As they walked—and Nami rolled—Adia understood why Thyme had never found her way out of this place. The Horrorbeyond was in constant motion. If anyone tried to retrace their steps, they would only wind up lost, left to wander until either an Energy Thief found them or they died from heat exhaustion.

"Wait! Please, wait for me!"

When Adia saw who was flagging them down, she was so mad she could spit. "You cannot be serious."

Sinachi approached them cautiously with her hands in the air, the picture of innocence.

"And who is this?" Gini sniffed.

"The Energy Thief who hurt Nami."

Gini and Thyme raised their weapons, and Adia jumped in front of Nami. He'd only just stopped babbling about washing dishes. She wasn't letting Sinachi have another go at him.

The power rushed through her blood again, and she clenched her fists to keep Gini and Thyme from seeing the small beams of purple light coming out of her hands. The blades of grass at her feet licked at her heels. They felt sharp. Like actual blades. That was new. But she needed to be careful. Calling up her dark power was coming to her easily now. Too easily.

"I'm not an Energy Thief!" Sinachi cried. "I didn't mean to hurt your friend! I just needed help. She said she had a boat but refused to take me off this island. Can you imagine? I'm sure you two will be more reasonable. After all, it's our duty as creatures of the goddess to help each other. If someone asks for help, you should give every bit of help you can. You should give a thousand percent of your energy, but she refused and—"

"Oh, good grief," Gini said in disgust.

Sinachi's mouth snapped shut so fast a rotten gray tooth fell out.

Adia reined in her power and the sharp blades of grass sank back down into the ground. Gini could handle this. Adia just hoped no one had noticed what she was doing.

"A *thousand* percent, you say?" Gini continued. "We all have precious little energy to spare, my dear. And I'll be keeping that thousand percent for myself, thank you very much. Find another, soulless one. You're wasting your breath with me. I *am* the goddess."

Fire shot out of Gini's eyes. Adia jumped back. She grabbed Thyme's arm without thinking, but Thyme didn't push her away. She was too busy gaping at the flames that now surrounded Sinachi in a fiery cage. The Energy Thief gave a few attempts at breaking free but backed up every time the fire singed her. All pretense of sweetness fell away as the creature hurled curses at them.

"Shall we continue?" Gini said, calmly walking past the screaming Sinachi.

"What is she?" Thyme whispered to Adia as she stared at Gini's fire.

"An Alusi."

Thyme's eyes widened. "One of the guardians? They walk among your people?"

Adia snorted. "They most certainly do not. These are unique circumstances. Although," she said, remembering what she'd overheard that night in the library, "she's not at her full strength unless she's in the stars."

"This is her in a weakened state?" Thyme asked. "Impressive."

"Hurry, girls. I can feel it," Gini called. "It's caught our scent now. The Horrorbeyond is about to fight back."

"It's because we're close to the shore," Adia said. "Look. You can see the water. We're almost out."

Adia was surprised to find Thyme blinking back tears.

"I never thought I'd be free of this place," she said with a sniffle.

Adia grinned and was about to speak when a terrible booming sound made her cover her ears. It was worse than all the thunder and lightning and hissing. Trees flattened to the ground at the detonation, then flew to the side as something crashed through them.

"What could be big enough to cut through trees like that?" Thyme said, notching an arrow into her bow. She spun around, trying to figure out where the threat was coming from.

The trees went still. Adia held her breath, waiting for the monster.

"Where are you going?" a sweet soprano voice asked.

Adia spun around in the direction of the voice.

"And why are you taking that stone? I like that stone. Who said you could take it away?"

The person attached to the voice stepped forward, and Adia stared into wide brown eyes. Eyes in a head . . . that was held in the hands of a headless girl.

Thyme, who Adia had thought unflappable, began wheezing. "What . . . what . . . what is that?"

"It's Hiroma," Adia moaned. "Hiroma the Headless."

FIFTEEN

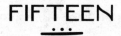

"Headless? Who are you calling headless!" Hiroma snapped. "My head's right here in my hands. What a rude thing to say. I spent all day and night working on my cornrows too. Aren't they pretty?"

Thyme was still wheezing like Bubbles with congestion issues, and Gini stared up at the sky, no doubt praying to Alusia to send a meteor and put them all out of their misery.

"They're . . . lovely," Adia said, a forced smile on her lips as one of her worst fears manifested in front of her. "Such . . . such straight parts."

Hiroma's head beamed and her eyes sparkled.

"Thank you! What's your name?"

Adia studied Hiroma for a second. She was small and looked no more than seven or eight, and wasn't trying to kill her. But Adia knew better now than to trust anyone in the Horrorbeyond. No matter how innocently headless they appeared to be.

"Adia."

"Adia. That's a pretty name! And your hair is so beautiful! So long and thick. Would you like me to braid it for you? I'm very good," Hiroma said, holding out her head and turning it around in her hands, giving it a spin so her braids could be examined from behind. "See?"

"Thank you for the offer," Adia said, backing up slowly, same as Gini and Thyme, who edged closer to the water, rolling Nami behind them. "But I'm afraid we must be going."

Ferryman rolled out and glided onto the water, the cloak blooming until the fuchsia boat reappeared. Nami lay at the bottom of it. He was blessedly silent but had a dazed look on his face. How was she going to explain any of this to him?

The smile dropped from Hiroma's lips.

"No one ever wants to stay with me," she said glumly. "That's why I have to *make* them stay. But then we have lots of fun together. You'll have fun too. Wait and see!"

"No, little girl," Thyme snapped. "We will not. You're the one turning this place into a maze and keeping everyone trapped here until they turn into a wraith?"

"Yes," Hiroma said with a blunt shrug as Thyme snorted. Her eyes turned back to Adia. "But you saw how I switched the trails and you figured how to get out. You're very smart. I like you."

She glared at Thyme.

"But I don't like *you*."

"The feeling's mutual, kid. Now, are you and your decapitated head going to move out of our way? Or do I have to make you move?"

"Thyme," Adia hissed, but the warrior girl already had a throwing star in her hands.

"Ahhh!" Hiroma screamed, and threw her head at Thyme.

Adia dove out of the way and hit the sand as the most hellish game of dodgeball she'd ever seen took place.

"Gini," she gasped as Thyme caught Hiroma's head and hurled it back at her headless body. "Can't you do something?"

"I think I'm already doing enough for your world," Gini muttered, climbing into the boat. "Besides, Thyme is an excellent distraction."

"Thyme!" Adia called, but Thyme was rolling around on the ground, Hiroma's head rolling right after her.

"I can do this all day," Thyme snarled at Hiroma, jumping over her head and spinning out of reach. "This is how they train champions on Nri. And we don't use heads or balls. We use rocks. Keeps us sharp."

Hiroma's braids grew longer and longer until braided ropes wrapped themselves around Thyme's leg and tripped her.

"You headless brat!" Thyme screamed, slicing through a braid with a finger knife Adia hadn't realized the warrior girl was wearing.

"My hair," Hiroma's head gasped, rolling away from Thyme. "You cut . . . my hair?"

A sound unlike any Adia had ever heard before came out of Hiroma's mouth. Adia quickly covered her ears.

"Nooooooo!" Hiroma wailed.

"My ears are bleeding," Adia groaned. "Or are they ringing? No. Definitely bleeding."

Hiroma's head was stomping up and down the sand. "I wasn't due for a trim!"

If Gini wasn't going to stop this, Adia would. She wanted this whole adventure to be over and done with so she could collect her money, buy a house in the middle of nowhere, and go back to having no one to talk to but Bubbles—that is, if he would forgive her for leaving him behind in her moment of despair. She cautiously approached Hiroma, who was literally shrieking her head off.

"Hiroma," Adia said as gently as she could, "Thyme didn't mean to cut your hair. But you can't tie us up and make us stay here."

"But how else will I have any friends?" Hiroma cried. "Everyone is afraid of me."

Adia couldn't believe she'd found sympathy for the headless.

"I know the feeling," Adia said honestly. She took a deep breath.

It was time to admit the truth.

"Where I'm from . . . everyone says I'm an ogbanje. That it's only a matter of time before I unleash hell onto the world."

She saw Gini sit up straight in the boat, and shame pulsed

through her. But Gini hadn't hurled a fury of fire at her yet, so that was a good sign.

Hiroma stared at her with wide eyes.

"You? But you're so nice and smart."

"And strange," Adia said. "I do strange things. I never forget anything I read; I always know what direction to go even if I've never been to a place, like in here. I'd rather be in the woods alone than talk to anyone." She thought of EJ, his body returning to the village shrouded. Of the missionary trying to give her Drops, and the way she caused the entire village to tremble until it began to fall. Of reading in the school library about the misfortune brought by ogbanje, and how perfectly those books described her. "And I've done bad things. I caused a lot of chaos. No one wants to be around me either."

She'd never said it out loud before. She had pretended it didn't bother her if someone crossed to the other side of the road when they saw her coming or if the other girls whispered instead of asking her to play with them. She wasn't sure if she even *liked* being alone or if it was just habit. A safe bubble of solitude where no one thought she was a freak.

"But if there *is* something dark in me, I'm choosing to fight it," she said firmly. "And so can you. And I promise that if you let us go, I'll come back and visit you. But someone needs our help, and we really do have to go now."

"You'll come back?"

"I promise."

"And I can do your hair?"

"If you'd like."

Hiroma picked up her head.

"All right. Only because I like you. You're the only one who talks to me like I'm a normal person. I won't turn you into a wraith."

"Thanks, Hiroma," Adia said, bending down and giving her head a kiss. "And your braids really are incredible."

"Well, it's easy to do when you can put your own head in your lap," Hiroma said shyly.

"Yeah, I'm sure they'll grow back in no time," Thyme muttered as she stomped to the boat.

"*If* you want to bring the bald one with you when you come back," Hiroma said with a glare, "you should tell her to get better at dodgeball."

"Why you little—"

"Come on, Thyme," Adia said, dragging the warrior girl to the boat.

Adia woke up with a jolt. She hadn't meant to fall asleep, but clearly her body had needed the rest. She sat up and rolled her stiff neck from side to side. They must have been sailing for a while now. The sun was setting, but she could make out a village not too far off, the first lights beginning to spark on along the water's edge in the dusk.

"We'll catch a ship back to the Academy from there."

Adia turned to see Gini watching her. She was about to ask the Alusi what the plan was when they got back to the school, how they would lure Darian away from his guards and how she'd capture him with the blood-stained stone, but before she could speak, Gini cleared her throat.

"What were you doing back there?" Gini asked. "With the Energy Thief?"

Adia didn't answer. She wasn't sure what Gini saw, or what she thought.

"I felt an interesting power coming off you," Gini continued. "And what was that you said to Hiroma. That you're an ogbanje?"

Adia fidgeted for a minute, unsure of how much she should say, but Gini wouldn't stop staring at her, and short of jumping off the boat and swimming to shore, Adia wasn't sure what choice she had.

"I am," she finally confirmed. "It's what everyone in my village says. And bad things *do* happen everywhere I go." She pointed to Nami as an obvious example. "That is, I cause them," she added apologetically.

"Is that so?" Gini murmured. "The plants were responding to you in the Horrorbeyond. They told you how to get out of the maze, didn't they? Is that a bad thing?"

"Not exactly," Adia said. She shifted, uncomfortable under Gini's penetrating gaze. "It's not like I heard voices in my head. . . ." Not this time at least. "It was more of an instinct. A gut feeling."

"Seems like more of a gift than a curse," Gini said.

"Shamans have gifts," Adia said. "Ogbanje have dark powers. They *are* cursed. They're the bringers of misfortune. They're even born sickly and miserable. I was. My uncle said when I was younger I kept the entire house up for a full year, coughing every night."

"Yes," Gini said. "And isn't that a convenient explanation when you're dealing with a sickly, unwanted child—it's not a real child at all, just a demon sent to torture us, so I don't have to treat it like a human!"

Adia was startled. Yes, that was how Uncle Eric treated her. How the whole village had treated her, as if she wasn't fully a person, but rather an inconvenient, miserable obligation cast upon them. But wasn't she?

Gini continued, softening her voice. "Most children who are declared malevolent ogbanje did nothing to deserve the label other than having the misfortune of being born sick. Or maybe not being as well behaved as their parents would like."

"So ogbanje aren't real?"

"Oh, I didn't say that," Gini answered. "Ogbanje most certainly are real. And yes, some *are* malevolent spirits, reincarnating over and over in the form of a child causing great chaos."

Adia looked down at her hands.

"But being different doesn't make you evil and having powers doesn't make you an ogbanje. Some people were meant to be gifts for the world," Gini said softly. "Shamans who can come and go through spirit realms as easily as walking through a door. And *their* only misfortune is being born into a family who won't accept them or is afraid of them. Afraid of what they can do."

It sounded nice, but Adia wasn't so sure. If ogbanje were real, and bringers of misfortune, and had dark powers, then surely she was one, no matter how much she might want to believe otherwise. No matter how nice it felt that Gini seemed to want to see the good in her, rather than the bad. She decided to move the subject away from her.

"Well, too bad there's nowhere for shamans to be trained. The Academy is a joke."

Gini snorted. "That's certainly true. It used to be an excellent school in its prime. I mean, it didn't hold a candle to Imo Mmiri, but it was a very good option for people whose abilities weren't strong enough to hear Imo Mmiri's call."

"Imo Mmiri?" Adia was so excited the boat rocked as she leaned forward, her eyes wide. "It was a real place?"

The mythic rain forest that had always had a lead role in Adia's daydreams was real! A land powered by water and full of mermaids and priestesses. The water spirits that lived there were so strong you couldn't even strike a match. Fire couldn't burn in Imo Mmiri, according to the legends.

"Yes. Very real," Gini said. "A gift from my sister Imo so shamans and channelers and priestesses would have a safe haven to live and practice. Rare for an Alusi to bestow one of the lower realms with so much power, but the energy on Imo Mmiri was comparable to the energy of a star. It's long gone now. Vanished into thin air one night. That's one thing your mortal legends got right. Even the Alusi can't figure out where it went."

Adia leaned back as the puzzle began to click into place.

"A place with the energy of a star. And fire can't burn there."

Gini said nothing as Adia worked out the terrible truth.

"That's why Olark-as-Darian is on a mission to consume Zaria in fire, isn't it? Because the only thing that would be left standing is a land that can't be burned. He's trying to find Imo Mmiri because it has the power of a star. But why? What does he want all that power for?"

"What does he want?" Gini repeated. She paused for a moment and closed her eyes.

"He wants the same thing as every other creature in the universe," she finally said, "human, celestial, animal. He wants to be happy. He wants to be loved and feel special. He wants a home."

Movement in the corner of the boat stopped Adia from asking more questions. Thyme was still sleeping, but Nami stirred. She prepared herself to tell him the lie that she, Gini, and Thyme had come up with.

"Adia? What's going on?!" Nami gasped. Adia took him in. He looked terrible. She supposed they all did. Her own hair was probably sticking out in fifty directions and full of thorns and twigs too. The Horrorbeyond had done a number on all of them. Gini was the only one whose appearance was obnoxiously perfect.

"Where are we?" he asked.

It was a fair question. On the shore, Adia saw lights from kerosene lamps flickering in the windows like stardust. And even though it was dark, the village was alive with noise.

She could hear it from here. People talking, music blaring, drummers drumming.

"We're headed into a town to catch a ship back to the Academy," she said, carefully moving in the boat until she was sitting next to him. "How are you feeling? You got hit pretty hard with that pawpaw."

Nami stared at her. "What?"

"You were standing under a pawpaw tree, and you got hit in the head when the fruit fell."

"Hit in the . . . No. No, that's not what happened. I was talking to someone. She was horrible. She did something to me. Dragged me through this decaying forest . . ."

Adia felt terrible lying to him like this, but what was the alternative? Tell him the truth about Sinachi and Olark and have him start scrubbing the bottom of the boat for an hour?

"You took quite a hit to the head," Gini said firmly. "Your brain is addled."

"Gini," Adia hissed.

"And who's this?" Nami said, his eyes wide.

"I'm Lady Gini. I've hired Adia as my assistant. She helped me retrieve my cousin over there," she said, pointing to the sleeping Thyme. "We're due at the Academy for Emperor Darian's arrival."

It was like Adia could see Nami's brain working. On the one hand, none of this made sense. But on the other, he wanted to impress someone he thought was rich.

"Ah. I see," Nami said, flashing Adia a look that made it clear he did *not* see. "Well, I guess I need to go back to the

Academy too. I'll need to explain myself and why I got off the boat. I might be in a bit of trouble."

Adia shot him a guilty look. If he got in trouble, it would be because he'd come after her.

"I'm sorry you got dragged into this," she said quietly so only he could hear.

He shrugged. "It's not like you wanted me to come after you."

"Still . . ." she said, worried about what would happen to him. "What happens if you get let go from of your post, same as I did?"

"Don't worry. It'll never be that bad. My dad's a mess, but everyone in the capital likes my mom. She's the sweetest person you'll ever meet, just too depressed to leave the house," Nami said with a small smile. "They'll keep me on out of respect for her. You'd like her. Maybe you and your parents can come visit us in the capital sometime? It might cheer her up if I bring a friend home."

"I don't have parents," Adia said. She could see Nami gearing up to launch into an *I'm sorry*, but she didn't want to talk about it. She didn't like bringing the few memories she had of her mother to the surface. Memories of a woman whistling around the house and singing. She couldn't even remember her mother's face, but thinking about her still made Adia want to cry. Would she have accepted Adia? Or would her mother have also reached the conclusion that she was too strange, too unfortunate to love?

"I live with my mom's half sister, but she never talks

much about my mom's side of the family. So I can't miss what I never knew," she said quickly, and hoped that would be the end of the subject.

Thankfully, Gini spared her from having to say more.

"We're here," she said just as the hull of the boat thunked against land. "Thyme, wake up." Gini moved to whack the warrior girl with her staff, but even with her eyes still closed, Thyme grabbed the staff in midair before it made contact with her shoulder, then yawned. Gini gave an impressed look and pulled her staff back.

"Oh. Is your friend awake?" Thyme said, glaring at Nami. "Not going to try to sweep the boat clean, are you?"

Nami's jaw dropped. "Huh?"

"Nothing," Adia said, shooting Thyme a warning look as they pushed the boat onto shore with an oar. Thyme was the first one to hop out of the boat, the loamy beach squelching beneath her shoes. She stared at the twinkling night lights of the small fishing village.

Adia quickly jumped out after her. This was the first place besides the Horrorbeyond that Thyme had seen in five hundred years. And judging from the shock on Thyme's face, it looked nothing like Nri.

"Thyme?" she whispered. "Are you all right?"

"But. . . this is all wrong," Thyme said. Her body was shaking. "There shouldn't be people here. I can tell where we are from the position of the stars, and there's no village here. Just active volcanoes."

The volcanoes of Zaria had gone dormant centuries ago

and villages built around them, but Adia didn't bother to say it. Thyme was finally facing reality.

"What you and Gini said is true," she said dully. "I'm not in Nri anymore, am I? The blood-stained stone took me to another time."

"It's true. I'm sorry."

"So my friends are all . . ." Thyme's face hardened. "This is all the Bright Father's fault. I might kill him myself before Gini gets the chance."

"Thyme, you can't take on Olark all by yourself," Adia began, but Thyme wasn't listening.

"And if I got taken out of my world, then there has to be a way for me to get back," she said, her voice now determined.

"Thyme . . . I don't think—"

"We'll discuss it later," Thyme said. "The boy is coming. Don't say Olark's name. I can't deal with another cleaning fit right now."

"Adia, are you sure about that woman?" Nami asked as he approached. "I mean . . . look at her!"

Gini was gesturing dramatically to Ferryman and pushing him back into the water.

"She's having a full-on conversation with a *boat!*" Nami said in disbelief. "Telling it to 'go on now, git!' like it's a dog she decided to set free."

Adia couldn't think of a response. What could she say? That Gini was probably a few days away from completely losing it?

"Don't mind my cousin," Thyme said. She stepped

behind Nami and herded him away from Gini. "She's always been unique like that."

"But—"

"Did you ever stop at this village when you were bringing luggage to the Academy?" Adia asked, desperate to distract him from Gini's bizarre behavior. "I've never seen it. Is it always so lively this time of night?"

"No, actually," Nami said curiously. "It's usually pretty dead here no matter the time of day."

A fisherwoman walked past them.

"Hey!" Nami called out. "Is something going on tonight?"

"The emperor sailed by in a great gold ship a few hours ago," the woman answered with a friendly smile. "The whole village made a celebration out of it. Everyone came out to wave at the flotilla. This party will go on all night. You're not from here?"

"No," Gini said, finally joining them. Adia glanced back to the water. Gini had sent Ferryman sailing off into the night, back to his post in the Serpentine.

"We're just staying for the night to catch a ship of our own."

"Eagle's Nest Inn should have a couple of rooms for you," the fisherwoman said. "Nothing fancy, but it's cheap and the food's edible."

Gini sighed, steam coming out of her mouth. Adia had a headache. Gini was even forgetting to hide her power now. Adia hoped it didn't mean her grip on reality was already beginning to fade.

"That sounds so dreadful," Gini said.

"What?" the fisherwoman asked.

"She said you're so helpful," Adia corrected.

"Better get a move on," the woman said, looking at the sudden burst of steam in confusion. "Not sure why it got so foggy all of a sudden. It's been such a clear night, but I guess rain might be coming."

"We will," Adia said, eager to get Gini out of sight. "Thank you, auntie."

"What?" Thyme whispered. "She's your aunt?"

"No, no," Adia whispered back. "Just call women her age *auntie* when you're here."

Thyme's nose scrunched up, but she nodded.

For a moment, Adia thought about her own uncle and auntie. She hoped the Swamplands were recovering. Maybe there was a chance she could help fix the destruction she'd caused last month. She just had to fix herself first. But for the first time since this all started, she felt a bit hesitant about getting rid of her power. She'd used it to save herself from Sinachi. And it had saved them all from wandering around the Horrorbeyond in Hiroma's maze forever. Yes, the first few times that power had come out of her she'd been destructive. But she was learning to control it now—She shook herself. No, it was still for the best to be rid of it.

"Do you think you'll be all right going back to the Academy?" Nami asked. "Even if you're with Gini . . ."

Adia knew why Nami was worried. She'd almost forgotten about getting expelled. Almost.

"I'll stay out of Mallorie's way. And Gini's only going to be there for the night to see the emperor. No one will notice me. Listen, Nami . . ."

Her voice trailed off, and she fidgeted her hands. She took a deep breath and started again. "Look. I'm sorry for how I've been acting. I was upset, and I took it out on you. I'd just gotten expelled and—"

"And *I* was pretty insensitive about everything that happened with Mallorie, wasn't I?" Nami said sheepishly.

Adia felt a rush of relief. She hadn't realized how guilty she felt about blowing him off.

"So . . . we're friends?" she asked.

"What was that?" Nami said, feigning disbelief. "Adia Kelbara has *friends?*"

"It's been an interesting week," she said, rolling her eyes. "I guess I picked up a few friends along the way. But you were the first one. I just didn't realize it back then."

"Well, I'm glad you figured it out now," he said, smiling at her. Her face went hot and she didn't know where to look, so she grinned and stared at the ground. She'd been more open in the past day that she had been in her entire life. And nothing bad had happened. In fact, maybe something good had happened.

SIXTEEN

A loud thump woke Adia from a deep sleep. It took her a second to remember she wasn't in the Swamplands or the Horrorbeyond, but safe at an inn just a few hours away from the city of Chelonia and the Academy. She sat up, untying her sleeping scarf from her hair. The source of the thumping was in front of her—Thyme, already up and exercising, of all things. Adia flopped back down. Hopefully Thyme didn't notice she was awake. She'd probably make her train too.

The next boat to Chelonia didn't leave until early afternoon, which meant they'd be back at the Academy by dinner. Hopefully before the kola nut ceremony welcoming Emperor Darian to the school. Emperor or not, everyone had to go through the ceremony. Adia wondered if the kola would break into only two pieces.

"Finally! You're awake!" Thyme jumped up from a plank

position in one fluid motion and bounced up and down in an excited jog. "Gini left early for the market. Do you want to do a few reps of—"

"No."

The day would be horrible enough without starting it by doing push-ups. Adia got out of bed and stretched.

"How long have you been awake?" she asked.

"A few hours," Thyme said. "I tried to wake you earlier, but you swatted me away in your sleep."

"Is Nami up?"

"He's out cold. I think the whole Horrorbeyond thing took it out of him," Thyme said casually. "But I'm ready to do this. Once we deal with Olark-as-Darian, I can figure out how to get back to my world. Now, come here so I can do your hair. You've still got twigs in it. Gini came in while you were sleeping and told me to make you look respectable."

Adia wasn't sure there was any hope of Thyme returning to her world. Her world was a different time, and it was called *the past* for a reason. But maybe there *was* a chance Thyme had some family left. When this was over, she could help Thyme try to find them.

For now, all Adia could do was help Thyme stay distracted, if that's what Thyme wanted. She made no protest when Thyme ushered her into a chair but winced at how roughly the warrior girl combed her thick, coiled hair.

"Stars save me, Thyme," she yelped at a particularly hard yank. "Start with the ends!"

Her hand gentled, and Adia sighed. "I should shave it off

like yours," she said.

"Don't you dare," Thyme said, going to work on the coils at the nape of her neck. "I didn't shave my head because I wanted to."

Adia was surprised at the harshness in Thyme's voice.

"It's a show of dedication when a girl is declared a champion of Nri. If you're a Chosen One, you renounce everything to focus on your quest. Your life, your possessions, your vanity. My hair used to grow down to my waist. Enjoy my shiny brown head while you can, because I'm not going to so much as trim it when it grows back."

Thyme stepped in front of Adia and smoothed out the front of whatever hairstyle she was creating, then went back to pulling on her hair. "So what's this Academy like anyway?"

"A joke," Adia said with a snort. "It's more rich students deluding themselves into thinking they have magic powers, less anyone with an actual shamanic ability. Although . . ."

She thought about the abandoned room where she'd hidden the broken vase. A student who'd shown potential and then left without even bothering to take their things with them. Why hadn't she realized how strange that was?

"Someone told me students with abilities do show up sometimes. But then they disappear."

"Disappear?" Thyme said, letting up on the hair pulling. "People disappeared in Nri too when the Bright Father showed up. Powerful people."

"Powerful? Like chiefs?"

"No, like the healers and wisewomen."

"Lebechi didn't make it sound suspicious," Adia said with a frown. "Just that those students got sick of dealing with the fakes and moved on."

"Do you think Olark has something to do with it?" Thyme asked.

She wondered. If those students hadn't returned to their homes, that would have been huge news. Children vanishing from a school? Their families would search for them, same as she'd searched for EJ before she had accepted that he was dead. Same as Thyme's family had probably searched for her. But she'd never heard even a whisper of such a thing.

"I don't know. I don't know how something like that could be covered up. But if he does have something to do with it, I guess we'll find out soon enough."

Adia touched her hair, wincing at how tight it was. Then she got up, thanked Thyme, and said, "Come on. Let's go to the market, see if we can find Gini."

The market was a mess of people, all crushing in at each vendor, jockeying to get the best piece of fruit, the freshest cut of meat. Thyme dodged between the shoppers easily, as instinctually as a fish returning upstream, but Adia had a little more trouble.

"You have to be agile," Thyme said.

"I'm agile of mind," Adia groaned. "I've never been any-where this crowded in my life."

But the markets were full of delicious food, and Adia had a little money left over from the school's final payment to buy a thing or two. They stopped at a stand selling bags of warm puff-puffs, the sweet aroma of freshly fried dough pulling them in. They gave each other a look. Adia didn't think twice about reaching into her bag and telling the vendor, "We'll take two." After all, when this was over, either she'd get paid enough by Gini that it wouldn't matter, or else Olark would have destroyed them all. May as well enjoy some puff-puffs while they had the chance.

By the time they were done eating, there was still no sign of Gini, but they had found a market stall selling some of the ugliest clothing they'd ever seen. Skirts the size of houses due to all the layers of petticoats, alongside tops that looked like they were made for dolls with their restrictive corsets.

"What in the world?" Thyme muttered. "Is this where fashion has gone over the last five hundred years?"

"It's the style from beyond the Sunless Mountains," Adia said with a snort. "It hasn't really caught on with locals, but I guess if someone wants to prove they're the pious, civilized Zarians the empire wants them to be, wearing the Sunless Mountain's clothing is a good start."

"Well, if we need to sneak into the emperor's dinner tonight, maybe we could get something here. Pretend we're rich friends of Sunless himself."

Adia laughed skeptically.

"C'mon," Thyme said. "At least let *me* try something on. All I've had to wear is this same dirty tunic for the last year. Or five hundred, depending on how you're counting it."

They spent the next hour driving the stall vendor mad,

trying on every piece of clothing they could, Adia's coins jangling in her pocket like a promise even though they both knew they probably couldn't afford anything here. Each time they'd show each other a new ridiculous outfit—hats ugly as sin, dresses so big they nearly drowned in them— they'd laugh, making the vendor lose a little more patience. When Adia found something that she hoped made her look at least respectable-adjacent, she stood in front of Thyme.

"What do you think?" Adia asked.

The vendor looked at Thyme hopefully.

Thyme looked her up and down, appraising the outfit. Finally she burst out laughing and said, "Maybe we'd better let Gini pick something. I'm not sure any of this screams, 'You should let me into the emperor's dinner.'"

Adia barely had time to pull the dress off before the vendor pushed them out of the stall. "GO!"

"I don't know why Gini needs me to look respectable," Adia grumbled as they walked away, back toward the inn. "I'm just going to lure him out to her. Although Gini never said how she expects me to do that."

"You're going to render him unconscious and bring him to me," Gini said, gliding up behind them with a basket of food and a bag tucked underneath her arm.

Adia jumped, then glared, though Thyme seemed unbothered. It was a lot easier to walk through the sea of people with Gini, because everyone just parted out of her way, clearing a path.

"I beg your pardon?" Adia asked.

"Don't worry. It will be simple. You'll just slip him this," Gini said, producing a kola nut. "I've laced it with that sleeping medicine you were so good to make me."

"I knew that was what you were up to," Adia snapped, but Gini carried on as if she hadn't spoken.

"After it takes effect, you and Thyme will bring him to me behind the Academy. The woods there are deep and powerful. No one with sense would venture into them. I'll perform the exorcism there."

Adia was going to kill her.

"So when you said lure him to you," Adia said through gritted teeth, "what you really meant was that you want me to *kidnap* the emperor of Zaria?"

"No. I want you to help set him free. Think of the boy, Adia. Possessed and devoid of all hope of ever being free of the demon inside him."

The portrait of Darian from the Academy swam in front of her. The trapped look in his eyes. Her exasperation faded. Yes. She could do this. She could help Darian. She gave Gini a curt nod.

Gini smiled, knowing Adia was officially on board.

"But how would we manage to drag an emperor out of the Academy without being spotted?" Thyme asked.

"I can take care of that," Adia said. "I have every map of the Academy memorized." Darian would undoubtedly stay in the grandest chamber at the school, the Red Room. Adia knew exactly where the escape passage in that chamber was.

"If this actually works, we can drag him out through one of

the passages and no one will see us. The trickiest part will be switching out his kola nut with the one that will make him fall asleep. I used to work in the kitchens, and I was there when they were making plans for his arrival. I might be able to pull it off."

"I'm glad to see some things never change," Thyme said. "You still have your guests break a kola nut?"

"It's still tradition," she confirmed as they reached the inn and went back to their room.

Even in the Swamplands, if someone entered your home, they were offered the excruciatingly bitter kola nut as a welcome and sign of friendship. Not even the Bright Father and his missionaries could do away with a custom that had existed for thousands of years.

"He'll be the first person to eat it tonight when he welcomes everyone. But I still say his guards will be a problem," Adia said nervously.

"We have Thyme now for that. Speaking of Thyme— here." Gini tossed the bag she had tucked under her arm at the warrior girl. "This is for you. Put it on once we get rid of that boy of Adia's."

"Nami isn't *my* boy," Adia protested.

"What is this?" Thyme asked in horror, pulling thick red robes from the bag.

"Adia is my traveling companion, which will allow her to walk around as a servant," Gini said. "But you will enter the Academy as a revered nun of the Hills. You'll be the last person anyone suspects of fighting with guards."

"But who's going to think I'm a nun?" Thyme cried. "What if someone asks me for advice?"

Adia thought about Nami's reaction to her Mallorie Amber encounter.

"It'll be easier than you think. If someone tells you they have a problem? You sidestep it with some positive statement and hope they don't realize you haven't said anything useful. Say someone asks for advice on dealing with a husband who drinks too much palm wine. All you have to do is look superior and say, 'It's all perfect. That's how we learn. Everything happens for a reason.'"

Thyme stared at her.

"It's all . . . What? But that's ridiculous. What's perfect about a husband who drinks too much?"

"Absolutely nothing," Adia said with a shrug. "But there's no way to give a response to that without seeming negative. It's an effective way to shut someone up if you don't actually want to listen to them. I'm sure the Hill nuns don't sound as ridiculous, but it's unlikely the nobles will be able to tell the difference between a sage and a complete fraud such as yourself."

"Hey!" Thyme said, but she was laughing.

"Trust me," Adia said with a grin, "people will nod as if you've said something wise because you'll *look* like you're supposed to be wise."

"Well, I don't see how anyone with a mind would think I gave them helpful advice if that's all I said, but I'll take your word for it. You're the Zarian, not me." Thyme fiddled with her new robes. "I suppose I'd rather avoid my problems too and pretend everything is somehow perfect and happened for a reason. Maybe I'm avoiding things myself. It's easier to join in another quest than to wrap my head around the fact that everyone I knew in Nri might be . . ."

Adia looked at Thyme in concern. She'd held herself together for days, distracted herself, but now sadness flooded her face.

"When I decided to take on the Bright Father, I knew what I was risking," Thyme continued. "I've always known that the next quest might be the last. And in the end, I thought I would die in the Horrorbeyond. But still, to come out of it and find the world is completely wrong and all my friends are gone . . . There's no way to go back into the past, is there, Gini?"

"I'm sorry," Gini said. She looked surprisingly sympathetic, maybe thinking about all the things she would change if she could go back in time. "The past is over and done with. There's no going back into it."

Thyme didn't respond—she just fixed her face, as though she were trying not to give anything away. Adia walked over and gave her a hug, flinching when she felt all the weapons strapped to Thyme's back. Thyme allowed the hug for a few seconds, then pulled away.

"So what am I supposed to do now? Where do I go when all this is over?"

"You can come with me," Adia said, surprising herself. "I mean, I don't have a home yet, but if we defeat Olark and he doesn't kill us first, Gini will make sure we're all set for life."

"When," Gini corrected. "Not if."

Adia continued, ignoring her. "We could buy a home in the mountains and never have to talk to anyone but each other and our cats. If you want to, of course."

Thyme's face finally cracked. She looked like she was close to tears, but she nodded, her eyes scrunched like she was trying to keep herself from crying. "I guess if I have to get stuck in some other time, being stuck with you isn't the worst," she said, wiping away a rogue tear. "But I'll need a dog too," she added with a smile. "Maybe a few."

"As long as they aren't wraith dogs, I think we can work it out," Adia said. She offered her hand, pinkie stretched out, and they promised on it.

Thyme's face turned serious. "But first I want revenge. I want to look the Bright Father in the eye when you banish him from this world. Gini, when do we leave?"

"In an hour," Gini said.

"All right, then," Thyme said. "I'll go wake up Nami. Thanks for putting up with my denial for this long."

"You're handling it better than I would," Adia said honestly.

Thyme gave them a sad smile and opened the door but then turned back.

"Here," she said, reaching under her collar and pulling out the chain. "You got me out of the Horrorbeyond, just like you promised. And you told me the truth from the start about Nri. I owe you this."

Thyme placed the blood-stained stone on a table and left the room.

Adia walked over to the stone. She reached out to touch it but then pulled back. "If I touch it, will it do what it did to Thyme and take me somewhere?"

Gini shook her head. "No, I'm in control of it now. You can touch it."

She didn't know what she'd expected, but it felt normal enough. She turned it in her hand, examining it from all sides.

How could something so small be enough to contain a demon? she wondered.

But she didn't doubt that Gini knew what she was talking about. Maybe the girl Thyme mentioned had known it could contain him too.

"Did Olark ever lose the stone before?" she asked Gini. "Or have it taken by someone else?"

"What?" Gini said. "No, of course not. I think Thyme's the only person who would have the audacity. Olark always had the stone until she ended up in the Horrorbeyond with it and inadvertently weakened him. Why do you ask?"

"Thyme mentioned that Olark came to Nri to look for a girl. He only burned it down after he realized she wasn't there. That he said he would have no choice but to burn the world down if she didn't come forward. A shaman named Viona. I thought maybe she'd stolen the stone from him too or something."

"Viona?" Gini was visibly startled.

"You know her?"

"I know *of* her," Gini murmured. "She was rumored to be the most powerful shaman Zaria had seen since Ovie, but I always assumed she died in one of the fires. What else did Thyme say?"

"That he threw out another curse. Though I suppose he thought it was a blessing or protection spell that would get Viona to trust him," Adia said, placing the blood-stained stone back down.

"Did he, now?" Gini said, narrowing her eyes. "I'll have to ask Thyme to tell it to me."

"No need," Adia said. "I memorized it."

"You . . ." Gini gave a small laugh. "Yes, of course you did. Recite it to me, please."

"Hear my words throughout the world and read them in the skies."

Adia felt a bit like Ikenga in the library. It made her feel ill to think of those words, let alone speak them out loud. But she swallowed and continued reciting to Gini in a shaky voice.

"She of Ovie is protected
By the good and wise.
Her name will be a Word of Power
In a world of lies."

She took a deep breath before speaking the most disturbing part of it.

"And anyone who brings her harm
Will be the one who dies."

Gini closed her eyes and shook her head.

"That poor girl. Wherever she hid herself, I hope she never had to hear that *blessing* from the creature who destroyed her people."

"Was she very young?" Adia asked.

"Yes. Probably around your age. And so much power. I heard she was close to mastery of all the shamanic realms."

Adia bit into her fruit. The teachers at the Academy were useless, but Gini wasn't. And who better to learn about the shamans than from one of the goddesses who gifted them their powers.

"What are the realms?"

"Water, fire, death," Gini said. "And plants. Ovie mastered all of them in his day. It's why he was the most powerful shaman in Zaria. Most would need a lifetime to even master one. Viona might have rivaled him if she was getting that close at such a young age. We'll never know." She pointed to a pot near the window. "Why don't you try touching that plant, Adia."

"What?"

Adia frowned. In the Swamplands, they would consider that plant a weed, but the trumpetlike white flower was pretty. She could see why someone had put it in the room as decoration.

"Why?"

"Just see what happens. Focus on nothing but the plant. Clear your mind."

She put her glasses back on and walked over to the plant.

The flower petals were soft like satin. But that was all. No light came out of her hands, no earthquakes. Then she hissed and pulled her hand back. There was no voice whispering this time, but she felt the same nervousness she had that day at the Academy when Mallorie was about to shove her face into a poisonous plant—but worse.

"What is it?" Gini asked.

"It's lethal," Adia said in shock.

"Jimsonweed," Gini said with a triumphant smile. "A garden pest to farmers, a study in poison to shamans. And a master plant. Powerful spirits from the stars live inside the master plants. And they get quite happy when they find a person who can hear them. Their language is too high a vibration for most mortals to hear, same as an Alusi's name. But some bloodlines can handle it."

"Gini, I don't know what to tell you," Adia said, backing away from the potted poison. "*My* bloodline is currently wailing over a Bright Father statue and singing hymns. And why are you acting like touching a plant and knowing how to kill a person with it is a positive?"

"Because," Gini said, "you would also know how to save a person before they poisoned themselves. It's just power—you can choose how you want to use it. But you've convinced yourself you're going to harm people."

Adia clenched and unclenched her fist a few times. The

flowers moved up and down as she did it. Turning up toward the window, then drooping down toward the ground. She held her hand still, and the flowers stayed pointing upward, taking in the sun.

Maybe she had more of a choice in this than she realized, but she had no idea what she was doing. She hadn't known she would cause an earthquake that day. And now that she knew she had power, it wasn't like she would ever willingly use it to hurt anyone. But . . .

"I can't control it," she admitted.

Gini nodded. She thought for a minute, then went to a table set up with cups, a water pitcher, and small bowls of sugar and salt.

She dumped the contents of the salt bowl into a napkin and folded it up tight.

"Well, you're going to need to learn," Gini said. "And we'll deal with that after the exorcism. But for now, if you ever feel yourself going too far like you did when you caused the earthquake, salt will help bring you back. Add a few pinches to some water and drink it down."

"Salt?" Adia asked, taking the napkin from Gini. "Why?"

"For the same reason too much salt kills plants or leaves people feeling thirsty. If the power is taking you too far, salt will effectively dampen that energy. Not for too long, but long enough for you to get ahold of yourself."

Adia nodded.

"Like how nothing will grow on salted earth?"

"Exactly," Gini said. "It's a temporary solution, but that's all we have time for right now."

Adia carefully put the napkin into her bag, trying not to spill a drop of the salt. It gave her some sense of security to have it, even though she was about to walk into the most dangerous situation she'd ever been in in her life. Because tonight she would come face-to-face with the demon emperor.

SEVENTEEN

Their strange party walked through the fishing village and to the docks, where dozens of small boats lined the water as fisherfolk brought in their hauls. Adia held her breath as much as she could. She'd never been able to stand the smell of fish, and the docks were lined with nets and barrels full of them as people haggled with the fishers over prices.

Thyme kept scratching at the headwrap now pinning down her ears. Nami hadn't noticed Thyme's pointy ears yesterday, but they would be too obvious in daylight. Adia was about to tell Thyme to stop scratching, but suddenly a chill went through her despite it being such a hot day.

It felt like someone was watching her.

Adia glanced around. Nothing looked out of the ordinary. It was just people buying fish. That, and a long line of children standing in an orderly fashion.

"Never thought I'd see those people again," Thyme muttered.

"You know them?" Adia whispered. She let Nami walk a bit ahead so he couldn't hear their conversation.

"Well, not *them*. But I know those outfits. The Bright Father's followers wore those awful black robes and called themselves his missionaries. They accused anyone who opposed him of being a witch. Myself included. They probably would have disappeared me too if I hadn't . . . disappeared myself," Thyme said with a roll of her eyes.

So that's where the missionaries came from, Adia thought.

Even when Olark disappeared, his missionaries from beyond the Sunless Mountains had carried on in his name. Mindwashing all of Zaria for centuries.

One by one, each child stepped forward, tilted their head back, and opened their mouth as a missionary dressed in black placed one Drop on their tongue.

"What's going on?" Thyme whispered. "What are they giving those kids?"

"They're call Drops," Adia said, keeping her head down as they walked past the missionaries. "It makes you . . . obedient."

Gini frowned. "Adia, do you know what's in that vial?" she asked under her breath so Nami wouldn't hear.

"Drops. Made from the agrias vine."

"What does the vine look like?"

"Thick and brown. As hard as wood too. It's not like a soft green vine climbing up a tree, even though it can definitely climb. You could use it as a bat if you wanted, it's so tough. Why?"

For the first time since she'd known her, Gini looked nervous.

"There are plants that are so strong, so revered, they can grow anywhere in the universe. On land, in space. We have a vine like that on Alusia. It has many healing properties but can also be used as a strong sedative of the mind. It would make someone easier to manipulate if they took it in liquid form. I didn't realize it grew here."

"The missionaries say it soothes the mind and opens your heart to better feel the Bright Father's love," Adia said. "They make everyone who's old enough take a Drop before sermons." She frowned. "At least, everyone in the poorer parts of Zaria like where I'm from. People who've been dosed will sit for five hours without moving a muscle, baking in the sun with a smile on their face while they get yelled at about how sinful they are."

"A smile on their faces, yes," Gini said. "But what do their eyes look like?"

"Their eyes?" Adia thought of her aunt and uncle. "Dulled. At least until the Drops wear off."

"Dulled and defenseless," Gini murmured. "Olark-as-Darian might be starting with the poorer regions no one pays attention to, but it won't stop there. He'll expand until he has an entire empire that would never question his rule or commands. Everything he's ever wanted."

Before Adia could say any more, Nami groaned.

"What's wrong?" Adia asked, walking up to him.

"Over there," he said, tilting his head.

A dozen Gold Hats were on the dock, looking as mean and intimidating as ever. Everyone hurried out of their way without making eye contact. Nami lowered his gaze when a man with muscular arms the size of small trees glared at him.

"That's one of my superior officers. I better go explain myself," Nami said nervously. "I might not see you again till we get to the Academy."

"Go," Adia said, relieved that the question of how to get Nami away from their dangerous mission was so easily solved. She just hoped he wasn't walking into something worse. But *would* she see him again at the Academy? Once this was over, they might never meet again.

"Nami, wait," she said on a whim. He paused, and she rushed up to him and gave him an awkward hug. "I really am sorry about everything."

He gave her a huge smile.

"It's all right. I'm sure everything will be fine. I'll find you at the Academy."

She waved goodbye. Maybe she would send him a letter later and explain everything. Or visit him and his mother in the capital someday. But for now, being with the Gold Hats was safer than being with her.

"Adia, why is that person staring at you?" Thyme asked.

"What person?" She'd almost forgotten the uneasy feeling of being watched earlier.

She followed Thyme's gaze. A missionary stared at her

with a fascinated expression, as though he recognized her. Adia knew it couldn't be for something good.

But then he turned back to the line and continued to place drops on children's tongues. Maybe she'd imagined it.

"He must have been looking at something else," Adia said.

If he'd recognized her as the girl who had destroyed the Swamplands, he would have sounded an alarm, and so far no one was coming to put her in chains. But still, he made her nervous.

"That's our boat," Adia said. "Let's get out of here."

She wanted as much distance between her and the missionaries as possible.

Ferryman had taken them closer to Chelonia than Adia had realized, and from there it was only a short boat ride before they were back at the Academy. While they were gone, someone had tried to beautify the entrance to the school for the emperor's arrival. White and yellow flower petals were strewn on the ground, and brightly woven tapestries covered the holes in the walls, as bronze statues aimed arrows into the sky.

It didn't help.

Mushrooms had already sprouted up and covered half the statues, and the Academy's ever-growing weeds strangled the tapestries. A professor appeared to be in the middle of a staring contest with one of the walls as if daring it to act up. It was all in vain, as a board sprang loose and whacked him on the head.

Thyme snorted with laughter as the professor clutched his head and ran away, howling. "This place would fit in well with the Horrorbeyond."

But Adia wasn't laughing. Along with the sad attempt at redecorating, a brand-new gate with fierce iron teeth now stood in front of the doors leading into the Academy. Two Gold Hats stood guarding it, their machetes shiny in the sun.

She turned her head away from the sharp blades, focusing instead on the nobles walking through the gate. She mimicked their demeanor, straightening her shoulders, pinching her eyes and lips, and looking down her nose.

After a few seconds, she lifted her glasses off to rub at her eyes. "How can they see when they're glaring all the time?" she wondered.

"I can't risk getting any closer," Gini said. "I'll meet you at the waterfall in the woods. I assume you know where it is?"

Adia nodded. The waterfall had been marked on the Academy map.

"Thyme, you go first. I'll stay here to make sure you don't have any trouble getting in."

Adia held her breath as Thyme walked down the flower-petal-lined path to the Academy. Hopefully, Thyme could walk in through the front gate without issue, but they couldn't risk Adia being recognized. Plus it was better for them to go separately so no one noticed *two* uninvited guests. But not only did no one stop Thyme, several people gave the sign of piety due to a member of the spiritual order. They touched their hearts, then placed two fingers in the middle of their forehead and bowed. Thyme performed wonderfully, giving the slow, benevolent, superior nod one would expect from a Hill nun, looking every bit the part in her dark red robes.

"They never suspect a girl," Gini said with a snort. "All right, Adia. I'll see you at nightfall. Go." When she saw Adia hesitating, she clapped her hands together twice, sparks flying. "Whoops, I promised Ikenga I wouldn't clap while I'm down here. One time I did, and it created a sonic boom so strong it flattened an entire forest." She winked, but Adia wasn't sure she was kidding. She bet that was how the great Alusian Plains—said to be given to humankind by the Alusi to help feed herds of livestock—were created. Adia was starting to suspect many of the "gifts" of the Alusi were just accidents.

"I'll see you in a few hours," she said, giving Gini a nervous nod as she rushed down a tree-lined trail.

Adia took a path only the servants used. It was blessedly empty. She didn't know whether to smile or glare when, after a few minutes of going down the trail, she came upon the library. A new wrought-iron gate stood in front of the library's entrance, with a thick chain wrapped around it.

Is that because of Olark-as-Darian? she wondered as she stared at yet another Academy eyesore.

She felt the same pull as last time, when she'd ended up overhearing the curse—but she wouldn't fall for that twice.

"Absolutely not," she muttered, thinking about everything that had happened since she'd last been inside the library and everywhere she'd been since then. EJ would have been impressed with her turning into a world traveler, even if her travels had been for all the wrong reasons. How would she have even described all this to him?

Everything floated around in her mind the way it did when she was drawing maps. The places she'd been and seen began arranging themselves onto an imaginary piece of parchment in her brain with a little footnote about what she'd learned in each location. Starting with her journey from the Swamplands and seeing the burned lands on the ship.

Olark-as-Darian had burned them trying to find where Imo Mmiri is. A land with the power of a star. Enough power to make him whole and let him go home again.

Then the Academy. That was obvious. Where she'd met Gini and learned Olark was back. It was the beginning of her being stuck on the cursed mission.

And finally the Horrorbeyond to get the blood-stained stone. A stone that he hadn't held for five hundred years, yet somehow he still had power.

And then it all clicked together. The map settled into place.

And Emperor Darian's invested a lot of time in the Academy. You might even get to see him. The rumor is he's got some project going on. Lots of shipments back and forth.

Nami had told her what she needed to know the day they met.

"Olark's power source," she said with a groan. "Why didn't I realize it sooner? It's in the Academy."

She had to warn Gini. The blood-stained stone might not be enough if he was this close to whatever his new source of power was.

Adia turned to run back the way she'd came to find Gini, but she stumbled when she saw two miserable-looking Gold Hats walking down the path. They glared at her as they approached.

"What are you doing standing here talking to yourself?" the taller one asked.

Adia swallowed.

"I'm sorry," she said after a few seconds. "I . . . I was brought on to help in the kitchens for the emperor's arrival."

The Gold Hats grinned at each other. Not a nice grin— the grin of two people who thought they'd just found an easy target.

One spun around, feigning confusion.

"Doesn't look like any kitchens are around here. Do you see any kitchens?"

"No, none," his partner said, moving his hand toward his machete. "This seems mighty suspicious. A young girl running around. What *I* think is that some peasant girl snuck her way into the Academy to get a glimpse of Emperor Darian."

Adia took a deep breath and did her best to channel the confidence of Thyme and Lebechi. She stood up straight.

"And what *I* think is that Maka is going to have my head if you delay me gathering the herbs she wanted. We can go to the kitchens if you need her to confirm that I work here. Although I can't imagine she'll take the interruption well, when the kitchen is so busy."

The sneers dropped from the Gold Hats' faces. The shorter one nudged his partner.

"You remember what happened last time you made Maka mad," he whispered anxiously. "She made our pepper soup with *ghost* peppers. My stomach's never recovered."

The other one cleared his throat.

"All right, then," he said. "Get on with it. But don't go sneaking around trying to get a glimpse of Emperor Darian. You're a servant, not a guest. Say it."

"I'm a servant, not a guest," she quickly repeated.

He waved his hand and let her go, but they stood still watching her. She had no choice but to walk a little off the trail and pick a few sprigs from a rosemary bush.

There was no going back to warn Gini now. Not without making these two even more suspicious. All she could do was carry on and hope that the exorcism would still go according to plan.

Adia cautiously walked into the Academy. She had to sneak in through a servants' entrance instead of the secret passageways in case those Gold Hats had decided to follow her. But now she was safely inside. All she had to do was find Thyme. It had barely been a week since her expulsion. The servants must have worked to the point of exhaustion to have the Academy transformed to this extent—and also been on constant watch to make sure the cranky school didn't undo their efforts.

The walls had been freshly painted gold, and hand-woven coconut palms covered the wooden floors. She tilted her head up to take in the colorful tapestries now hanging from the ceiling, all the way to the floor. The fabric had to be over forty feet long, with complex embroidery depicting scenes of the emperor in what she assumed were heroic acts of bravery. Olark-as-Darian was many things, but subtle wasn't one of them.

Someone brushed against her dress. Thyme, doing her best to look serene. "Ah, don't I know you? Did your father not request my counsel last summer?"

Adia tried not to cringe at Thyme's best attempt at sounding pious. "You honor me by remembering, wise one," she said before lowering her voice. "There's a false wall near the grand staircase. Underneath a painting. It leads to a bunch of secret passages we can use to sneak around without anyone seeing us. I used them after I got fired. The tunnels were so full of cobwebs I kept getting stuck. No one else knows they exist."

"I think I see it," Thyme said. "That painting over there? Next to that giant yellow bird wearing a girl as a hat?"

"The *what*?"

Thyme nodded her head to the left, and Adia snorted as she spotted who Thyme meant—a girl in a monstrosity of a yellow dress and drenched in pearls, uglier than any outfit they'd tried on at the market stall. The eyesore of a garment was probably considered the height of fashion in the capital—a clear example that money couldn't buy taste. Adia groaned. There was only one person who would wear something so ridiculous. Someone she'd been hoping to avoid.

"Stars save me," she muttered. "It's Mallorie Amber."

"Who's that?" Thyme whispered anxiously. "I didn't think you'd bump into anyone you knew outside the kitchens."

"I hardly *know* her," Adia replied. "She's a student who terrorizes the staff. The one who got me expelled."

Thyme chewed her lip. "What's she going to do if she sees you back here?"

Adia shrugged dismissively and tried not to let her emotions show. But being in Mallorie Amber's presence made her feel humiliated and angry all over again.

"Don't worry about it," Adia said, aiming to sound nonchalant. "I can't imagine she'd remember me. To someone like her, I'm nothing more than an inconvenient piece of dung she stepped on once."

"Are you sure about that? Because it looks like she's staring at you."

To Adia's shock and dismay, Mallorie's eyes *were* focused on her. And she was headed straight toward them.

Please don't recognize me. Adia's heart raced as the girl went crashing through the crowd, pieces of yellow feathers flying off her hideous dress as she barged through people without so much as an *excuse me.* Adia closed her eyes, waiting for Mallorie to start yelling. But she didn't yell. She shoved Adia out of her way and beamed at Thyme as Adia caught herself from falling on the floor.

"What an honor!" she said, giving Thyme a huge smile. "I'm Lady Mallorie Amber."

She paused as if waiting for her name to mean something, but Thyme only raised an eyebrow, unimpressed.

"And?" Thyme said.

Mallorie cleared her throat, obviously annoyed that her name hadn't produced the reaction she'd hoped for.

"*And,*" Mallorie said, her smile less bright than before, "I've been trying to get an invitation to see the monasteries of the Hills for months, but my father says invites are practically impossible to come by. I have a great interest in your teachings. I'm planning to start teaching myself soon. I'd like to share my wisdom as well as my shamanic power. I was thinking of charging thirty-five hundred gold coins per guest, and I'd like to see how the Hill nuns host people."

Thyme opened and closed her mouth, looking a bit like a caught fish.

"Thirty-five hundred gold coins . . . for what?" Thyme asked, giving Adia a dumbfounded look.

Mallorie's eyes narrowed. Adia knew that look.

"For my wisdom and power, of course. To teach the people of Zaria the way of the shaman."

Adia couldn't help laughing. A spoiled brat from the Sunless Mountains charging people to listen to *her* talk about shamanism. Mallorie really was one of a kind.

"Well . . . true wisdom has no price," Thyme murmured.

That wasn't the answer Mallorie wanted to hear.

"Don't be ridiculous," Mallorie snapped.

Thyme lifted her hand, but Adia nudged her in the back.

"No weapons," she whispered.

She knew it was taking Thyme remarkable self-restraint not to pull out whatever sharp object she'd been reaching for in her robes, but her look of serenity faded.

"Besides," Thyme continued, "where I'm from, nobody *chooses* to be a shaman. The universe chooses *them*. Chooses them and their bloodline. And most of them are pretty miserable about it. You think it's easy having to walk between worlds?"

Mallorie's face turned as red as a ripe ackee. Her mouth flattened into a thin angry line.

"You don't know what you're talking about," Mallorie said. Her nasal voice was shriller than ever. "Shamanism is for *all* of us. Once I graduate, I'll have my certificate. And since I'm kind enough to share my wisdom and love, it's your duty to help me with that task."

"Energy Thief," Thyme growled.

"Thyme, calm down," Adia whispered again.

"What did you call me?" Mallorie said in shock.

As painful as the situation was, Adia turned her head to hide her laughter. Mallorie had clearly never been spoken to like this in her life.

"An energy thief," Thyme repeated. "You're a mess. Shamanism isn't for everyone, and anyone telling you otherwise is selling you something. Not everything is for you."

With that, she walked away from the sputtering Mallorie

without a backward glance. Adia fell in step with Thyme.

"That could have been handled better," Adia said, shaking her head.

"We don't have time to deal with nonsense, Adia. We should try to get eyes on the emperor. I'm sure he doesn't really look like *that*," Thyme said, gesturing to yet another new tapestry of Olark-as-Darian, handsome as ever, sitting on a horse and wearing a crown with at least a hundred jewels on it.

Adia glanced at it as they walked by.

"He might," she admitted. "His portrait looks like that too."

The crowd grew animated, jostling her. People clamored over each other as they rushed toward something.

"This way," she said, tugging Thyme's arm and following the crowd. She wished she had a fan. The heat was getting to her. "Stars save me, when did it get so hot in here? It's worse than the Horrorbeyond."

Thyme raised her eyebrows.

"Really? I think it's pretty chilly today. We're going to get rain before the day is over."

"I guess it's just me," Adia said, fanning herself with her hand. "Oh no!"

"What? Another one of your enemies? You really made a reputation for yourself."

Adia ducked behind a statue to avoid the girl carrying a huge basket on her head.

"No, not an enemy."

Sadness overcame her as Lebechi rushed by.

"A friend, I think."

She wanted to say hello, but she knew it was impossible. She had tried not to think about her and Maka because it hurt too much, but she missed everyone in the kitchen. And she missed Bubbles. Maybe she shouldn't have left him behind. But her future wasn't as bleak now. He was probably still sleeping with Lebechi in their old room. When this was all over, she'd bring him to live with her and Thyme.

The crowd was growing agitated, stirring Adia from her thoughts. She realized Lebechi had been rushing to get out of the way of the small stampede that was happening.

"Come on," Thyme said. She shoved her way into the crowd, dragging Adia behind her.

Adia pushed up her glasses and squinted. It took her a moment to see what was going on.

Attendants fawned over Olark-as-Darian as he walked down a trail leading to the dining hall. One attendant paused to talk to another, and for a brief moment, the emperor came into full view.

Adia's breath grew shallow. The heat that had been building up inside her from the moment she set foot in the Academy was now an inferno. She'd thought it was Mallorie who was making her feel primed to explode. But now that she saw him, she knew who the source of the fire was.

Darian.

EIGHTEEN

...

Olark-as-Darian didn't look like an ancient, terrible demon. In fact, he was as handsome as his portrait. Tall and strong, with perfectly thick eyebrows and skin that glowed with health. An elaborate headdress lay on his head, crowning him. But even without it, his presence was commanding.

And familiar.

Maybe it was because of all the garish portraits of him hanging all over the Academy, but if Adia hadn't known it to be impossible, she would have sworn they'd met before.

She took deep breaths to calm herself, but nothing quenched the inexplicable urge that filled her to smash her way through the crowd and scratch his eyes out. She was overheated to the point where she might faint and her vision was blurring more than usual. Everything around her was growing dark and shadowed. If no one were around, she would have jumped into the cold water of one of the fountains.

"Adia, you're swaying on your feet," Thyme whispered as she helped steady her. "Are you sick? Come on. We got a good look at him. I think this crowd is suffocating you."

Thyme was right. And she wasn't the only one feeling the heat now. The crowd around them started to murmur, distracted by the sudden and inexplicable rise in temperature.

"Why is it so hot all of a sudden?"

"Did someone light a fire?"

"I feel like I'm melting."

"Adia," Thyme said, staring at her in shock. "We have to get out of here."

Adia glared at Darian's retreating form but let Thyme drag her out of the garden and into another section of the Academy. The student section. She was about to tell her they couldn't be in there when a door flung open. Thyme instantly had a weapon in her hand, but Adia walked to the door.

"It's fine. The Academy is like this."

"Like this? Like what?" Thyme said, staring incredulously at the door as it closed itself behind them.

"Alive."

Adia looked around her. They were in a classroom. She'd never seen the inside of one before. It was as ridiculous as she would expect. Every desk had a gold pitcher of water on top of it and a velvet footstool underneath. Nothing but the best for the nation's least talented.

"Alive?" Thyme repeated. "The *school* is alive? I don't have time to unpack that. What happened back there? You're so hot I'm amazed this place hasn't burned to the ground. I thought Gini was the one who could start fires, not you!"

"I can't," Adia said. She slowly rolled her neck from side to side.

The room blurred like a mirage. It felt as if she was moving in and out of it. Like she was being pulled somewhere else. She could almost hear people calling her, spirits telling her to let go and join them. Thyme was right. She bet she could set the room on fire if she wanted to.

Why had she been suppressing this power? All she had to do was think of everyone who'd made her angry to make it come out. Her family, the missionaries, Mallorie. But most of all, Olark. She'd never felt such hatred in her life.

"I'm ready to take on Olark. Forget Gini." She walked toward a stunned Thyme. "I don't need her."

She held out her hand, letting the purple light come forth easily. It was a darker purple than before, with streaks of red in it. She smiled at how pretty it was.

"In fact, I'm beginning to wonder if I even need *you*."

Thyme's eyes narrowed. She went to a desk and picked up a golden pitcher of water, calmly walked back to Adia, and dumped the water on her head.

Adia gasped as the cold water met her skin. Steam came off her skin. She shook herself, splashing water everywhere as the fog she'd been in cleared. The room wasn't a mirage anymore. Everything was solid again.

"Thyme," she gasped. "What—what did I do?"

"I think you were about to burn me alive," Thyme said. "Did anyone talk to you? Give you something to eat or drink? You acted like you'd been drugged with something. Even your voice changed. And your eyes looked so . . . so cold and cruel."

Adia backed away, scared of what she'd done. Thyme's expression softened.

"Whatever just happened, it wasn't you, all right? Now focus. Did someone give you something to drink?"

"No," Adia said, feeling no less guilty for all of Thyme's kind words. "Everything was fine. I didn't start to burn until . . ."

"Until?" Thyme prompted.

"Until I saw the emperor." She didn't understand it. When Darian walked by, it was like when a scent reminded you of something, but she couldn't quite place the memory that had been triggered.

Thyme's jaw dropped. "I don't like this. I don't like this one bit. He must have done something to you. It still feels like there's a furnace coming off your skin. The whole room is at least twenty degrees hotter than it is outside. I'm burning up in here."

Adia continued backing away, afraid of hurting Thyme. "Is there any more water in this room?" she asked. If she didn't get ahold of herself, and fast, they would miss the kola ceremony. The plan would be ruined, and all this would be for nothing. "I mean, any water you haven't already dumped on me? Thanks for that, by the way."

"No problem," Thyme said with a concerned smile before rushing to a desk and grabbing another golden pitcher.

Adia lowered her head in shame as Thyme poured a glass of water. She didn't want to admit how close she'd been to giving in to the darkness and hatred she'd felt. She'd wanted to burn down everyone in the Academy if it meant burning Olark down with it. Thyme, who had already survived hell, could have gotten hurt all over again.

Thyme handed her the glass. Adia raised it to her lips, then paused, quickly digging into her bag.

"What's that?" Thyme asked as she pulled out the napkin and unfolded it.

"Salt," she said, adding a few pinches to the cup. "Gini said it would help me regain control if I ever go too far. Maybe she knew something like this would happen."

She took a gulp of her drink as Thyme opened the window, motioning Adia over.

"Here. There's a breeze."

Adia practically hung outside the window. Thyme took a palm fan sitting on a student's desk and fanned her as she downed the glass.

"Look, Adia, I don't know how things work in Zaria, but in Nri, no one has this much heat coming off them unless they're a fire starter."

"I'm not going to combust," Adia said, "But . . . I do feel like I need to smash something. Or scream. Or kick a door in. I need more water."

"Where's Gini when we need her?" Thyme muttered.

She cautiously touched Adia's forehead with one finger, then with her palm when she didn't get singed. "You're starting to cool down. But you're still hotter than any person has a right to be. Are you feeling better?"

"A little," Adia said. She was still overheated, but it was becoming manageable. "I don't know what happened."

"Me either," Thyme said, lowering her hand, "but in the end you were able to control it."

"This time," Adia said nervously. "I was able to control it *this time*. Whatever's happening to me, it's like Olark makes it stronger. Like he's waking something inside me. Before you dragged me away, it felt as if I was getting dragged into another realm. A shadow realm. I could feel darkness clawing at me. Wanting me to join it."

A drum banged, and they both jumped. It was followed by another and another. The beating was so strong Adia could feel the vibration through the floor.

"What's that?" Thyme asked.

"The welcome ceremony will start soon," Adia said. "We have to get the laced kola nut onto the emperor's plate."

"If you're sure you're all right . . ."

Adia nodded.

"I'm myself, don't worry."

"Then let's go," Thyme said. "I'll cause a distraction. And you'll make the switch."

The Academy dining hall had undergone the most dramatic transformation of all. Dozens of tables with silverware and green silk napkins, and a space cleared for dancing. Drummers played as the crowd moved around in excitement, and guards stood at every corner, including the back door, where the servers would enter.

"There are more guards than I expected," Adia said, worried. One of the Gold Hats glared at her, and she quickly turned away.

"Don't worry about that," Thyme said. "Just focus on swapping the kola nut. I'll make sure no one is paying any attention to you."

"They may not pay attention to me, but they're paying attention to that tray."

A server came through the back door carrying a gold tray with a goblet and small saucer. A guard with an angry scar running down his cheek was practically glued to the server's side.

"It must be Darian's," she whispered. "There's no other reason for a guard to be assigned to a server. They must be there to make sure no one slips him poison, which is basically what I'm about to do."

"It's not poison," Thyme said. "Just a sleeping potion. A very strong sleeping potion. Come on, we have to do it now or it'll be too late. We'll improvise!"

"No, wait—" Adia whispered, but Thyme had already jumped in front of the server.

"Excuse me, when is the food being served? I haven't had a single thing to eat or drink since arriving. I'll have that glass."

The server looked aghast and held the tray away from Thyme as she tried to grab it.

"This is for the emperor!" the guard snapped. Thankfully he hadn't reached for his blade, but his annoyance was clear.

"Oh, surely you can pour him another," Thyme sighed. "I'm about to faint from thirst. Help a nun out."

Thyme lunged for the tray again. The flustered server lost his balance, and the guard, Thyme, and Adia all reached out to catch it before everything on the tray crashed to the floor.

"Let me help you," Adia said, grabbing the kola nut out of thin air as the server grabbed the saucer just before it hit the ground. The guard snatched the kola nut from her and put it back on the tray and she tossed a disapproving frown to Thyme. "You'd expect a Hill nun to have more decorum, wouldn't you?"

She walked off and hoped that none of them would remember her. That she'd just be another servant in the crowd. She touched her pocket and sighed in relief. The normal kola nut was in there. And the laced one was on the tray, heading straight to Darian.

She pushed her way through the sweaty crowd that stood shoulder to shoulder in the grand hall, waiting to kneel before Olark-as-Darian. She had no choice but to join the line. Thyme would find her soon enough. Once the sleeping agent began to kick in, the emperor would have to go to his room unless he planned to take a nap in front of the crowd. They'd sneak in through a secret passage, and hopefully no one would realize he was missing till morning. By then, this would all be over. Darian would be free, and Olark would be contained forever within the blood-stained stone.

Adia would have done her job, and Gini would have to pay out her fee. She would have a future again. All of Zaria would.

Her eyes went to the high table. The server quickly set out the emperor's plate, the kola nut sitting in the middle of it. She let out an exhale.

It's done.

The drumming stopped. Olark-as-Darian entered the room, and everyone fell to their knees. Much as it pained her to kneel before him, Adia lowered herself to the ground as her blood once again began to boil.

"You're heating up again," someone whispered behind her. Thyme had found her.

"I'm getting hot, but I'm not on fire," she replied. "Everything's in place. And next time warn me when you want to improvise."

"Oh, it all worked out," Thyme said. "Look."

Olark-as-Darian waved his hands, and everyone rose to their feet. Adia backed up and stood next to Thyme.

"This is it," she explained. "The kola nut welcome ceremony."

"Esteemed citizens, distinguished guests," Olark-as-Darian said in a booming voice, "let us raise our glasses. Join me in asking the Bright Father to bestow his blessings unto the great empire of Zaria."

Adia didn't have a glass, so she mimed the gesture as Olark toasted himself.

"And now," he said, laying down his glass, "for the kola nut."

She swallowed nervously as Olark-as-Darian picked up the kola nut off the small plate, touched it to his lips, and held it out.

"Onye wetere oji, wetere udo."

"'He who brings the kola nut brings peace,'" Thyme snorted in disgust. "He really is the Bright Father. As deluded as I remember. He swore he'd come to save us all from our heathen ways. Glad to see some things never change, no matter what century you're in."

"Thyme, hush," Adia hissed, elbowing her to be quiet as she stared at Olark-as-Darian, who had crushed the nut in his hands. "Can you see how many pieces it broke into?"

"Don't your glasses work?"

"Not really," Adia sighed. The first thing she'd buy once Gini paid her were new glasses.

Thyme squinted at the high table. "Two pieces."

"Just what I expected," Adia said. "Nothing but sinister intentions."

"You needed a nut to tell you that?" Thyme scoffed. "All right. Let's get out of here and get to the passageway under his chambers."

One task down, one more to go. Adia's part in this story was almost over, and she couldn't be more relieved. The emperor sat down. She almost imagined that his eyes were locked onto her. As if he could peer into her soul and know what she was up to.

"Adia . . . is he looking at you?" Thyme whispered nervously. "And good grief, stop glaring. You look like you're about to leap forward and stab him in the eye."

It wasn't her imagination. Olark-as-Darian *was* looking at her. And for reasons she couldn't comprehend, he looked as terrified at the sight of her as she was inexplicably furious at the sight of him. He turned and spoke quietly to the Gold Hat with the scar running down his cheek. The man nodded and moved toward her, his hand trained on the hilt of his machete. How did he know what she'd done? It was too early for Darian to feel any effect from the sleeping agent.

"Thyme," she gasped.

"Whatever is happening," Thyme said quietly, "stay calm. I'll be close by, I promise. I won't let anything happen to you."

Adia barely heard her over the blood pulsing in her ears as the Gold Hat grew closer. Olark knew what she'd done. Maybe he'd known all along and had switched out the laced kola nut with another. Somehow he knew. And he'd sent a Gold Hat to deal with her.

The Gold Hat was so tall that the shiny machete at his waist was almost at eye level with Adia.

"The emperor has requested your presence in his chambers," he said in a cold voice.

She didn't know what was about to happen to her, but she could at least try to stall. Olark had eaten the nut. If she stalled long enough, maybe he would pass out before things got too bad and she could escape. She forced herself not to give in to the fear threatening to take over. To not stare at the Gold Hat's machete. To not even consider the possibility that she was minutes away from getting an arm chopped off. What had Thyme just said? That she wouldn't let anything happen to her?

You're not alone, Adia reminded herself. *Just buy everyone some time.*

She raised her head a notch and fixed the Gold Hat with a steely expression.

"Is that a request or an order?" Adia asked, trying to sound like Gini.

The detached look in the Gold Hat's eyes faded for a moment. He gave her a surprisingly sympathetic look. She hadn't thought the soldiers capable of sympathy.

"I imagine it's an order. If you'll follow me?"

He might have phrased it like a question, but she knew she had no choice in the matter as he subtly but firmly pushed her forward.

Thyme disappeared into the crowd. Adia trusted her friend to keep track of her. She followed the Gold Hat, still unsure if she was following him to her death. Snippets of conversation reached her ears.

"—but does anyone know who she is?"

"—and Darian can't take his eyes off her. She's so lucky! I wish I was her."

"Well, you can't deny she's beautiful for such a dark-skinned young girl."

She wanted to jump through the crowd and claw the eyes out of whoever had made that last comment, but she schooled her face into a stillness she didn't feel. The catty whispers were doing nothing to calm her rage.

She kept her eyes straight ahead, but the intensity of someone's stare made her turn. Her mouth fell open, matching the shocked expression on Nami's face.

He wasn't wearing his green-and-gold apprentice regalia, but if he was at the welcome ceremony, it meant he hadn't been sacked for leaving his post and following her into the Horrorbeyond.

At least he didn't get in too much trouble for trying to help me, she thought sadly as she was led out of the hall. No one could help her now.

The Gold Hat took her up the winding staircase.

She had never entered this part of the Academy. She had no reason to. Only senior servants were allowed up there to clean. The walls of the upper level were gilded to the point of distraction. It was like staring into the sun. This floor was reserved for dignitaries and the highest of high society who blessed the Academy with their patronage and donations. People like Mallorie's father, no doubt.

The Gold Hat stopped in front of a burgundy door that was at least four times taller than her. This must be the Red Room.

"In here," he said. He seemed to want to say more but sighed and opened the door, nudging her inside.

The distinctive sound of a lock clicking into place

cemented her fate as the Gold Hat crossed his arms and stood in front of the secured door. What if Thyme wasn't able to find her way through the passages without her? How would she ever get out?

All right, then, what would Thyme do? she thought.

Not stand there like a helpless baby, that's for sure. Adia took in her surroundings.

The room was hideous. Dismembered heads of dead animals hung on brown walls, their eyes frozen in terror, forever staring at the hunter who ended their life. Adia covered her mouth to stop herself from gagging. Turning her gaze away from the taxidermy animals, she took in the strange and sharp angles of furniture that looked like it could have been decor from the Horrorbeyond.

Find a weapon.

There wasn't much she could do with the Gold Hat at the door, but there was a table a few inches behind her with a sharp letter opener. She rocked up and down on her feet, as if she was nervous, backing up a little bit with every rock until finally she hit the edge of the table. She put her hands behind her.

"How long is this going to take?" she asked, hoping he'd focus on the question and not on the way she was fumbling around behind her.

"He should be here any minute. I think I hear him now." The Gold Hat turned to open the door, and Adia quickly grabbed the letter opener, wincing when she pricked her finger on the tip. She slipped it into her pocket.

And just in time. The door opened and Olark-as-Darian entered the chambers. The Gold Hat bowed, then exited the room.

The emperor stared at her for a minute before closing the door behind him. She gripped the letter opener and narrowed her eyes as he stalked toward her. If he thought it would be easy to throw her in a dungeon or worse, he was in for a surprise. She wasn't going down without a fight. And then, when he was a few inches away, he fell to his knees, hands clasped in front of his heart.

Adia stared at him in shock.

Was he . . . crying?

He looked up at her, tears and snot running down his face.

"I've waited five hundred years for this moment. I had started to believe I'd never find you, but the stars have delivered you to me. And when my missionaries told me of a girl causing chaos and destruction in a small village, I knew it was you. Nothing could break our bond, not even time."

Adia froze to the floor. The missionary in the fishing village. It wasn't her imagination that they were watching her.

"You've had people following me," she said slowly.

"To keep you safe, of course!" Olark-as-Darian said. He got to his feet and held his hands out in a placating gesture. "And here you are. Reincarnated after all these years so we could fulfill our destiny. When I realized you were heading to the Academy, I came straightaway. I'm so glad to see you again, Viona."

NINETEEN

Adia gaped at the blubbering Olark-as-Darian. Tears trickled out of brown eyes made even more striking by the black kohl lining their lids. Those piercing eyes were fixated on her as he continued his weeping. He didn't realize she'd switched the kola nut; he'd dragged her up here because he thought she was someone else. Viona—the descendant of the first shaman, Ovie—reincarnated five hundred years later?

"Your Majesty," she said slowly, "my name is not Viona."

What was going on? Olark had known Viona. He had to realize they weren't the same person. But he was staring at her with a hungry expression, worse even than an Energy Thief. Like he'd finally found the solution to all his problems.

Olark-as-Darian wiped his tear-streaked face and stood up, shaking his head dismissively.

"You're confused. That's my doing, I'm afraid. I cast a

ward of protection on all mortals."

"A ward of protection," Adia repeated. *That wretched curse that almost made Lebechi claw her eyes out was a ward of protection?*

"Yes. You see, Viona—"

"I'm *not* Viona."

"—vile rumors led Zarians to believe that I am a demon. A demon! Can you imagine, Viona—"

"That's not my name."

"—that these people, who I love more than my own life, are now afraid of me! I had to make it so that they don't know who I am. But surely *you* know. You can recognize my celestial frequency, just as I can recognize yours—"

"I've never seen you before in my life."

"Viona! Please. You must stop interrupting."

He approached her, quick as a panther. Adia jumped back.

"Don't be afraid," he said.

And Adia realized she wasn't. Not anymore. Her heart had been thudding loudly in her chest, but now it went stone-still. She had taken on Sinachi, and Headless Hiroma. Good or bad, Adia knew that she was at least a little brave now.

"You were so angry back then," he continued, "but you must know I would never hurt you. Didn't you see my proclamations? The blessing I've already bestowed upon you? You'll be provided with more wealth than any queen who ever lived if you'll only give me what I want. Now, where did you hide it?"

She knew this wasn't about the stone, so what in the stars had Viona taken from him?

"Hide what?" she asked, genuinely baffled.

"Imo Mmiri," he said.

Imo Mmiri? Wasn't that why he was burning everything down, since Imo Mmiri couldn't be touched by fire? What did he want her to do? Hold his torch for him? She wasn't sure what he'd do to her if he found out she couldn't help him. She'd just have to keep feigning ignorance.

"Why? What's there?"

"Why?" Olark repeated. "Don't play coy with me, my dear. You know how powerful the land is, and the people who reside on it. There is said to be more celestial energy generated by the shamans of Imo Mmiri in one minute than the rest of Zaria generates in a thousand years. Imagine what you could do with that. What *I* can do with that. The Alusi never wanted me to be one of them. They didn't think I was good enough to be in their sphere. But if I harness the power of Imo Mmiri, I'll become more than Alusi. I'll rule over them."

It always came down to power.

"And you were so clever, hiding it with a shamanic glamour. But I know you can still see it—let me use your eyes. I've tried to find it the other way, but it will take centuries trying to find one small bit of land that won't burn. Maybe longer. And that's time I don't have. But if I use your eyes? We can find it in an instant. We can go there together. Once we get there, I promise, I'll let you have your body back."

This was what he wanted? This is what he was doing here?

Looking for Viona's soul so he could possess her in order to find Imo Mmiri? And he thought *she* was Viona?

He opened his mouth to say more but suddenly doubled over, wheezing and gasping.

"This foolish boy," he snarled. "Now is when he tries his tricks? Stop fighting me, Darian."

Darian. Adia was startled. He was still in there, trying to fight. *You can do it,* she thought, willing him to beat the monster possessing him. *Keep trying.*

Olark regained control, once again turning his fevered eyes to Adia, but now she knew Darian was still in there, that he was still trying to fight. And so would she.

She moved toward a table where a truly bizarre statue stood. It was brown marble and in the shape of a deer, but it was missing one of its legs. Olark-as-Darian must have tried to fix it by sticking a branch on the missing limb. It was a ridiculous sight, but the statue looked to be a good size for smashing the emperor's head in.

She was done stalling. The laced kola nut had been designed not to take effect until the welcome ceremony was over and he was back in his chambers so that his sudden loss of consciousness would go unnoticed—it wouldn't happen soon enough. Which meant she would have to render Olark-as-Darian unconscious some other way if she wanted to make it out of this room alive and unpossessed.

He straightened, seeming to have caught his breath for a moment.

"Viona," he began, but Adia held up a hand.

"Majesty," she implored, reaching her hands behind her back, "I truly have no idea what you're talking about. I don't know anything about Imo Mmiri or where it is. I'm not sure if it even exists. My name is . . . Peggy," she said, thinking of the peg-legged deer statue her hands were frantically feeling around for behind her back.

She channeled Mallorie Amber and gave what she hoped was the vapid giggle of a noble whose greatest desires in life were for money, mansions, and whatever meaningless materialism people like that cared about.

"I'm afraid I don't know anyone named Viona, though I certainly wouldn't turn up my nose if you offered me enough riches to let me live like a queen."

"I told you," Olark-as-Darian said, his voice still polite but growing more clipped, "you're just confused by my protection ward, and maybe by all those years of reincarnation. I get it—I become a little disoriented every time I change bodies too," he said with a small, closed-lip smile, as though his murderous spree of possessions would make him slightly more sympathetic to her. "Even our powers are similar. You hid yourself and Imo Mmiri from me. I hid myself from the world for five hundred years while I regained my strength. But now—"

His voice choked and he wheezed again, beating at his chest as if he was trying to clear a cough.

"You stopped trying to fight me months ago, Darian. Why are you so lively today?" Olark gasped as he struggled to catch his breath.

Adia's hand finally connected with the marble deer statue. She only had a second before whatever Darian was doing stopped distracting him. She'd never hit anyone before. A murderous demon was one thing, but it was Darian's body she would have to knock out. Her heart raced. It had to be just enough force to stun Olark so she could escape, but not enough to permanently harm Darian.

"Do you not see that our souls have been reembodied so that we may, at long last, make peace with one another? Give me your forgiveness so I can finally leave this foolish boy," he snapped, dropping any pretense of kindness. "Once I can see through your eyes, I'll find where you've hid Imo Mmiri and I'll finally have enough power to claim my rightful place as a benevolent ruler of all. I'm not doing this for my sake, but for the good of the entire universe. Give me your eyes, Viona."

This time he wasn't asking.

Adia lowered her gaze and bit her lower lip, taking a deep breath.

"Your Majesty, I will give you exactly what you deserve."

As Olark-as-Darian smiled and reached out his hands, *her* hands swung up with all her strength, slamming the deer into his head.

There was a satisfying clunk, and then Olark-as-Darian crumpled to the floor. Blood gushed from where the sharp edge of the deer's missing leg had cut him. Gazing at him now, helpless on the ground, he looked like Darian-just-Darian. She supposed he *was* rather nice to look at, even with the drool collecting at the side of his mouth. She only hoped she hadn't hurt him too badly and that he would be all right once Gini exorcised him.

Adia dropped the statue and ran to the closet where the Red Room's trapdoor should be hidden. She made quick work of the boxes and heavy rug concealing it. The door was there. Just like the maps said it would be.

She pulled it open, then ran back to Darian, hooking her arms under her shoulders and dragging his deadweight to the closet.

She shoved him through the trapdoor, hearing the thud as his body hit the tunnel below.

"Thyme," she whispered. "Thyme! Are you there?"

"I'm here," Thyme answered. "Are you all right? I've got him. Jump."

Adia stuck a leg down, then pulled herself back up. The peg-legged deer statue was still on the floor.

"I have to clean up first," she said. "I left blood on the rug."

"What is with you Zarians and cleaning?" Thyme snapped.

A sound at the door made Adia turn.

"Someone's coming," she whispered. "Go. I'll catch up." She quickly kicked the trapdoor shut with her foot and pulled the rug back over it.

She rushed back into the room to hide the evidence, but it was too late. Someone was already inside, staring at the blood-stained carpet with a ferocious expression and a sword in his hands. His eyes turned to her. Eyes that had always looked at her with cheer and kindness now fixated on her with shock and horror.

"Nami," she whispered. "I can explain."

Nami's eyes went back and forth from the blood on the carpet to the blood on her hands.

"I saw a Gold Hat take you away," he said slowly. "Not even Mallorie Amber could order the emperor's guards to kick you out of the Academy."

Nami's nosiness and obsession with raising his status was about to ruin everything. She was scared and angry, and so didn't bother to curb her tongue.

"So you followed me again?" Adia snapped. "Why? To see if I could help you make a connection with the emperor?"

Nami's face went red with anger.

"Why do you always have to be so *foul*?! Where's the emperor, Adia? Whose blood is this?"

He stared at Adia as though she were a stranger.

"Look, Nami, I don't understand why you came, but you should go. I'll explain it all later."

He shook his head.

"No, it's best if you tell the Gold Hats directly. You have no idea how much trouble I got in because I left the boat and went after you. I'm not making the same mistake twice. Wait here."

"I can't. Please just trust me. I didn't hurt Darian. I'm trying to help him."

"How could you help an emperor?" Nami asked, bewildered. "You're not making any sense. Adia, I can't let you go when you won't tell me what happened. What would the Gold Hats think if I did that?"

"Oh, would you forget about the stupid Gold Hats?" Adia said. She couldn't hide her exasperation. "Why are you so desperate to earn the praise of monsters?"

Nami's face flushed even deeper. When he spoke, his voice was thick with barely concealed anger. "The Gold Hats are the protectors of the empire. And as a future Gold Hat, I'm ordering you to stay here while I get my commanding officer."

"Would you just listen—"

"No. I don't want to hear it."

"Nami," Adia cried, unable to comprehend how he'd gone from her friend to someone who could dismiss her so easily.

He stormed out of the room, locking the door behind him.

She stared at the door in horror, kicking herself. If she had only mentioned Olark's name, she could have sent Nami into a fit, but she'd been too shocked to do anything. There was no time to waste. She ran back to the trapdoor and jumped down. As she fell into the dark tunnel, she heard the Gold Hats rush into the room above her.

"She was just here!" Nami said.

"She must have picked the lock. Close the gates!" a Gold Hat yelled. "No one goes in or out until we find the emperor! What? Why won't this door open! Did you lock us in from the outside?"

"Of course not!"

"The wood is completely warped! What is wrong with this school?"

Adia could have cried in relief. The Academy was on her side. Good. She needed all the help she could get.

She struggled to see in front of her as she ran through the dark tunnel, but her eyes soon adjusted to the blackness. Plus there was a soft green glow helping to illuminate her path—bioluminescent mushrooms and plants. More lit up with every step she took.

"Thanks," she whispered to the plants, and she could have sworn they glowed even brighter.

Under normal circumstances, she doubted she would have been able to catch up to Thyme. But the warrior girl had Olark-as-Darian hoisted over her shoulder, the extra weight slowing her down. Adia reached her in only a few minutes.

"I was just about to get lost," Thyme said in relief. "Get us out of here."

Adia took the lead. The passage grew narrower the farther down they went. Water from the river that ran through the Academy grounds had almost reached her knees when she saw a sliver of moonlight. If her map was correct, they should be at the entrance to the woods behind the Academy.

She peeked her head out of the passage. Thorny bushes and acacia trees that were undoubtedly full of fire ants stood as a barrier, daring anyone to enter past the tree line.

"We're here."

"Adia," Thyme hissed, dumping Darian to the ground and pulling out a double-edged ida blade. "Look out!"

Adia whipped around and saw a Gold Hat running toward them, machetes in both hands.

"Get the emperor out of the way," Thyme said.

Adia grabbed Darian's arms and lugged him toward the thorny entrance to the woods.

She winced as his head bounced against a rock. But she was more concerned about Thyme battling a Gold Hat than she was about Olark-as-Darian's head wound. She looked back at the fight in progress.

Their blades moved at an impossible speed, but the fight belonged to Thyme. Even weighed down in her nun robes, Thyme had a sparkle in her eyes and a wicked smile on her lips. Adia sighed.

She's enjoying this.

Thyme delivered a flying kick that sent the Gold Hat crashing into a tree. "Is that the best you've got?" Thyme taunted, positively gleeful.

"Thyme, come on!"

Thyme sighed in disappointment, but she gave up her fun and ran to Adia.

She glanced at Olark-as-Darian, still bleeding, drooling, and unconscious.

"What happened back there anyway?" Thyme asked as she slung him over her shoulders. "Why'd he drag you away?"

"I have no idea. He lost it. Kept calling me Viona. Then

Nami showed up for some reason. And he—he—"

She couldn't continue and blinked back tears. Nami had set a mob of Gold Hats with machetes after her. How could she have been so wrong about him?

"I don't understand it. Nami's always been obsessed with status, but I thought he was my friend. I can't believe he would do something so . . . Thyme? What's wrong? Are you hurt?!"

For the first time since she'd know her, Thyme looked afraid.

"*What* did you just say?"

"I said Nami's always been obsessed with climbing the ladder and meeting rich people but—"

"No. Before that. Olark-as-Darian called *you* Viona?" Her voice was heavy with shock.

"Thyme, what is it? You're scaring me."

"That's who the Bright Father was searching for," Thyme whispered. "The girl who stole something from him."

Adia felt sick. Was another friend about to betray her?

"I know," she said. "*She of Ovie.* The girl you told me about. Viona, the descendant of the first shaman. But I'm not her."

"He said he would burn Nri to the ground if we didn't bring her to him," Thyme said, her eyes narrowed. "But no one knew who he was talking about. Then I touched the blood-stained stone, disappeared for five hundred years, and found out he did exactly what he said. Destroyed my world because we didn't bring him Viona."

"Thyme," Adia said nervously. "Viona's been dead for

centuries. I'm not five hundred—I'm twelve."

Thyme stared at her, then rolled her eyes. "I didn't think you were her," she snorted, "but clearly *he* does. He destroyed a world the first time she escaped him, and now I'm carrying his drooling self on my back, traveling with the girl he's been on the warpath to find all these years?" Thyme adjusted Olark-as-Darian on her back. "We have to get to Gini."

Adia couldn't agree more. They needed to get Darian exorcised as soon as possible.

And *she* needed to figure out why Olark thought she was a girl who had died five hundred years ago.

TWENTY

Just when Adia thought she couldn't run anymore, Thyme slowed down.

"We're getting close. I can hear the waterfall."

"There she is!" Adia said.

The moon hung directly over the falls, lighting up the pond the water emptied into. Gini stood underneath it.

"You're late," Gini said.

"There was an incident," Thyme said, dumping Olark-as-Darian on the ground. "We had to improvise."

"What incident?" Gini said, placing the blood-stained stone on the ground.

"He thinks I'm Viona," Adia said. She waited for Gini's jaw to drop in shock, but Gini only frowned. "Why don't you look surprised?" asked Adia.

Gini shrugged. "You've been in such denial about your power. I was waiting for the right time to ask where you think it comes from."

"What are you talking about?" Adia asked. "Trust me, no one in my family is a shaman. You'd know that if you laid eyes on my aunt and uncle for more than two seconds."

"But what about your parents? I heard you in the boat. Your aunt is only your mother's half sister. So you're missing information about a decent chunk of your lineage."

Before Adia could say anything else, before she could wrap her head around the thought that she and Viona were related and that she was descended from Ovie and the shamans of Imo Mmiri, a low laugh cut through the air.

"Get behind me," Gini said.

Adia scooted back, dragging Thyme with her as her stomach dropped. Olark was awake. He stared at her with fevered eyes.

"Vi . . . o . . . na," he said, lingering over each syllable of the name he insisted on calling her, like it was a spicy bowl of groundnut stew. He looked up, and at the sight of Gini, a quick expression of confusion rippled over his face. "Good to see me after all this time, Ginikanwa?" he said.

"Good to see you for the last time," Gini responded.

He turned back toward Adia. "You never fail to surprise me, recruiting the so-called leader of the Alusi. Very clever of you. But you've aligned yourself on the wrong side of history. It's not too late, though, Viona. Come. Help me get out of here."

"Do not speak to him," Gini said, moving in front of Adia. She pointed her staff at him. "I won't make the same mistake again," she seethed. "I may not be able to kill you outright, but I will force you back into the shadows. The blood of all the lives you stole is waiting to bind you. Be silent."

His face contorted with rage, and he struggled to open his lips. Gini had done something to keep him from speaking. Adia was glad of that—but he still clawed at the ground and foamed at the mouth as he tried to get to her. She moved closer to Thyme, who, naturally, had an arrow aimed at the emperor's throat.

As Gini knelt next to the blood-stained stone, Olark's focus immediately switched. His eyes glowed red to the point that Adia wondered if he could shoot fire out of Darian's possessed body.

"Ahh," Gini said in a mocking tone. "Recognize this, do you?"

When he saw the stone, Olark-as-Darian flung himself forward. Gini placed her long flowering staff on the ground, and violet light shot out of it, circling the stone. Adia and Thyme flew back at the force.

Adia scrambled up and shook her head. Spots danced in front of her eyes, and her ears rang.

Olark-as-Darian's body slammed to the ground, then was flung up again. He floated in the air, limbs dangling and shaking in a way no human limbs could move. Adia wanted to turn away from the disturbing image, but she needed to see it. She needed to see a demon exorcised from a body. It had only been a few hours ago when she'd almost lost control and hurt Thyme.

Please free me too, she thought, willing Gini's power to wash over her. She flinched as Aunt Ife's singing suddenly came to her head. *Wash me so I can be whiter than snow.* No. It wasn't like that. She hadn't been mindwashed like the rest of her family; she didn't want to be anything like those people. But there *was* an evilness in her that needed to be purged. She took a deep breath and tried to be as receptive as possible to whatever Gini was doing. There were two people who needed to be exorcised tonight.

The stone began to pulse and shake.

"Leave this body!" Gini yelled. "May all those you've killed find justice and may your soul find peace."

The stone on the ground shook along with Olark-as-Darian's body. His body trembled . . .

With laughter.

Adia took a step back and glanced at Thyme, who looked just as unnerved as she felt.

"You think that will be enough?" he hissed in a warbly voice, not even trying to sound human anymore. "I'm not as weak as I was five hundred years ago. I have the most delightful source of power now to fuel me."

The ground began to shake. Adia looked at her hands. No purple lights were coming out of them. But a red glow *was* coming off Olark-as-Darian—*he* was doing this, not her. He caught her eye and smiled. Adia knew what he was thinking. Their powers were similar. Too similar. And unlike her, he was in control of them.

"Adia, get back!" Thyme shouted.

Adia barely got out of the way as a shadowed hand came out of the earth where she had just been standing. Dozens of them were popping up, and they didn't seem to be attached to bodies.

"What are those?"

"He shouldn't be able to do this when he's not in his true form," Gini gasped.

"But what are they?" Adia repeated sharply.

"Malevolent spirits he's calling to him," Gini said, holding her staff tighter. "Don't let them touch you."

Purple fire shot from Gini's eyes, briefly lighting up the entire forest. The entities Olark had been trying to call to him were quickly snuffed out. Adia covered her ears as Olark let out a high-pitched, blood-curdling, inhuman scream.

There was a singer in the Swamplands who could reach a note so high that glass shattered from the frequency. That's what Adia was reminded of as Olark screamed. But still, he held on to his possession of Darian.

Gini didn't let up.

"Leave this body!" she shouted again, more force blasting out of her staff.

Adia recoiled as something oozed out of Darian's ears. Looking closer, she saw that it wasn't liquid—it was a shadow. It moved slowly but then sped up as the blood-stained stone sucked it in. Darian groaned and collapsed, completely still.

The shadow was gone.

"It's over!" Thyme cried. "We did it!"

Adia grinned. What Gini had done had been so strong. She was certain it had worked on her too. But she'd wait until Gini was gone to test it out and make sure her own demons had been cast out.

"So what will you do now?" Adia asked. "Throw the stone into a volcano? The bottom of the ocean? Or maybe you can take it with you and fling it into space."

"I say you let me go to town on it," Thyme said, rubbing two daggers against each other. "I'll turn that rock into dust in no time."

When Gini didn't reply, Adia turned to look at her.

"Gini?"

"Be quiet, both of you," Gini whispered.

That's when Adia noticed how tense Gini still was. She hadn't moved and was poised like a snake about to strike, her eye trained on the blood-stained stone.

"Something's wrong," the Alusi said.

"What do you mean?" Thyme said. "What else is there to do?"

"Stay back," Gini hissed.

That's when Adia saw it. A drop of blood ran down the center of the stone. She gasped.

"Is it supposed to be leaking?" she asked.

"Of course not," Gini snapped.

"What's happening?" Thyme said. Her bow was back up, but Adia didn't know what she planned to shoot at.

"I don't know," Gini whispered, cautiously picking up the bloody stone.

Before they could say any more, a flash of lightning struck. It was like something out of a painting—one perfectly crooked, jagged trident of light illuminated the night sky. The rain that had threatened to fall all day finally unleashed itself. The trees swayed to the point of snapping as a wild wind tore through the forest.

Adia was about to say they needed to move before the storm descended when a voice shouted through the woods.

"I see them!" someone shouted. "That's her!"

"No one with sense would come into these woods at night," Gini said, aghast.

"You're in the least sensible place you'll ever know." Adia parroted Maka's words as she spun around. At least fifty Gold Hats charged toward them, machetes raised. With a familiar face in the lead. Her jaw dropped.

"I can't believe him," she gasped as Nami rushed forward.

"I'm about to end that boy's existence," Thyme snarled, a large battle-ax in her hand and an angry glint in her eye.

"Thyme, even you can't fight off fifty Gold Hats," Adia said, holding her friend back. "We need to run. And where were you hiding an ax?"

Something bright caught her eye. It was the moon, reflecting off one of the gaudy jewels on the crown that had been knocked from Darian's head. When he woke up, he'd tell everyone what had happened to him and they would, justifiably, think he was out of his mind.

"Adia," Thyme hissed. "Let's go."

Agrias vines crept over her feet and into the river, swimming toward Darian's body. Forming a line that connected them.

"We need to take Darian."

"Forget that," Thyme said. "What if your pal Nami convinces him that you're an assassin? He'll send the entire empire after us!"

"Which is why he should be with *us* when he wakes up. Gini?"

She turned to Gini. The Alusi looked to the sky and closed her eyes, then sighed and pointed her staff. A line of fire formed between Darian's unconscious body and the charging Gold Hats.

"Quickly, now. Go get him."

Thyme sighed and followed after her.

When Adia got to his unconscious body she flinched, but not because of Darian. Nami had reached the other side of the fire.

Their eyes met through the wall of flames, and he glared at her. She wanted to glare right back, or better yet, slap him upside the head, but she didn't have time for a staring contest with her former friend.

"Grab Darian's legs," she said to Thyme, turning her away from him.

"You can run, Adia, but I'll find you!" Nami yelled.

"Go," Gini said.

Adia risked one more look behind her as they ran deep into the forest. The Gold Hats were tackling the fire, trying to beat it back. But she didn't see Nami. He must have gone around it.

She couldn't believe he'd gone this far. That he'd assumed the worst about her and reacted in such a murderous manner. Who *was* he? Certainly not the friend she'd thought him to be. But she couldn't think about that now. Not when everything had gone so wrong. She didn't say anything until she was sure there was enough distance between them.

"I need to catch my breath," she wheezed, taking in big gulps of air. Gini and Thyme stopped too.

"Why didn't it work, Gini?" Thyme asked.

Gini didn't answer her. Just stared up into the stars with a shocked expression, so Adia answered for her.

"He's using something as a power source," she said. "He's stronger than we realized. The blood-stained stone probably won't be enough to stop him if we don't find and destroy whatever this other object is."

The Alusi shook her head in disbelief and gave a short laugh. "And I mocked him for *his* arrogance. I made a mistake again. I didn't think whatever's been keeping him alive in this world would be any match for a celestial object like the stone. But whatever this boost of power is, the stone can't contain it. Or won't. We'll need to find and destroy whatever this source is to weaken him enough for this to work," Gini said.

Her eyes narrowed, and she pointed at Darian.

"And I'll bet he'll have some answers. That's why I wanted to bring him along. Put him down, girls."

Thyme huffed as they carefully lowered Darian to the ground. "You didn't want to do anything. Adia's the one who—"

"Oy!" Gini screamed, thumping her staff against the trunk of a tree. "Warlord Baby, wake up! Oy!"

"Oh, Gini . . ." Adia sighed.

She was about to suggest they throw some water on him when Darian groaned. Unsurprising, as Gini's voice could wake the dead. She hoped the fire was still keeping most of the Gold Hats at bay.

He slowly sat up and touched the giant lump on his head before staring at them.

"What is going on? Who are you people?"

None of them answered.

Darian sat up. He moved his arms slowly, watching the motion in shock. Adia was still as he pieced it together.

"I'm free?" he gasped.

Then he fainted all over again.

Every minute they spent waiting for Darian to wake up felt like a lifetime as the blood-stained stone continued to drip. A small crack ran through the middle now and grew deeper every second. Adia didn't take her eyes off it. If they didn't find and destroy Olark's extra power source—and fast—it wouldn't be long before he would break free and possess the person he thought would give him everything he'd ever wanted.

Her.

Adia turned to Gini. "Why did you spare him?"

Gini blinked. "What?"

"When you were sent to the star to destroy Olark, why'd you send him here instead? You never told me *why* you didn't just kill him." Adia asked. She didn't mean to blame her. She just wanted to understand.

Gini looked at the stone for a moment intently: at the blood of Olark's victims, Olark somewhere within it. It was one of the few times Adia had seen such a human expression cross the Alusi's face—this time, one of pain. Of heartache. *Grief*, Adia realized.

"Every celestial spirit is the creation of an Alusi," Gini said. "We spin them from star matter to help manage the celestial realm, and all our creations. At least that's what they're supposed to do. And when we create a particularly powerful celestial spirit, we train them."

She paused and looked for a moment up toward Alusia, but it wasn't visible behind the clouds.

"Olark was mine. I had spun him from star matter, raised him and trained him from his creation to one day have his own star—or tried to. It's my fault he wanted it so badly—I made him feel like it was his only purpose, and then when he asked for the star, I told him he couldn't be trusted." She paused, and for the first time, Adia wondered if an Alusi could cry. "Even if I didn't properly show it," she continued, "I loved him. In my way."

"It might not have been the right choice," Adia said, "but at the time, maybe it was the only one you could make."

To her surprise, Gini didn't rebuff Adia's kindness.

"Deep down, I guess some part of me hoped he wasn't beyond saving," Gini said, her voice now more clipped. "But I won't make the same mistake twice."

A few minutes later, Darian shifted and opened his eyes.

"Finally," Adia sighed. Now that he was Darian-just-Darian, Adia felt guilty about the head wound she'd inflicted on him. But she pushed it aside. They had no time; guilt would have to wait.

"What's happening?" Darian asked as he sat up.

"I'm sorry, but we don't have time to explain," Gini said, cutting him off. "Yes, you're free, but you're still in danger. All of us are. What do you remember? What do you know about the last year of your life?"

Darian hesitated.

"You can trust us," Adia said.

Her voice seemed to snap him out of the last of his fog. He stared at her for so long she started to fidget.

"Something . . . something dark took over my body," he said, his gaze not lifting from hers. "I tried to fight it at first, but every time I did, it was like being drowned. My body would gag and gasp for air. I'm pretty sure the demon found my attempts to break free funny. Nothing rattled him.

"Until you," he said. "For the first time since he possessed me, he was afraid of something. He's afraid of *you*, Viona."

Adia pushed her glasses up in exasperation. "My name's not Viona."

"What? Then why was he calling you that? So your name's really Peggy?"

"No, I was just trying to stall him. I'm Adia. That's Thyme and this is . . ."

"Ginikanwa of Alusia," Gini said, giving a grand flourish of her hand.

Darian's mouth fell open, and he scrambled to his feet. Adia held her hands out and helped steady him. He really wasn't in any condition to be anywhere but a sickbed.

"Will someone please explain to me what's going on?"

"Quick version?" Thyme said. "You were possessed by Olark, Adia kidnapped you so that Gini could save your life, and now we need to—"

Darian screamed. His voice carried through the forest, probably alerting every Gold Hat and missionary within a five-mile radius of their location.

"Oh no," Adia groaned.

"Olark? What do you mean? Olark disappeared centuries ago. You dare spin such lies to my face and—"

Thyme leaped on top of him, trying to cover his mouth.

"Keep him quiet!" Adia said as Darian flailed around.

"You just had to bring him with us, didn't you?" Thyme said as she sat on one of Darian's arms and glared at him. "We don't even have Ferryman this time. We can't trap him in a carpet and roll him out of here."

"I'd hoped that since Olark possessed him he wouldn't be under the influence of the curse," Gini said. "Adia remains the only Zarian who can get around it. Refer to Olark as *the demon* from now on. Darian knows well enough he was possessed. We just can't mention who did the possessing."

The screeching came to a sudden halt, taking Adia by surprise. Thyme cautiously released him.

Lebechi had gone on for almost five minutes. And Nami had been out of it for a full day. Darian looked confused, but he was himself again in a matter of seconds.

"Forgive me. I might still be feeling the effects of the head wound," he said.

"Unbelievable," Thyme muttered, but Gini gave a nod of approval.

"Now *this* one is strong," she said, staring at Darian intently. "I see why he was chosen as a placeholder for you, Adia. The two of you . . . Well, never mind that."

Darian rubbed his forehead.

"What was I saying? Ah, yes. The demon was afraid of Adia."

He stared at her. "When he saw you at dinner, he was terrified. I saw you the way he saw you—you looked like you were on fire. I could feel it too. The heat coming off you. You glowed."

"I felt angrier than I've ever felt in my life when I saw you for the first time," Adia admitted.

"She was burning up," Thyme added. "I could feel it standing a foot away from her. It started the second she saw Olark."

Adia covered her face in her hands.

"Uh-oh," Thyme said, realizing her mistake as Darian

launched into another round of indignant screeching.

"Olark? What do you mean by this? Who even is this bald fool? As if Olark could ever return to the realm of mortals and—"

Thyme grimaced. "Sorry, sorry. Won't happen again."

"Forgive me," Darian said, coming back to himself even faster than last time. "I must have lost my train of thought."

"You've lost something all right," Thyme snapped. She looked like she was going to say more, but then her ears moved.

Adia and Darian both started at the motion. Thyme's ears were strange, but Adia hadn't realized they could move! They swiveled in a half circle as Thyme frowned.

"I think some of the Gold Hats got through the wall of fire. I'll go to high ground and take them out."

She climbed up a tree faster than a cat and disappeared into the night sky.

"What . . . is she?" Darian said slowly.

Adia wasn't entirely sure, so she just gave a bewildered shrug. Several arrows flew from the tree and howls of pain lit up the forest.

"Thyme," she called, "try not to kill anyone."

"I don't know what all the fuss is about," Thyme said from high up in the tree. "I'm just aiming for kneecaps. You Zarians are so weak."

"Where is she from if not Zaria?" Darian said, gaping at Adia.

"That is a very long story."

"Retreat!" someone shouted. "The girl must have an army with her!"

Adia rolled her eyes.

"Right. Adia's Deadly Army. Gini, we need to get out of these woods. The storm's getting worse."

"Yes," Gini said. "You'll have to slow them down."

Adia blinked.

"Me? How can I slow them down?"

"Do what you were beginning to do in the Horror-beyond. Hiroma wasn't the only person in there who could turn a forest into a maze, was she?"

Darian gaped. *Headless* Hiroma? The Horrorbeyond?"

Adia ignored Darian and stared at the ground, studying the trees and plants all around her. There was no denying it anymore. She had powers—she just hoped they were strong enough to be useful.

She knelt down and put her hands on the ground.

"Thyme should probably get down from that tree," she said, her brow furrowed in concentration.

Gini pointed her staff, and a bolt of fire shot up. Darian jumped back.

"This is a nightmare," he said as if none of them were there. "I'm still possessed, and this is a nightmare."

"Hey!" Thyme said, falling to the ground with a thump. She swatted out a flame on her robes.

Adia ignored them and dug her fingers into the dirt.

"What is happening?" Thyme asked in shock.

Adia glanced up. Willow trees shifted the direction of

their weeping, their limbs moving to cover trails. Grass grew tall and dense, obscuring the river. It would be easy for someone to fall into the water, thinking there was still solid ground beneath their feet.

Everywhere she looked, the forest was rearranging itself to become an impenetrable maze. Yet she could still see the way out.

"What are *you?*" Darian asked.

She stood up and dusted her hands off on her dress. She expected Darian to be looking at her in fear and disgust, but he seemed amazed.

"I'll let you know when I figure that out. Darian," she said, "he's been in your body for a year. Is there somewhere he's taken you when he was weak? Or is there something he has that gives him a power boost?"

Darian shook his head miserably.

"When he possessed me, I still slept when I normally would have. *He* never did, but there were always seven or eight hours of the day I couldn't account for. I think he waited till I was asleep to cause the most chaos."

It had been a long shot that he'd have the answer, but Adia had to stop herself from stomping in frustration.

"Whatever this source is, it could be anywhere in Zaria," Darian said.

They were running out of time. A steady stream of blood now oozed out of the stone.

"We shouldn't have to go far," Adia said. "Whatever's going on, I think it's in the Academy."

"This would be the perfect place to hide something," Gini said. "All right, Adia, is there a dungeon or a crypt or somewhere hidden away? Somewhere none of the teachers and students would ever go?"

Adia didn't need to pull the map of the Academy into her head. It was obvious. A place where no one who paid their way into this prestigious school would ever dare enter? A section of the Academy that would immediately give the students a headache if they tried to process what was inside? And that now had a locked gate in front of it to keep people out?

She knew exactly where Olark had hidden his power source.

"The library."

TWENTY-ONE

"Was it really smart to leave Gini behind?" Darian asked.

Adia shivered. She could barely see through the rain dripping down her glasses, so she sighed and took them off. Low vision was better than no vision right now.

"If there's some power source making O . . . the demon stronger," Adia said, catching herself before saying Olark's name. "It wouldn't make any sense for Gini to carry him right to it in her pocket. It's better that she and the blood-stained stone stay separate from us."

She kept her other reason for wanting distance from Gini to herself. No need for everyone else to be scared. But Gini was running out of time too. She could surpass her limits any second now and become untethered. And if Gini lost herself and went on a rampage, there was no chance of ever stopping a power like hers.

"Plus," Thyme said, unaware of the other danger they were facing, "he's finally found the one person he needs to possess. The second he breaks free from the blood-stained stone, you think he's running to possess you or me or anyone else here? No. He's coming for Adia."

"Thank you, Thyme, for that comforting thought," Adia said, but the truth of it made her run faster.

"But are you sure you know where you're going?" Thyme asked.

"I'm sure," Adia said, ducking under a fallen tree. They were on the trail behind the student quarters. She glanced up at the dorms. Mallorie Amber might be tucked away in her bed right now. Probably dreaming about marrying Darian and becoming an empress.

"No one but the staff uses this trail. If you went that way," she said, pointing down the path she'd used to use to deliver the breakfast trays, "you'd reach the kitchens. But this way leads to the libraries. Now that I think about it, no one was ever sent to clean there. I assumed it was because no one who goes here reads, so why waste the manpower, but maybe when Darian was possessed, he told the headmaster it was off-limits."

After a few minutes, she could make out the run-down enclave that housed the libraries ahead.

"It's there," she said, pointing.

"How many libraries are there?" Thyme asked.

"A few dozen according to the maps," Adia said. "The enclave is two levels. There's a bunch of rooms, but I only had time to go into one before I was expelled."

They reached the newly wrought gate.

"We'll have to climb over."

Thyme was over the gate in a matter of seconds, and Adia and Darian dropped down after her. Darian was a little unsteady, but he just nodded and grinned when Adia gave him a worried look. If he'd left them to go rest or find a healer after everything he'd been through for the past year, she wouldn't have blamed him. But she was glad he'd come along.

The library had been a comforting presence the last time she was here. But in the storm, with Gold Hats and a demon wanting to possess her, every shadow made her want to jump.

"We should probably split up," Thyme said, drawing a dagger. "I'll take the top, you take the bottom. Adia, stay with Darian. One of us needs to protect him."

"I *can* fight, you know," Darian said, but he looked amused. "Though I did end up possessed for a year because I was distracted from my training by a book, so fair enough."

"You'll have to tell me about that one day," Adia said as they walked down the stairs.

"Careful," Darian said. "It's slippery from the rain, and there's no handrail. You want to take my hand?"

It *was* slippery. She also hadn't eaten anything since breakfast and was starting to feel dizzy. Adia grabbed Darian's outstretched hand, and they carefully walked down the stairs.

"So what was it like?" she asked. "Living with a demon in your body? Having no control."

"Horrible. I tried to fight him at first, but I stopped a while ago. Until he brought you to the Red Room."

"I know," Adia said, remembering Olark's anger at whatever Darian had tried to do to stop him. "I would have been in serious trouble if you hadn't done that. Thank you."

"You don't owe me any thanks," Darian said. "It was the first time I've ever seen him rattled. Usually, my heart rate stayed exactly the same, even when he was doing something terrible, like sending his missionaries to take over a village that sat on top of an oil reservoir when he needed more funds. But when he saw you at the welcome ceremony . . ." He shook his head. "You *glowed*. At least to him you glowed. And his—that is, *my* heart raced for the first time in a year. I thought he was in love or something. You were the prettiest girl in the room, so it was a logical guess."

Adia rolled her eyes. "Pretty for a dark-skinned Zarian."

"You're pretty for anyone," Darian said. He cleared his throat as Adia looked away. "But then I could feel something else mixed in with his excitement. Panic."

"Panic?" Adia said, incredulous. "Why would the sight of me make him panic?"

"I think he's afraid of you."

"If he's afraid of anyone, it's Viona. I can't do anything to him."

Darian snorted. "I just watched you make an entire forest bend to your will. I'd be afraid of you if I were him. How did you do that, by the way?"

"I don't know," Adia admitted. "I wanted the forest to help me, and it listened. It's . . . just a part of me, I guess."

"Who's Nami?" Darian asked suddenly.

"What?" she said. She stumbled on the slippery floor, startled. She'd been trying to keep Nami's betrayal buried deep in the back of her mind so she didn't start to cry. Or punch something.

"Careful," Darian said, tightening his grip on her hand. He cleared his throat. "I heard you all mention him when I was coming to. He's someone you know?"

"He's someone I thought I knew," she said through gritted teeth.

"I see."

And she thought maybe he really did see.

"I'm sorry," he said.

"What do you have to be sorry about? You and Thyme are the most innocent people in all this."

"And you're not? You saved my life. Now you're risking everything to save more people."

"I'm not as good as you think I am," she said bluntly. "The demon is after me for a reason. I've done things. I've come close to being exactly what my family thinks I'm destined to be."

"And what's that?"

"A bringer of great misfortune. Every time I think I'm not, every time I think I can fight whatever's wrong with me, something comes along to confirm that I can't," she said. "Like a demon thinking I'm just the girl to host his twisted soul."

Darian snorted. "I think you're giving a demon way too much power over your life. Besides, I've always thought good and evil don't exist. Just ignorance versus wisdom."

She was shocked. If anyone would believe in good and evil, she'd thought it would be a boy possessed by a demon for a solid year.

"You sound like Gini," she said after a moment of silence.

Darian shrugged. "Even that thing possessing me thought he was doing me a favor, not harming me. I guarantee you, he doesn't see himself as the villain of this story. He's too ignorant."

"His missionaries are like that too," Adia admitted. "It's not an act. They really think they're saving our souls and making us civilized when all they're doing is making the demon rich. They're completely mindwashed."

"Obedience without question," Darian said grimly.

Adia gave him a startled look.

"One of my favorite catchphrases, wasn't it?" he shuddered. "The entire world thinks I actually said things like that. I'm going to have to change my name and disappear after this is over."

"I think you're giving a demon too much power over your life," Adia flung back at him.

Darian snorted. "Fair enough. But I don't know what I'm going to do when this is all over."

"What about your family?"

"My mother would never believe any of this. Or let me

give up the throne. I've finally lived up to the Edochie family legacy. I swear my family puts a sword in your hand as a baby instead of a bottle. My mom always thought I was weak because I didn't like fighting—I'm good at it, but I don't like it."

Adia finally realized why Darian felt so familiar and easy to talk to. He reminded her of EJ.

They reached the bottom of the stairs, where a dozen doors lined the stone halls.

Darian stepped forward, but she jerked him back.

"Hang on," she said.

She reached out her hand and touched the walls. The school had a life and will of its own. You felt that the second you arrived. But this was different. The walls were shaking. She jumped back when a brick fell from the ceiling, exploding in front of them.

"The Academy's furious," she whispered.

"At us?" Darian asked nervously.

"No. At whatever's going on down here," she said, softly stroking the wall. "You recognize me, right? I used to work here. I'm trying to help."

The walls creaked and groaned in the way old houses do, but the sound was eerily human and heavy with despair. Whatever was going on down here, Adia knew it had everything to do with the Academy's constant mood swings. Olark had been hurting it somehow.

"We're going to check the rooms," she said, cautiously taking a step forward. "Don't fight us—we're here to help."

Darian followed her, and she sighed in relief when the floorboards didn't beat them up. They got to the first door. Darian opened it, peered inside, and shook his head.

"No one's been here for a long while. The cobwebs are so thick I can barely see inside. Doesn't anyone read at this school?"

She opened another door and shook her head. "Nothing in this one either."

They worked fast and in silence until there was only one room left to check. When they reached the door, Adia clutched her head. She'd thought she'd felt dizzy from skipping lunch and dinner, but now her head was throbbing too. This felt like more than hunger pangs.

"What's wrong?" Darian asked, worried as she hunched over. She held the wall to steady herself, surprised at how rough it was compared to all the others. Like it was made from a completely different material.

"I don't know. This door is different. This whole section is different."

The Academy had always pulsed with unseen energy to the point that even someone as shamanically dense as Mallorie Amber could feel it. But this part of it felt cold and devoid of its usual energy. It felt dead. And she felt sick.

Darian touched it. Then to her surprise he stuck his tongue out and licked it.

"It's salt," he confirmed.

Behind them, moss covered the stone walls and weeds shot out in between cracks in the ground. But there was no sign of life anywhere near this section. She touched the napkin Gini had given her. In her pocket, the small amount of salt was a tool to help control her power. But someone had used that tool another way—to *suffocate* the Academy's power. To make sure that even if someone with shamanic ability was nearby, they wouldn't be able to feel what was going on behind this door. No wonder the school was furious.

"The demon did this," she said. "He's hiding his source in here."

"Should we get Thyme?" Darian asked, but Adia wasn't waiting. It was her soul that was on the line. Every minute that passed was a minute Olark got closer to breaking free of the blood-stained stone.

She pushed the door open and stepped into the room.

There were no books. There were no shelves. There was nothing.

Adia's feet crunched over the pink rocks that covered the floor. No, not rocks—

"It's nothing but salt," she said.

Darian followed her inside. He picked up a block from one of the piles that lined the walls. After several minutes of tossing salt blocks out of the way, she saw it—iron bars protecting a drainpipe made of cut stone, large enough to crawl through. This must be what they were looking for! If Olark had gone to this length to hide something, it had to be the source of power. If he hadn't been hell-bent on possessing her to use her eyes to find Imo Mmiri, Adia would have thought the magic land was somehow hidden in the Academy's drainage system. But it had to be something else. Something it felt like she should be able to piece together. An answer that had always stayed just out of reach but was now on the other side of this pipe. And if she destroyed that, she could help save two worlds from a murderous demon—her own, and the stars he was so desperate to return to.

"Darian," she whispered.

She lifted the heavy latch keeping whatever was on the other side from getting out and pulled the door open.

"I'll go first," he said, crawling into the dark tunnel.

She crawled in after him, wincing as her knees scraped against the stone surface.

"There's something up ahead," Darian called over his shoulder. "It's a bit of a drop. Be careful."

Then Darian yelped in pain. She quickly dropped down after him, landing with a thud.

"Did you hurt yourself?" she asked as she stood up. Darian didn't answer, and she squinted in the darkness.

"Stay back or I'll slit his throat," someone whispered.

Adia froze. She could make out Darian now. His hands were pulled behind his back and someone had his mouth covered. She was about to charge the person holding him when she saw dozens of eyes trained on her in the dark. Her heart started racing. They were completely outnumbered.

"I don't know who you are or what's going on," the shadowed person said, "but since you've been good enough to open the gate, we're getting out of here."

Getting out of here?

Maybe whoever these people were, they weren't the enemy.

"We're not here to hurt anyone," she said, holding her hands up in the air. "Who are you? Why don't you step into the light so we can see each other?"

"Wait." The person covering Darian's mouth stopped whispering and spoke clearly. He sounded shocked. "Who are *you*?"

The air left Adia's lungs.

His voice was familiar. It wasn't possible, though. She might have imagined it a million times. But the dead didn't speak.

"Step into the light so I can see you," she said hoarsely. "Now."

This had to be some trick of Olark's.

The boy didn't let go of Darian, but he backed up until he was standing underneath a dimly lit candle that was close to dying out. His glasses were broken down the middle and held together with a piece of twine, and two scars that hadn't been there before ran down each of his cheeks, but his eyes were the same as they'd always been—sharp and slightly sad.

"EJ?"

TWENTY-TWO

Adia burst into tears.

EJ let go of Darian and caught her in a bear hug. She couldn't speak for several moments, trying to process that this was really happening. She was scared that if she released EJ, he would disappear, but after a moment, he pulled back from her.

"I never thought I'd see you again," he said.

"I thought you were dead," she said.

"Dead?" EJ said in horror. "So no one searched for me?"

Adia's guilt consumed her. She'd given up her search too soon. In her heart, she'd always known she should never have stopped trying to find him.

"Of course I searched for you! The entire village did. Your parents. Ericson. But then the missionaries said they'd found your body, and we had a funeral and . . . Is it really you?"

"It's me," he said, giving her another hug. For months, Adia had tormented herself with all the things she could've done differently the day EJ disappeared. She went over every little choice that had led up to EJ vanishing, and wondered what might've been if she'd made different ones: Maybe if she hadn't insisted they skip breakfast (Ericson usually took most of hers anyways), they would've gotten to the lake later, when it was hotter and the alligators were less likely to be active. Maybe if she had prayed more to the Bright Father—or prayed to him at all, really—then EJ would've been protected by his blessing. Maybe it could've been her, instead of him.

She lived in a world of maybes, but the biggest was *maybe he's still alive.*

Adia had stopped tormenting herself with that possibility months ago—it hurt too much to want something so badly and feel like it could never be.

But here EJ was.

Alive.

"I don't understand," EJ said when they had finally both stopped crying enough to speak again. "Adia, how did you get here? Were you kidnapped too? I don't know how they missed you when they took me."

"Why would anyone kidnap me?" she asked, baffled. "Why would anyone kidnap *you*?"

"But then how are you here?" EJ asked, just as confused. "My parents would never let you come to the Academy of Shamans, even though you obviously should be a student."

"What a terrible thing to say," Adia gasped. "Have you seen the kids who go here?"

She wanted to tell him everything that had happened in the year since he'd been gone, but Darian was pacing nervously around the room and children were coming out of corners, staring at them with wide, panicked eyes.

"EJ, I'll explain everything later, but what's going on?" she pressed. "What happened? You were swimming, and then you were gone. I didn't hear anything. Did they knock you out before you could scream? Who took you?"

EJ crossed his arms. She'd seen him do that a hundred times when Uncle Eric shouted at him and called him too delicate to be any son of his. EJ always tried to fold in on himself when he was embarrassed.

"No, no one hit me. I got lured away. You were reading, and she was really quiet."

"Who?"

"Sister Claudia," EJ said, grimacing at the memory.

"That horrible woman," Adia said. "One of these days I'm going back to the Swamplands to deal with her. But why would she kidnap you? And why are all of you down here?"

"She had her orders," EJ said. "I ended up here with all these other kids. She said we had a special gift that we needed to share. Shamanic gifts."

Adia felt a chill run through her. The students Lebechi had mentioned, who seemed to have an ability, then disappeared, never to be seen or heard from again. They hadn't bailed on the Academy, leaving all their things behind in their rooms—they were kidnapped children with shamanic abilities.

EJ was Olark's extra source of power. All these children were. Children like her, stolen away and hidden in this dark prison all so he could have the fuel to hunt for Viona. Her body was heating up again, like it had the first time she'd laid eyes on him.

"You probably won't even believe me when I tell you who's behind all this," EJ said, not noticing how hard she was fighting to keep her anger in check and not slip back into that dark space. She could already feel it calling to her again. "But it's . . ."

His voice trailed off, and he shoved Adia behind him.

"What is it?" she asked, peering over her cousin's shoulder. She only saw Darian.

Darian. Who they thought was the person who'd trapped them here.

EJ glared at Darian with a hatred she'd never seen come out of her cousin's eyes. And the rest of the children moved forward, circling them.

"Knock him out, EJ!" someone yelled, flinging a lead pipe that EJ caught.

"No," Adia said, jumping in front of Darian. "No more head wounds. It's a miracle he hasn't fainted again."

It was a miracle she hadn't fainted either. Every second she spent down here left her feeling exhausted and drained.

"Adia," EJ said slowly. "Move away from him. Trust me."

"No, EJ," she said firmly as she shoved herself between

them. "You need to trust *me*."

EJ stared at her in surprise, and she knew why. He'd always distracted Uncle Eric when his rants about Adia's demonic nature went on for too long. And he'd always put himself in between her and Ericson when Ericson got it in his head to fling Adia into the compost heap or whatever other torment he had cooked up on any given day. EJ took care of her, and she followed his lead. But this time he would have to listen to her.

"I know someone who *looked* like Darian has been coming down here," she said, "but it wasn't him."

"No. He's put a spell on you," EJ said, shaking his head. "You can't trust a word that comes out of his mouth."

"It's true," a small girl said, glaring at Darian. "I was a student here. He cornered me one day and told me he needed my help with a secret project. That I was the Academy's strongest student and only I could help him. But I would need to take Drops first. A huge dose. Next thing I know, more power than I've ever felt ran through my body, but before I could do anything, he put his hands on the side of my head and inhaled, like he was trying to suck out my soul. I ended up half-dead on the floor, and he walked out of here, never looking better. My powers never came back."

"Every few months, he shows up with a new kid and keeps those of us he's already drained locked away down here," EJ said. "And apparently the schools or the missionaries or whoever works for him tell our families we're dead so no one bothers to search for us."

"It wasn't Darian," Adia said. "If you can't trust him, trust me. He's my friend."

EJ looked confused. "Friends? You don't have any friends except stray cats and books."

Darian raised an eyebrow, and Adia felt her cheeks heat up. She'd almost forgotten EJ's complete lack of filter.

"Well, I do now," she muttered.

"It wasn't me," Darian said. "I don't know how to prove that to you. I don't even have *time* to prove it to you. And I'm really glad you two are reunited, but we need to get out of here—all of us. That thing that was possessing me? We slowed him down, but we don't have much time before he snatches another body—Adia's. She's the one he's been looking for all this time."

"He's not looking for Adia," EJ scoffed. "He's looking for a girl. Some shaman who hid a huge source of power from him. He's always going on about her. He says if he finds her again, he can ascend and rule us all. Her name is—"

"Viona," Darian and Adia said, cutting him off.

EJ blinked. "How do you know about her?"

"He thinks I *am* her," she said.

EJ finally lowered the pipe. The other children didn't look any happier, but they stopped crowding Darian.

Adia stepped deeper into the room. Barrels were stacked high on top of each other, almost touching the ceiling. She lifted the top of one and peered into it.

"Is this—"

"Drops," EJ confirmed. "He had us make them too. All

we do is beat agrias vines and boil them into Drops."

Adia took in the barrels of Drops lined up all around the room. *Obedience without question.*

"Darian, find Thyme and get everyone out of here." She ignored the fact that she had just barked an order at an emperor, and marched purposefully to the barrels. She wasn't going to leave a single drop of Drops for Olark. If he didn't have this, he couldn't drain any more kids. She didn't know how much power he had left on his own. For all she knew, he'd already escaped from the blood-stained stone. But at least this would buy Gini time to bind him again.

"What are you doing?"

"Just go. I'll be right behind you. If he doesn't have Drops, he can't bring out your powers. Or anyone's. He needs them to drain you. Get everyone out of here."

She shoved the first barrel. It was heavier than she'd expected. She gritted her teeth and dug her heels into the ground, and down it went. The dark brown liquid spilled onto the salted ground.

Everyone stared at her.

"He'll kill her," someone whispered.

"Let us help," EJ said, ignoring the panicked whispers.

"You can help by getting out of here. Stop wasting time."

EJ pursed his lips but nodded, then rushed to the other children. Someone had already stacked barrels to climb to get into the drainpipe, but they looked too scared to leave on their own.

"Darian, you need to show them where to go," Adia said.

"Find Thyme and get them to Gini."

Thankfully he didn't fight her.

"I'll lead them out, then come right back down to help you."

She nodded at him as she tipped over another barrel. She was still dizzy, but she wasn't going to tell Darian or EJ how weak she'd been this entire time or they'd never leave.

Darian led the way, and EJ stood at the rear as the children scrambled up the drainpipe, leaving her alone in the room to her task.

Adia worked as fast as she could, but the dizziness was overwhelming now. The room started fading in and out, the shadows turning into a mirage. The same as when she'd first seen Olark. She was being pulled away again. And Thyme wasn't around to dump water on her.

"Get ahold of yourself," she said, but trying to will herself to not feel sick was proving pointless.

She hadn't finished spilling the Drops, but she couldn't hang on any longer. Maybe she could make it upstairs and out of the library enclave and catch up with Thyme, Darian, and EJ. Maybe they could get her to Gini before she lost control again.

Adia stumbled forward, trying to make it to the drainpipe, but she was so dizzy she fell to her knees. The room went in and out of focus as shadows swam in front of her. Not just shadows. She screamed when she realized she was no longer alone.

A face loomed in front of her. Three white lines were

drawn down the sides of their cheeks and their hair was in braids, but she'd know the face peering down at her anywhere.

It was her own.

The girl with her face, but no glasses, watched her with a solemn expression. Adia moved her hand, wondering if the girl would lift hers up too, like a mirror reflection. But the girl stood still. That was when she realized that, yes, they looked eerily similar, but they weren't the same.

This girl's eyes weren't as wide, and she wasn't as tall. Vines weaved their way through her hair and down her back. One of the vines snaked forward and touched Adia. When it did, she felt as if she'd been shocked. And suddenly she knew who was before her.

"Viona," she whispered.

A ghost. She'd already seen gods, a headless girl, a possessed emperor. Why wouldn't a ghost show up too?

"Yes," Viona said.

"Am I dead too? Did Olark get me?"

"No. You're journeying."

"I'm what?"

"Journeying," Viona repeated slowly. "Through the realm of spirit. Look around you."

Adia had been so shocked by her mirror image that she hadn't realized the makeshift prison was now different. She knew she hadn't left the cellar, but every part of it was covered in colorful lights that shifted in and out of shapes. Geometric patterns one second, then animals the next. For one brief moment, they shifted into the forms of three women drumming. But while she could still make out parts of the room around her, she couldn't say the same for the ceiling. It was gone. Replaced with a dazzling display of lights that went up and up, climbing so high she felt dizzy trying to follow them, like a living cathedral dome that had no end, not even the sky.

"The realm of spirit," she repeated in shock.

"It's the only place we can talk," Viona said. "I've been trying to reach you. I came close a few times. The day you caused the earthquake, the orientation ceremony."

Adia blinked. "Someone warned me at orientation that Mallorie was about to poison herself. Then agrias vines were moving around on the ceiling. And that day in the Swamplands, the vines smashing through the window when Sister Claudia was about to dose me—that was you?"

"Actually, the warning at orientation was all you. Your power. But the vines on the ceiling were me. I tried to write your name on the ceiling with them, but you never saw."

Adia's jaw dropped. The vines that looked like the letter A. Viona had been trying to contact her. A spirit . . . had been trying to communicate with her.

"Agrias is one of the strongest plants there is. Olark twisted its power and turned it into *this*," Viona said in disgust, pointing at the spilled barrels of Drops, "but agrias itself is not bad. He just chose to use it in a bad way. I've been using it to reach you whenever I could."

"If you've been watching me, then you've seen what I've done. I almost lost control. I could have hurt my friend. The first time I saw Olark—" she began, but Viona waved her hand.

"You were half journeying when you first saw Olark. Seeing him triggered your ability, and you went in and out of a spirit realm. The first few times are always chaotic. We usually go in with our teacher and *only* after we've gone through initiation, which you haven't yet. You're lucky you were able to pull yourself back. Dark entities are drawn to a shaman on their first journey through spirit. We're easy prey. You felt something scary try to pull you away, right?"

Adia nodded. "Something tried to take control of me."

"But you pulled yourself back. Why?"

"What do you mean, why?" Adia said in surprise. "Because I didn't want to hurt Thyme. I don't want to hurt anyone!"

Viona raised an eyebrow and gave her a knowing look, and finally, Adia understood.

Yes, she had power. And, sure, her family and the missionaries saw it as evil. But she wasn't possessed by an evil spirit, and she wasn't doomed to bring misfortune to everyone who crossed her path. It was like Gini had said: power wasn't good or evil, until someone used it to that end. There was nothing wrong with her and nothing to exorcise. She wasn't cursed. She wasn't a demon.

She was a shaman.

"I knew he'd come for you," Viona said. "Same as he

came for me. But you've been fighting your gift up until now, so I couldn't talk to you. I needed you to meet me halfway. You only became fully open when you saw EJ again."

Adia could understand that. Seeing all those children. Knowing there were other kids like her—or would have been if Olark hadn't stolen their powers. It was easier to accept what she was when she realized she wasn't alone.

Viona tilted her head, listening to something Adia couldn't hear. She frowned and turned back to Adia.

"We don't have time," she said. "He could break free from the blood-stained stone in a matter of seconds."

"What can I do?" Adia said, quickly standing up. "He's never going to stop. He thinks I'm the key to regaining his power. That if he possesses me, he'll be able to use my eyes to see where you hid Imo Mmiri."

"He's right," Viona said. "Your eyes would be able to see it because we share the same blood. Anyone else would see an ordinary forest, get confused, and end up lost. But Imo Mmiri is just as much your home as it is mine. Anyone descended from the first shaman would be able to see it. Ovie was my grandfather, and I was his apprentice. And now you're the only living descendant of our line left. You have more power in your little toe than all those kids combined. You're the only person in the world who would be able to find our home and reopen the circle of shamans."

Viona was starting to fade in and out. The mirage too. The room was going from hazy to solid.

"How do I fight Olark?" Adia asked quickly.

"You don't have to fight him. He's already destroyed himself. He's bad at curses, at Words of Power. There's a loophole—"

"I already discovered the loophole," Adia said. "That's how I learned he was back and possessing Darian."

"No—" Viona suddenly stopped talking, looking nervous, as if something in the distance, a distance Adia couldn't see, was calling her.

"He's broken free," she said. "He's coming."

Adia's heart stopped. She started to shake, but Viona whistled sharply. The high-pitched sound made her jump but also pierced through her the way it did when Gini had whistled at the sadness leaving her in the Horrorbeyond. It wasn't just a tune—they were doing something with energy when they whistled. Her shaking stopped.

"There's no time for you to freeze, Adia," she said. "Find the loophole. I have to go before you end up trapped in a spirit realm. If you stay in another realm for too long, it's hard to find your way back. And you don't know how to properly come and go yet."

"I don't know how to what?"

"How to come and go. It's what shamans do. We walk between realms. Shadow realms, star realms, death realms. There's really no place that's off-limits for the children who come and go. And now," Viona said, placing two fingers on Adia's forehead and giving her a shove, "you need to *go*."

The world went black, then back to light in the span of a second. Viona was gone. Adia was out of the world of spirit.

She finally understood why her body turned to fire whenever she saw Olark. He'd hurt her family, her ancestors. It was like Maka had said about the ancient sea trees: *the ax forgets, but the tree remembers.* Her blood remembered too.

The sound of voices made her jump. Someone was above her.

"Has anyone checked down here?"

"No one goes down there. I think it's where they keep *books.*"

"Which would make it a clever place for someone to hide," the other voice answered. "Who'd want to look at books?"

Adia ran for the drainpipe, then stopped. She turned around and quickly spilled the last barrel over, sloshing the black liquid all over her dress.

There. If they failed, at the very least Olark wouldn't be able to dose anyone any time soon. And the kidnapped children had been freed.

She sprinted the last few steps to the drainpipe and quickly crawled back up. The dizziness got even worse the second she was back in the room with too many salt blocks, but she shook it off and rushed back into the hallway.

She held her breath as she hugged the walls and tiptoed along the corridors. The stairs were just in front of her.

"What's this?"

She'd been caught. It was all over.

At least I got EJ and Darian out.

Her eyes closed as she waited for the cold kiss of a Gold Hat's blade.

She could feel his breath on her forehead, but she didn't open her eyes. She didn't want to see the swing of the machete.

"It's just a stairway to nowhere," the other voice grumbled. "Told you this was a waste of time. There's nothing down here."

She didn't understand what was happening. She slowly opened one eye.

The Gold Hats were standing right in front of her, but she might as well have been invisible. She looked down and understood why. The walls had changed color to camouflage her brown skin and green dress.

The Gold Hats turned around and ran back up the staircase.

Adia waited a minute before prying herself off the wall. The walls that always took care of the servants at the school. "Thank you," she whispered.

She hurried up the stairs and ran outside. No one was around. Good. It was terrifying being out here by herself, and the moon was hidden behind dark gray clouds, making the night even darker, but if no one was here, that meant Darian and Thyme should be on their way to Gini. Or already with her. She quickly climbed back over the gate and dropped to the ground. But before she could steady herself, someone shoved her, sending her crashing into a tree.

She groaned in pain and rubbed her head, alarmed to

find blood gushing from her temple. The Gold Hats must have realized something was off and doubled back.

One grabbed her roughly and spun her around. She gasped and tried to reach for her dagger, but it was knocked to the ground. Cold sharp steel pressed against her neck. She lifted her gaze, meeting the eyes of the person who'd captured her.

"Nami."

TWENTY-THREE

Nami led her through the dungeon, which reeked of mold and misery. Clearly this dungeon hadn't been built for students. If a student here got in trouble, their parents would probably send money as a bribe to get their record washed clean. This must be where the headmaster threw servants accused of stealing.

Nami had bound her hands with rough rope that cut into her wrists as he pulled her along.

"It's better if you don't struggle," Nami said. "That— that was quite a head wound you took."

A head wound *he'd* inflicted! She would have said as much, but Nami also had her gagged. She couldn't even say Olark's name and send him into a fit. She jerked free and tried to tackle him but only fell on the cold stone floor, painfully scraping her knee. He tried to help her back up, but she recoiled at his touch.

"I'll put you in a cell and go get my superior officers," Nami said, ignoring the way she'd cringed. "You'll be interrogated until you tell us where the emperor is and—and then you'll be put on trial."

He didn't meet her eyes as he spoke.

"If you have an explanation for all this, you'll be fine." He sounded strange. As if even he couldn't believe how far he'd gone, and needed to justify his behavior. Words poured out of him. "Look, Adia, I have to do this. Leaving my post, letting you escape? They can't look the other way if I mess up again. And I have to become a Gold Hat—my family *needs* this. And like I said, you'll get a fair trial. It'd probably help a lot if you just tell everyone what you did with the emperor."

Exorcised him and saved his life, you bloody fool.

But Nami had effectively made sure that he didn't have to listen to her, lest she say something that made him realize how wrong he was. It was a lot easier to see the world as you wanted to see it if you forced everyone who might tell you differently to be quiet.

They reached a cell. He didn't look at her as he pushed her forward.

"I—I'll have someone bring you some water."

With that, he slammed the bars shut and left her in the dank cell. A mouse scurried into a corner away from water that was dripping from the cracked ceiling. The hole it disappeared into was the only way out that Adia could see. Four walls, iron bars, and no windows. There wasn't even a bench to sit on.

The only thing she could do was hope that Gini, Thyme, and Darian would save the day. This mission was always going to come down to the heroes anyway, not her. The most she could do was try to talk her way out of getting executed before it was over. She sat in a corner and buried her head in her knees.

The bars creaked open.

"I can't believe a criminal was working in my kitchen," someone sniffed.

Adia's face shot up.

Maka?

The head cook glared down at her. A guard was with her, also looking at her in disgust.

Adia's eyes watered, and she put her head back down. Nami's betrayal was one thing. She may not have listened to her gut, but she'd sensed something was off with him. But Maka and Lebechi? They had always been kind to her. Everyone in the kitchens must be talking about her right now. Adia Kelbara, the great disgrace.

"Don't know why we have to give her any food at all after the chaos she caused. I've never seen the Academy in such a state. All those poor, dear students. They're so sad about what's befallen our beloved emperor. To miss their chance to see him. It's not like any royal will ever come this way again."

Poor, dear students?

Adia lifted her head up again but schooled her face to betray no emotion. What was Maka talking about?

"Well, we can't have her dying of hunger before interrogation," the guard said.

Maka sighed. "I suppose not. But I'm not giving her anything but scraps. The way this child used to eat the Academy out of house and home. Always stealing the best cuts of meat for herself."

At that, Adia's tears dried up.

Stealing *meat*? She couldn't even stand to be in the room when Lebechi was plucking chickens.

Nothing coming out of Maka's mouth made sense.

"Only the kindness of my own heart kept me from not tossing her out on her ear. I should have known better. Her kola nut ceremony? The kola broke into two pieces. I knew exactly who she was from that moment on. A bringer of misfortune."

Her nut had broken into six pieces—a bringer of light. Maka had been impressed. She took the old ways seriously.

Adia allowed herself a glimmer of hope. The cook was trying to tell her something.

"Here."

Maka slammed down a tray by Adia's feet. She reached out and undid the gag tied around her mouth.

"Eat quickly. We'll be back in ten minutes to get this tray, so if you're not finished by then, it'll be too late. You understand me?"

Adia finally looked up. Everything about Maka's expression was cruel and heartless, but her words had been enough.

"Say it," Maka said urgently.

It took everything in her not to jump up and give Maka a

hug for the risk she was taking.

Ten minutes to escape.

"I understand."

"Good." Maka exited the cell and turned to the guard. "Come on. I can't breathe down here. You should have her scrub these piss-stained walls." Maka cackled, the echo of her laughter bouncing off the walls.

Adia waited until she was sure they were gone, then knocked the cover off the tray. There was a small cup of water and a stuffed banana leaf. She quickly tossed back the water, since she *was* incredibly thirsty, then ripped open the leaf.

The smell of moi moi hit her nose, but hungry as she was, she didn't have time to eat her favorite bean cake. She squished the soft cake between her fingers and touched metal.

A key.

She jumped up and shoved the key into the lock. At that moment, a high-pitched scream pierced the air, startling her so much that she fumbled the key. Olark must have reached the salted library and found it deserted. Her hand shook, but she tried the key again. This time there was a satisfying click as the bars sprang open.

Thanks, Maka.

"Now, which way is out?" she whispered. She had no bearings in the dungeons whatsoever. They hadn't appeared on any map she'd ever seen.

Something furry brushed against her leg, and she bit

back a shriek as she peered down, expecting to see a rat. But instead, a chubby orange surprise swatted at her ankle.

"Bubbles!"

She scooped him up, and he yowled in protest at the tight hug.

"I've missed you! Did you come to help me get out? You're such a good boy! Show me the way!"

Bubbles jumped down and took off. She took off right after him, running to freedom. Any second now and—

Bubbles meowed happily and darted through a hole in a massive pile of stones—a hole so small only a boneless cat would be able to squeeze through it. She could hear his purrs from the other side.

"Oh, you wretched animal," Adia said, stomping her foot.

The stones were too big to move. She bent down and peered through the hole Bubbles had gone through. It was the right direction at least—she could see a familiar patch of forest outside. Gini was barely five minutes away, but she was trapped by a wall of stones.

Adia frowned and clenched her hands. She knew how to use her power now. It wasn't that she had to make any great effort to bring it forward. It was that she had to relax and not suppress that side of her. She just hoped it would be enough.

The memory of sweeping under her bed every morning to make sure Uncle Eric didn't find an ogbanje's stone made her let out an exhausted laugh. If only her uncle could see her now! But if the forest was on the other side of this wall of stones, so were the roots of the trees.

She unclenched her hands, let the light come through, and felt the roots on the other side.

"We need to move the stones."

The ground underneath her shook. She peered out of the hole again, and yes, just like that day in the Swamplands, the roots of the trees whipped the ground. Only, this time she wasn't afraid of her power. She was choosing it. Choosing to use it—and it felt good, like releasing something she'd bottled up for far too long.

One of the large stones rolled away. Then another as the roots obeyed her command, moving the rocks out of the way as if they were an extension of her own two hands.

Enough space cleared, and she shimmied through. When she reached the other side, she rolled onto her back, breathing heavily. She hadn't stopped running since Sister Claudia had showed up that day at her house. Only a few weeks had passed since then, but it felt like a lifetime.

The rain slowed to a drizzle, and the clouds parted enough for the stars to shine through. She could see Alusia, brighter than all of them.

"How could she escape *again*?" someone shouted.

Would people never stop chasing her?

"Get up," she groaned. Her only chance was to find Gini in the forest before Olark or the Gold Hats found *her*. Maybe Gini could hide her in a ring of fire for the rest of her life so he couldn't possess her.

The ground around her popped like corn kernels hitting a hot frying pan, and it turned black, as if scorched by invisible flames. She shot up. Had Gini heard her thoughts? No. It wasn't Gini.

Even though the earth was scorched, the air around her turned cold as a shadow with yellow eyes slowly crept toward her. It was too late to find Gini now.

"I've waited five hundred years for this."

Her legs were shaking, her glasses were missing, and she suspected blood was dripping down her head. But she pushed herself up. It was over. She had no one to help her and no chance of survival, but she would face him head-on.

"Yes. I suppose you have," she said coldly. "Hello, Olark."

TWENTY-FOUR

"**B**ut where are your friends?" Olark asked.

He seemed to be making a sad attempt at holding a form, but the result was ghoulish. Like a monster from the Horrorbeyond, his limbs were too long and reeked of decay. He made a strange motion with his mouth. Adia shuddered as she realized he was trying to smile. But his teeth were twice as long as they should have been and kept falling out and growing back, a forked tongue appearing between the gaps. No wonder he was so desperate to possess bodies if this monstrosity was the alternative.

"Has the great Ginikanwa finally realized it's pointless to try to stop me? And no Darian either, I see. I made that boy an emperor, and this is how he repays me."

Adia was so disgusted, she forgot to be afraid.

"You're the most arrogant person I've ever seen," she spat out.

"So quick to criticize," he snapped. "Why do you keep fighting me? Don't you understand why I'm doing all this?"

She sputtered. "Understand? Of course I understand. Sending your missionaries to keep everyone too subdued with Drops to realize you've taken over. Letting rich people from the Sunless Mountains prance around charging money for the traditions they stole from us. Kidnapping children who have real power. Tormenting my ancestors because they had a power you wanted? All of it's connected to one thing."

"My desire to make the world a better place," he said, his voice dripping with condescension.

Adia snorted. "Not even you could believe that. You weren't given a star, and you've been throwing a five-hundred-year-long tantrum about it. Trying to prove to the Alusi that you don't need them, when clearly everything you do is to get their attention."

"Always with something to say," Olark growled. "Aren't you tired? Can't you see how much easier it would be for you if you joined me instead of fighting?"

Yes. She was tired. It had been a night full of nightmares. Of course it would be easier not to fight him. Maybe that's what Viona was trying to tell her. That it was time to give up. Let him possess her and become exactly what everyone in the village said she was. A bringer of misery and misfortune.

"My methods might seem harsh," he said, sounding a lot calmer than he ever had before, "but that's because I had no other choice. I'm not the greedy monster Gini's led you to believe. All I've ever wanted was to help others. Don't you want the same thing?"

Adia backed up as he came closer. Even in his diminished form, she could feel his power. It *would* be a remarkable thing if somebody directed that power and used it for something good. But he was too far gone.

"If you join me, you'll go from being a savage to an enlightened being. We'll rule the stars. You are the last person in the universe who I would ever wish to harm. Just trust me and do as I say. Obedience without question. Say it, Viona. *Say it.*"

His voice was hypnotic, but his words were nothing but hatred and entitlement. She shook herself, clearing the fog seeping into her brain. If this was the end, she would go down fighting.

"I'll never say it," she spat out. "All you care about is power, and you'll bleed anyone dry to get it."

All pretense of kindness fell away. Olark snapped his teeth at her, and Adia bared her own. She wasn't above biting him either if it came down to it.

"Fine. We won't discuss it any further, since you refuse to see that I'm right. You were always meant to bear my power. And now you will."

He rushed at her, a blur of rotting limbs, but she spun out of reach. She bent down, picked up a stone, and hurled it at his head. It missed but gave a satisfying thud when it landed on one of his shoulders.

As he recoiled, she pulled Thyme's dagger out of her belt.

Olark rushed at her again, knocking the dagger out of her hands, but she rolled out of his reach before he could touch her and grabbed another stone. Thyme would never be without a weapon, and neither would she.

But she knew this dance couldn't last for much longer. She wasn't a warrior like Darian or Thyme. She wasn't a goddess like Gini. She was Adia-just-Adia. The girl who tagged along with the heroes. Her only special power was an extraordinary ability to end up in the wrong place at the wrong time, being able to talk with plants, and a freakish memory.

Memory.

The stone fell from her hand. The curse of having a brain that needed to remember everything it learned had made her commit Olark's curses to memory. Both of them. The one he'd spun over Zaria. And the one Thyme had told her about in the Horrorbeyond. Viona said to find the loophole. Adia had thought she already had that day in the library. But there was another. . . .

Her eyes flooded with tears. The answer had been in front of her all along. Darian was right. Olark didn't know he was the villain of this story. He thought it was his divine purpose to make the world a more civilized and enlightened place. In his twisted mind, dosing everyone with Drops and possessing bodies, forcing people to change everything about themselves to become the version he thought was best, was all helping the world. Not harming it.

"Viona," she whispered. "You were right. He's already destroyed himself."

Hear my words throughout the world
And read them in the skies.
She of Ovie is protected
By the good and wise.

She of Ovie—not just Viona.

She was a descendant of the first shaman too.

"Have you finally decided to stop fighting?" Olark snarled.

Her name will be a Word of Power
In a world of lies.

"You don't need your body. You don't need your voice. You don't know what to do with all the power you've been gifted," Olark said, his voice rough and hoarse and twisted. The pathetic attempt he'd made to give himself a body started to cave in on itself as he let himself turn back into a shadow with yellow eyes. "But I do, Viona."

"I will say this one last time," she said, standing taller than ever as an agrias vine wrapped itself around her ankles. "My name is *not* Viona."

And anyone who brings her harm
Will be the one who dies.

The shadow shot out toward her like a spear, aiming for her heart.

"MY NAME IS—"

He smashed into her. And she knew this must be what it felt like when a star exploded. After years of compressing her power into something small, a pressure had built up that was too intense to contain. She felt Olark's soul connect with the shamanic blood of her wronged ancestors and prayed she hadn't made a mistake. That she had found the final loophole. If she was wrong, this would be the last word she ever spoke with her own voice.

Olark's essence slowly took over her. It ran up her legs, into her stomach, coiled around her arms, and choked her throat. As her airway constricted and she gasped one last inhale, she used the exhale to utter what might be the last word she would ever say. To say a Word of Power.

She would Say. Her. Name.

"ADIA!"

TWENTY-FIVE

"**S**he's waking up!"

Adia was scared to move. Had she been right? Was she still herself, or was Olark in there too? Her head still throbbed from Nami shoving her into that tree. Hopefully being able to feel pain meant she was alive and unpossessed. It didn't feel like anyone else was in her mind. Slowly, deliberately, and with the greatest of intention, she opened her eyes.

Bubbles peered back at her and yawned in her face.

"Adia?" Thyme asked frantically. "That's still you in there?"

Thyme, Darian, and EJ loomed above her with identical looks of worry on their faces.

EJ. In the past few weeks, she had accepted the fact that a lot of things she had once thought to be myths were real: the Alusi, Olark, Headless Hiroma. But believing that EJ, her cousin, was here and alive—that was almost too much for her heart to handle.

"It's me," she said, wincing as she tried to sit up. "Where are we? What happened?"

"We're in the Academy. They gave you a room that's almost as nice as mine," Darian said. "We found you on the outskirts of the forest lying on a bed of agrias and flowers and seedlings. A whole botanic garden, really. I've never seen so many different types of plants in one space. You've been unconscious for two days. That cat hasn't left your side, by the way."

"He has his moments," Adia said, giving Bubbles an affectionate pat on the head.

"And Olark?" she asked. She cringed as the name escaped her lips, waiting for EJ and Darian to lose it.

Nothing happened.

"The curse. It's broken," she said, sagging in relief. "Does that mean he's really gone?"

"That's what Gini says," Thyme said. "But I still can't wrap my head around it. Adia, how did you do it?"

Darian helped her sit upright, and she took in her surroundings. Plants were in every corner of the room. Growing out of the floor, hanging from the ceiling, some were even in bed with her.

"He possessed me too," she said, gently brushing leaves off her arms. "I let him."

She told them everything. About Nami, her other-worldly chat with Viona, and the final loophole. About her name being a Word of Power.

"And . . . you really still feel like yourself?" Thyme asked worriedly. "Because everyone is talking about you. Darian and Gini didn't give all the details, but everyone knows you saved the emperor's life. They're all clamoring to talk to you. I've been fighting off anyone who tries to get into this room. Especially that wretched boy."

Adia froze.

"Nami? What does he want?"

"A full pardon, no doubt," Darian snorted. "Technically, I'm still the emperor. Gini decided it would be best *not* to tell everyone a demon has been ruling Zaria for the last year. I've been dealing with advisers for the past two days. They want a full pardon for all Gold Hats since they thought they were protecting me. Thyme here has refused to pardon them on my behalf unless they go through extensive training in de-escalation."

"A ten-year-old warrior on Nri would have received that training," Thyme said in disgust. "What's wrong with them? They did almost as much damage as Olark, trying to res-cue an emperor who didn't need rescuing. And that Nami of yours is the one who sent everyone after us. I want his head."

"He most certainly is not *my* Nami," Adia said, getting out of the bed. "And no one's head is getting chopped off."

"We were waiting till you woke up," Darian said. "What do you want us to do with him?"

"I'd like to talk to him. Where is he?"

As they walked through campus, everyone fell to their knees.

"Who is that girl?" a shrill voice shrieked. "And why is Darian walking with her?"

Adia choked back a laugh as she spotted the curly blond head of Mallorie Amber. Mallorie's eyes went wide with recognition, and her jaw dropped in disbelief.

"*That's* who saved the emperor?" Mallorie sputtered. "But . . . but she . . . she . . . SHE DOESN'T EVEN GO HERE!"

"Shut up, you silly girl. Lower your head and show some respect," a professor said, shoving Mallorie into a bow.

"Give me a second," Adia said to her friends. "There's something I need to say to that girl."

Mallorie, still dressed in her tacky yellow bird dress and drenched in jewels, rose from her bow as she approached.

Adia took a deep breath, straightened her shoulders, and looked Mallorie straight in the eye. "My cat vomited in your face cream."

Mallorie clutched her chest and fainted.

Adia rejoined the others, a smile on her lips as Mallorie's friends ran over to fan her. But the smile fell from her face when she saw Nami.

Gold Hats surrounded him, and not one of them looked happy.

"Your Majesty," a Gold Hat said. "Here is the boy who sounded the alarm and falsely accused this girl of murder."

Adia gasped.

"Seriously, Nami? You accused me of *murder*?" Adia said.

"Without an ounce of proof?"

Nami went pale.

"I went into the room and there was blood on the floor and the emperor was missing and you ran . . ." he stammered. "I just thought—"

"Thought?" Darian snapped. "I doubt any thinking was happening. Did it never occur to you that *she* was the one in trouble who needed protecting? She was, by the way. So was I. She saved both our lives, and you sent a squad of goons after her for her trouble!"

A crowd gathered, eager to get the gossip. Knowing Nami, this was the ultimate punishment. A public shaming.

"And why were you in my chambers in the first place?" Darian said, glowering at Nami. He was poised like a lion about to attack. Adia was nervous he would order Nami to be whipped through the streets, he looked so mad.

She touched Darian's arm. Some of the tension left his body, and he gave her hand a quick squeeze. Everyone in the crowd gasped. But no one looked more aghast at the sight of her and the emperor of Zaria holding hands than Nami.

"Adia's a friend," Nami said frantically, though he didn't meet Adia's eyes when he said it. "I was concerned. I wasn't sure if she'd done something wrong to be called to the emperor's chambers."

"A fine way to treat your friends," EJ snapped.

Nami finally met Adia's eyes. His shame seemed genuine, but Adia couldn't tell if it was for her, or because he was being made to look a fool in front of half the nobles of Zaria.

The people whose connections he so desperately wanted. Knowing everything he was dealing with, why he was so desperate to bring honor to his family, she couldn't help but feel bad for him.

Darian's annoyance was plain, but he took a breath and turned to her. "I know what I'd like to do with him, but it's up to you, Adia."

An agrias vine crept past her and disappeared into the bushes. She sighed. She'd made mistakes on this journey. Several. At some point, she and EJ would have to go home and see what was left of the Swamplands. And she hoped no one would call for her head because of what she'd done.

"He was motivated by some concern for me, but he came to the room for his own agenda," she said slowly. "He caused unnecessary chaos. And he hurt me."

Nami's eyes filled with tears.

"You hurt me," she repeated.

"I'm sorry," he whispered.

"Pardon him with the others," Adia said, turning away. "He didn't know what he was doing."

"A generous and kind decision," Darian said through gritted teeth. "Kinder than I would be if the situation were reversed. Her wishes stand. Nami is pardoned."

"Wait," Nami cried out, and Adia turned back to him. "So . . . do you forgive me?"

Adia had never seen someone look so lost and pathetic.

"I don't know yet," she said. "I stopped them from throwing you in a dungeon like you did to me, but that doesn't mean I trust you, or like you, or that we'll ever be friends again. Being your friend turned out to be a dangerous thing. I'm not going to set myself on fire because you feel a chill."

Nami's head hung low as Adia turned away.

"Are you all right with leaving things like that?" Thyme asked.

"It's the best I can do right now."

She didn't want to give Nami any more of her energy.

"Where's Gini?" she asked. She didn't know what concerned her more: that Gini might be losing her mind and destroying the world, or that she might've returned to the celestial realm without Adia getting the chance to say goodbye.

"Dealing with the advisers," Darian said. "They can't seem to grasp that I'm not actually an emperor. I tossed the crown at them, and they practically wet themselves. She's been spinning lies to cover up what really happened. But she wants me to stay on the throne until they find a suitable replacement."

"It sounds miserable," Adia agreed, "but that's probably the most practical thing to do."

Practical. This was supposed to be her year of practicality, but so far, it was the most impractical year of her life to date.

"We'll see how practical it sounds when she tells you her plans for you," Darian said.

"Plans?" Adia said surprised. "What plans? Did she get me my job back?"

"Don't be ridiculous. I want you to attend the Academy of Shamans as a student!" The Alusi stepped out from behind a rosebush and smiled at them.

"Gini!"

Adia surprised herself and ran up to Gini, giving her a big hug.

Gini cleared her throat and awkwardly patted her on the head. "Yes, yes. Good child."

Adia pulled away, rolling her eyes. The divine daughter, she full of love and song, didn't have a maternal bone in her body.

"Why would you want me to go here?" Adia asked. "I'm in control of my power now. See?"

She reached her hand out, and every flower near them turned to face the sun. Thyme gave her a huge grin, and EJ looked like he was about to fall over.

"Yes, you are," Gini admitted. "But you also tend to burn hot. I told you Ovie was the most powerful shaman in his day because he mastered all four shamanic realms. Plants, water, fire, and death. And if Viona was able to reach you from a spirit realm, so did she. You're the last of that bloodline, and your powers are only just starting to awaken. You need to be trained."

Adia had to admit she was curious to see if she really could find Imo Mmiri like Viona had said she could. A magical rain forest powered by a river created by an Alusi? She assumed she'd learn all about the water realm if she found that place. But she had no interest in learning anything about fire. And certainly not about death.

"That's beside the point, Gini. You know this place is full of nothing but frauds. I can't study here."

"My thoughts exactly," EJ said, coming to stand beside Adia. "Besides, we're not splitting up again. We need to go back to the Swamplands."

Adia closed her eyes. EJ wasn't wrong. Uncle Eric and Aunt Ife needed to know their son was alive. But what kind of welcome would be waiting for her when she showed her face again?

"She doesn't belong there," Gini said.

"Well, she doesn't belong here either. Besides, Adia," he said, turning to her, "we still need to get rid of the missionaries. Maybe Olark is gone, but that doesn't magically erase all the mindwashing that's been going on. Or give anyone back the land the missionaries have been stealing and taxing."

"The Academy is a safe space for Adia to explore her powers," Gini said, staring down at EJ as though he was an irritating bug. "Yes, there's still much to be corrected, but she can help more effectively if she's reached her full potential. Besides, it's a terrifying thing, waking to shamanic abilities. You'll find that out soon enough. I suspect real teachers will arrive any day, now that a student is ready. Perhaps I'll come down from Alusia and teach for a semester as well. You all have benefited so much from my warmth and caring. I should share that with other children."

They stared at Gini in silence. Not one of them was brave enough to contradict her.

"In any case, you'll be safer here than back in the Swamp-lands."

Adia wasn't so sure about that, if the events of the last few weeks were any indication, but she didn't say anything. "Safe from what?" she asked. "Olark is gone?" She didn't mean it to be a question, but it came out as one anyway.

"Gone where, though? That's the question you should be asking," Gini said. Then she clapped her hands. "Whoops!" She looked around to make sure she hadn't inadvertently destroyed half of Zaria. "Anyhow, for now I must continue discussions with the advisers before I return to the stars. Someone has to take the throne since Darian insists on being difficult."

"Gini," Adia said, trying to keep the exasperation out of her voice. "Don't you think there's something more impor-tant you need to be doing right now?"

Gini gave her an approving look.

"Ah, your payment. Don't worry. Someone will meet you in a few days with your money."

Adia had almost forgotten that she was now wealthier than even Mallorie Amber. But that wasn't what she was talking about.

"No, I meant you heading back home before you surpass your limits."

"I couldn't agree more," a deep voice said.

Two shadows appeared on the wall behind them. One of which had two long horns coming out from the head.

EJ looked like he was about to faint. "That . . . looks like my statue of Horned Ikenga."

A man stepped out, horns blessedly gone, but Adia didn't need to see the horns to recognize Ikenga's imposing figure. Mbari was with him, looking even more cranky than he had that night in the map library.

"Ginikanwa," Mbari said through gritted teeth. "You did what you came here to do, and we're very proud of you. Zaria is safe. Or at least it's safe for the next ten minutes because that's how long you have before you go over your limit. I suggest you say your goodbyes and get a move on before you burn this continent down."

"Ten more . . ." Gini blinked. "I could have sworn I had three more weeks. Oh, very well, then. Give me five minutes."

"You have two," Ikenga snapped.

EJ's jaw was still on the floor, and even Thyme and Darian, who had seen so much, were speechless at the sight of three Alusi standing together. But Adia wasn't afraid of them anymore.

"I'll make sure she leaves," Adia said.

Ikenga nodded. "I'll leave it to you, then. Thank you, Adia. For everything." With that, he and Mbari vanished.

"He knows your name?" EJ gasped. "I'm one degree of separation from Horned Ikenga? Does he know I'm your cousin?"

Adia rolled her eyes at EJ, then gave Gini a pointed look.

"All right, all right. I'm going. Just let me try to deal with Darian's advisers as best I can before I do," Gini said. "But never fear, children, I'll be back soon enough."

She paused, staring at Adia with a thoughtful expression.

"What happened to Olark could have happened to me," Gini said. "That's the problem with living in the realm of the gods. We get so accustomed to having everything we want, when we want it. We forget not everything is for us.

"I've learned quite a lot from you, Adia Kelbara."

EJ shook his head in disbelief as Gini walked off. "And you mean to tell me that's Gentle Ginikanwa? What an impossible creature."

"She grows on you. But study at the Academy?" Adia said, bewildered as she watched Gini's retreating form. "Absolutely not."

"Oh, why not?" Thyme said, linking her arm through Adia's. "You're all famous and powerful now. You can make everyone who treated you like dirt bow down to you. I'm still not sure where I'll go or what I'll do. At least you have options. It could be perfect."

Perfect?

She thought of Nami, with his head in the clouds, telling her "it's all perfect" as her life got ripped out from under her feet. There was only one thing that was perfect, and it was why she was still standing. She stayed quiet for several minutes, mulling it over. EJ was right. They weren't splitting up again. None of them were, if she could help it.

"I'll only consider going there if you can come with me. We can all be together now," she finally said. "I love you guys, you know."

"Of course we know," Thyme sniffed. "You went and let yourself get possessed to save us. We love you too."

EJ muttered something that sounded suspiciously like *Love you too*, as Darian looked at the group thoughtfully but remained quiet, smiling.

Love, Adia thought. She hadn't loved much before she left the Swamplands, not even herself. But now she knew there was nothing wrong with her that needed to be fixed. Now she had friends she loved and would do anything to protect. Because love was the only thing in the universe that was perfect.

She cleared her throat and straightened her shoulders. No need to get too sappy about it.

"All right, let's catch up to Gini," Adia said with a frown. "I think someone's making her mad. I smell smoke."

ACKNOWLEDGMENTS

First and foremost, the biggest thank-you to the self-appointed president of my fan club, my beloved agent, Pete Knapp, for his tireless work, support, protection, and kindness. I couldn't have put this book into the world with anyone else by my side and I'm forever grateful.

Thank you to everyone at Park and Fine Literary and Media, especially Jerome Murphy, (vice president of my fan club) for all the brainstorming sessions and laughs, and Stuti Telidevara, for constantly helping me organize my chaotic life. Thank you to Abigail Koons, Kat Toolan, Ben Kaslow-Zieve and the foreign rights team for helping bring Adia to readers all around the world.

Thank you so much to my incredible agent across the pond, Claire Wilson, for helping usher this book into the UK. And thank you to everyone at RCW.

A massive thank-you to my absolutely brilliant editors,

Kristin Rens and Rebecca Hill. From my first calls with each of you, I knew that you understood what I wanted to say with this book. It's such a privilege to learn from the two of you and I'm so proud of the work we've done together.

Huge thank-you to my mentor and one of my favorite people in the world, Sylvia Liu. Seeing my name as your pick for Pitch Wars mentee remains one of the happiest moments of my life. From day one you understood me so well that you explained how plot structure works in terms of the Lord of the Rings so I could wrap my head around how to write a book. I'm so grateful to call you a friend and I couldn't have done this without you. (Yes, the hobbits are clapping.)

Massive thank-you to everyone at Balzer + Bray and Usborne. I'm constantly blown away by how much goes into getting a book on the shelves and I have the best publishing teams behind me.

At Balzer + Bray, thank you to Jessica Berg and Gwen Morton (Managing Editorial), Robby Imfeld and Sabrina Abballe (Marketing), Anna Bernard (Publicity), Patty Rosati, Mimi Rankin, and the team in School and Library Marketing, Sean Cavanagh and Vanessa Nuttry (Production), Amy Ryan (Design), and Kerry Moynagh, Kathy Faber, Jennifer Wygand, and the team in Sales.

At Usborne, thank you to cover designer Will Steele for Adia's beautiful UK cover, Sarah Cronin (Interior Designer), Hannah Reardon Steward (Senior Marketing Manager), Nina Douglas (Lead freelance PR), Jessica Feichtlbauer (Inhouse Publicity Executive), and Christian Herisson, Arfana Islam,

Louise Ward and Sabrina Yam (UK Sales team).

I've been so fortunate to have found the greatest friends in the writing community. There are too many to mention by name, and many who I met after this book was written, but a very special thank-you to my critique partners, Alli Carvalho, Heather Murphy Capps, and Nadi Reed Perez, who helped shape this book in its earliest form. Your feedback was genius and invaluable. And thank you to my earliest readers and hype squad, K.A. Cobell, Myah Hollis, María José Fitzgerald, Tyler Lawson, Jordan Link, and Dani Parker.

Thank you, Jessie, for your friendship, wisdom, and for literally saving my life in the Amazon. I love you.

And most of all, thank you to everyone who read this book and went on this adventure with Adia! More adventures to come!